SWORD
OF THE
GRAY
CHAMPION

CATE —

Enjoy —

Domenic

SWORD
OF THE
GRAY
CHAMPION

BOOK TWO

THE SWORDS OF VALOR

DOMENIC MELILLO

Phase Publishing, LLC
Seattle, WA

If you purchased this book without a cover, you should be aware that this book is stolen property. It was reported as "unsold and destroyed" to the publisher, and neither the author nor the publisher has received any payment for this "stripped" book.

Text copyright © 2019 by Domenic Melillo
Cover art copyright © 2019 by Domenic Melillo

Cover art by Tugboat Design
http://www.tugboatdesign.net

All rights reserved. Published by Phase Publishing, LLC. No part of this book may be reproduced or transmitted in any form, or by any means, electronic or mechanical, including photocopying or recording or by any information storage and retrieval system, without written permission from the publisher.

Phase Publishing, LLC first paperback edition
February 2019

ISBN 978-1-943048-76-2
Library of Congress Control Number 2019932054
Cataloging-in-Publication Data on file.

DEDICATION

This book is dedicated to my wife, Susan, who has always stood by me during my own battles and encouraged me to deal with them with virtue and valor.

Her love, strength, and faith in God inspires me every day to be a better man.

JOB 41: 1-34

Can you draw out Leviathan with a fishhook or press down his tongue with a cord? Can you put a rope in his nose or pierce his jaw with a hook?

Will he make many pleas to you? Will he speak to you soft words? Will he make a covenant with you to take him for your servant forever?

Will you play with him as with a bird, or will you put him on a leash for your girls? Will traders bargain over him? Will they divide him up among the merchants?

Can you fill his skin with harpoons or his head with fishing spears? Lay your hands on him; remember the battle—you will not do it again! Behold, the hope of a man is false; he is laid low even at the sight of him.

No one is so fierce that he dares to stir him up. Who then is he who can stand before me? Who has first given to me, that I should repay him? Whatever is under the whole heaven is mine.

I will not keep silence concerning his limbs, or his mighty strength, or his goodly frame. Who can strip off his outer garment? Who would come near him with a bridle? Who can open the doors of his face? Around his teeth is terror.

His back is made of four rows of shields, shut up closely as with a seal. One is so near to another that no air can come between them. They are joined one to another;

they clasp each other and cannot be separated.

His sneezings flash forth light, and his eyes are like the eyelids of the dawn. Out of his mouth go flaming torches; sparks of fire leap forth. Out of his nostrils comes forth smoke, as from a boiling pot and burning rushes. His breath kindles coals, and a flame comes forth from his mouth.

In his neck abides strength, and terror dances before him. The folds of his flesh stick together, firmly cast on him and immovable.

His heart is hard as a stone, hard as the lower millstone. When he raises himself up, the mighty are afraid; at the crashing they are beside themselves.

Though the sword reaches him, it does not avail, nor the spear, the dart, or the javelin. He counts iron as straw, and bronze as rotten wood.

The arrow cannot make him flee; for him, sling stones are turned to stubble. Clubs are counted as stubble; he laughs at the rattle of javelins.

His underparts are like sharp potsherds; he spreads himself like a threshing sledge on the mire.

He makes the deep boil like a pot; he makes the sea like a pot of ointment. Behind him he leaves a shining wake; one would think the deep to be white-haired.

On earth there is not his like, a creature without fear. He sees everything that is high; he is king over all the sons of pride.

PROLOGUE

Once again, I am called upon to tell you a tale. Freedom and liberty hang in the balance.

It is a tale I did not believe that I would need to tell, but as always, I must do my duty as the Prophet of Remembrance.

Heroes are again required to act, as evil does not relent, it just assumes a new form. Though time changes, the nature of evil does not. It is voracious. It is relentless. It is adaptable. Once having been subdued, it morphs. It alters its methods and draws new souls to its cause.

Evil cannot exist without willing adherents and requires that they give it their soul. They must worship it, and they must idolize it. This idolatry is infectious, corrupting even the innocent and righteous, for evil is a deceiver. It appears as good to those whose spiritual eyes have been blinded to the truth.

This blindness falls slowly and with subtlety. It overtakes those that are content, apathetic, and unchallenged. It comes in the guise of security, dependency, and pleasure. But its true nature is bondage and enslavement. It enslaves the body, mind, and spirit. It is a cruel master.

It is my duty to sound the alarm! To that end, I issue a warning and tell this tale. The Leviathan awakes! No one is so fierce that he dares to stir him. Who then is he who can stand before him? On earth there is not his like: a creature without fear.

He sees everything that is high; he is king over all the sons of pride. - Job 41:34

CHAPTER ONE

THE RETURN OF THE MEGLIO

Pulling his golf bag over the small grassy rise, Joseph Melillo smiled as he saw his son and grandsons waiting to tee off. It was good to see them smiling and happy again. The last time he'd seen them was just before…

Frowning just a bit, he tried to recall what had happened after he'd died. For him, it was as if no time had passed. Yet, he sensed that much had changed.

Just then, the starter pointed at him and said, "Good, here comes your fourth, just in time. The first group can start."

Joseph continued his slow trek to the tee box, grinning as he heard Joe sigh.

"Looks like a long day," his grandson murmured. "This guy is really going to slow us down."

Grandpa's grin broadened as he responded, "Sounds like someone needs to teach you youngsters some humility!"

Joe's head jerked up and he squinted. The other boys stared as well.

Their grandfather laughed aloud when he saw recognition finally dawn. A mixture of shock, disbelief, and a fair bit of hope filled their expressions.

"What are you guys staring at? You would think that you've never seen your own grandpa before."

He reached into his golf bag and drew out the Sword of Don Quixote. "Anyone up for a little adventure?"

Simultaneously, they dropped their golf clubs and ran to him.

"Grandpa! Is it really you?" asked Joe. "Is this real, or are you a holograph?"

The Meglio responded, "It's me, buddy, and as always, *I'm better than good!*"

They all hugged him at once. After a moment, they stepped back to allow the prophet to greet his father.

As Rob stood before him, Joseph saw the indecision in his son's eyes. The returned Meglio Di Buono of the Cincinnatus and Arimathea Family of the Swords of Valor, smiled and raised his arms, inviting a hug.

Rob stepped into his father's arms, and the two men hugged long and hard. The Meglio felt his son's shoulders shake with unspoken emotion. He found himself blinking back a few tears, too. After a few moments, he patted Rob's back, gave him one last squeeze, and stepped back.

When they stepped apart, Nick stepped up. "I don't want to interrupt, but I don't understand. How is this possible? How did this happen?"

The prophet reached for a handkerchief, wiped his tear-filled eyes, and replied, "Well, Nick, it's really rather simple. You guys changed history by a day, and anything can happen in a day. *Anything.*"

"I know we changed a day in history when we saved King Leonidas from being killed at the battle of Thermopylae, but how did that result in Grandpa's return?" Nick asked his uncle, bewildered.

"That is something we will need to ask the quantum

computer," replied the prophet. "There are too many variables for me to even begin to guess, but as you can see, changing history by even one day can have far-reaching consequences. Let's get everyone together and head back to the house to sort this all out."

As they walked back to the parking lot, Joseph observed, "It seems that all is well, Rob. I assume the mission was a success?"

Rob looked confused. "Yes. I mean, obviously. I mean, don't you know that? After all, you are here with us now after having…" His voice trailed off.

His father finished the sentence for him. "After having died?"

"Well, yes, after having died," repeated the prophet. "The last time I saw you was in the hospital just before it happened. Do you remember that? Do you remember anything we talked about? The plan? The Apostles? The Swords of Terror? Your office?"

"I remember everything up until that point," his father replied. "What I do not know is the result of your actions since then. I must assume that if you have taken our heroes out for a day of golfing, that all must have gone well, or you would still be in the Keeping Room, working feverishly to save the world from destruction. Am I correct?"

"Yes, Dad, you are correct. But there is more to the story than that. There are a lot of things that happened because of our victory. We need to bring you up to speed. All did not go as I thought you'd planned." He sighed. "It appears that you withheld some vital information, which I, for one, did not appreciate."

The Meglio smiled. "But you succeeded regardless! I'm sure you learned some very interesting lessons because of it. Believe me when I tell you that challenging

5

your abilities was an important part of the plan."

Then he turned to his grandsons and said, "I'm very proud of all of you. I knew the hero in each of you would rise to the challenge. Now you can catch me up on your adventures."

Robbie's eyes lit up as he bragged, "Guess what, Grandpa? I got us into Windsor Castle!" Billy and Joe just rolled their eyes.

Billy said, "Okay, Fabio, I guess the rewriting of history has already begun! Grandpa, don't listen to his version. We'll have the quantum computer tell you the real story."

"Don't worry, Billy," replied the Meglio. "I know all of you well enough to know when I'm being played. Remember, it was me who chose you, and that took a lifetime of very careful observation. I know you better than you know yourselves. I hope you realize that I may have been dead, but I was not born yesterday. Well, not technically anyway. By the way, I'm hungry. Is there any food left in the house, or did you barbarians eat it all?"

"We put a pretty good dent in it, Grandpa," replied Jeff, "but there is still plenty of chicken cutlet parmigiana left. Uncle Rob wouldn't let us eat that. He was keeping it for himself."

"Well," said the Meglio, "it looks like your uncle will have one more thing to deal with because of my return."

They all looked at Uncle Rob, who had a big smile on his face, and laughed.

When they arrived at the family compound, the cousins unloaded all the golf bags, including their grandfather's, removed their replica swords and the Sword of Don Quixote, and put the replicas in the storage room next to the Keeping Room under the barn. Their grandfather's sword, they put in the glass case where it belonged. While the cousins headed to the house, the Meglio and his son had a chance to speak alone.

"It really is good to see you, Dad," said the prophet. "You can't imagine how hard it was to watch you die like that, knowing that I had not done everything I could to heal you."

"I know, Rob," said the Meglio, "I am sorry for that, but it had to happen that way. There was so much at stake. Believe me, if I could have done it any other way, I would have never put you all through that. I hope that at least the holographic image I left for you helped to ease the pain."

"Yes, it did. That was a stroke of genius, Dad," replied the prophet. "It felt like we had you there right by our side, guiding and directing us. It was very comforting, but not as comforting as actually having you back with us. Of course, there is no worldwide catastrophe to deal with now, so we can just focus on relaxing and getting on with our lives."

"Are you sure of that?" asked his father.

"Well, yeah," said the prophet. "I mean, we destroyed the Swords of Terror, so what could cause trouble now?"

The Meglio stopped. He looked the prophet in the eye and replied, "Have you destroyed Azazel?"

The prophet looked surprised and responded, "No, but we have taken away his most powerful weapons, the Swords of Terror. All the Swords of Valor have been returned to their rightful owners and proper place in time, and the timeline changes appear to have had an overall positive effect."

"Changes to the timeline you say? Tell me about that," queried the Meglio. "I realize that something significant has been altered, since I am here with you, but significant timeline changes were *definitely* not part of my plan. But as you know, changes in the timeline are deceiving. They are never what they appear to be. I have taught you that, so I don't understand your cavalier attitude."

The prophet put his arm around his dad's shoulder and said, "We can talk more about this later. Why don't we get something to eat first, and then we will lay it all out for you? You will see that I am right, and that your plan worked to perfection despite, or maybe even because of, the timeline change."

"We shall see," said the Meglio, not feeling reassured. "Just remember, evil never changes its shape, just its form. As long as Azazel exists, we must be ever vigilant."

They arrived at the house and entered the kitchen where the cousins were busy preparing a feast for them all. The wine was already poured, the chicken cutlets were warming up, and the sauce was simmering.

"Smells like old times!" declared the Meglio as he entered the bustling kitchen. "I remember walking into my mother's kitchen. The smell of the sauce simmering and the sausage and meatballs frying almost put me into a trance. I also remember being beaten mercilessly whenever I took a piece of bread and dipped it into the sauce cooking on the stove. You would have thought I committed a felony. Of course, she never beat me with her hand. It was always with her beloved wooden spoon that never left her side. Ah, the good old days!"

"What are you talking about, Grandpa?" Ty placed his napkin around his neck. "Good old days? Grandma did that to us until the day she died. 'The beating of the sauce stealer'. It's a family tradition!"

The Meglio laughed. "I guess some things never

change. Speaking of traditions, something else that never changes is the oldest person at the table saying grace. Looks like it's up to me."

He bowed his head and began. "Dear Lord, we thank you for this food and drink. We thank you for your protection and provisions, and we thank you for our family. Strengthen and encourage us in our trials to come. We pray this in the name of Jesus Christ. Amen."

Everyone echoed his amen and began to dig in.

Joe spoke up. "Grandpa, it's so good to have you back! We really missed you. Can you tell us anything about what you experienced when you, you know, when you passed?"

Everyone looked at Joe, their expressions horrified.

"What?" Joe asked, throwing his hands in the air. "Don't you guys all want to know?"

The prophet said, "Joe, you don't ask someone who died what it was like."

Joe looked at him incredulously. "Really, Uncle Rob? Where is *that* rule written? I don't think there are rules for this sort of thing. If *we* can't ask Grandpa, who can?"

Unable to refute his argument, his uncle just shook his head.

The Meglio responded. "Joe, I wish I had a satisfactory answer for you. All I remember is closing my eyes and feeling at peace. I remember knowing that I had left nothing undone in my life. I had accomplished my goals and done my duty. I remember thinking that was the greatest gift. Then the next thing I know, I was walking up to the tee box, saw you all there, and heard Joe's smart remark. The rest you know. That's it. Take from it what you will."

"So, you remember nothing in between?" asked Jeff. "Interesting. It is as if all you did was transition from one

9

reality into another. That's what happened to the rest of the world when we changed time. The only difference between you and them is that you remember the past and don't know anything about the present timeline. They, on the other hand, don't remember the old timeline, but only know the new timeline. I wonder what it all means?"

"That is *way* beyond my paygrade," the Meglio replied. "I'm just happy to be 'on top of the grass', as I always say."

They finished their meal and headed into the living room. The prophet once again stood in front of the fireplace and addressed the group.

"Today is a memorable day for many reasons. We celebrate the return of our father, grandfather, and Meglio. We feel indescribable joy at his return. That only increases the sense of celebration and relief we have because of the amazing victory over the Apostles of Azazel. The same emotion that Grandpa described to us at lunch is what I know you must be experiencing now; the sense that you have given your all, been victorious, and left nothing undone. Enjoy that feeling and remember it. Live your life so that at the end of it you can experience the peace and joy that your grandfather felt at the time of his passing. No man can hope for anything more. Now, I want us all to gather in the Keeping Room where we, and the quantum computer, can fill Grandpa in on our missions. That will be a fitting conclusion to this whole episode."

As they stood to move to the Keeping Room, the Meglio spoke. "Rob, I hate to delay the meeting, but could I ask an urgent question?"

"Sure, Pop, anything. What is it?" Rob replied.

"Your very inspirational and heartfelt speech affected me greatly. May I take a minute or two to go the bathroom before we head to the Keeping Room? After all, the last time I went, I had a catheter you know where."

Rob stood there speechless for a moment, then shook his head. "Like grandfather, like grandson," he remarked as he looked at Ty.

"Way to go, Grandpa!" declared Ty. "They always get mad at me for that. Now I have you on my side. See, everyone? It's not just me! My father's speeches have the same effect on Grandpa!"

Grandpa high-fived Ty on his way to the bathroom. When he returned, they headed to the old barn out back where the Keeping Room was hidden.

On the way, Nick asked, "Grandpa, Uncle Rob told us all about this place, and I have a question. Did you and a group of friends really dig this out and build it yourselves, or was that just what you told everyone?"

"That is a true story, Nick," replied the Meglio. "Back then, I was still very wary of the local people and didn't want to set off any alarms. So, I had separate groups of Guardians join me up here on two-week rotations. We carefully and precisely did the work ourselves. Remember, these were men who had fought in World War II and understood demanding work and the need for secrecy. There was a camaraderie that is hard to replicate today. I had more volunteers than I could accept. Everyone wanted to contribute to the effort. It was that cooperative and selfless attitude that won the war, and what I believe is missing in today's world. Today, it is everyone for himself or their own special interest group. We have lost the desire to contribute to the greater good. It's a big problem. I hope that the changes that you and your cousins have instigated have influenced that. If not, then we still have work to do."

Before entering the Keeping Room, the prophet

punched in the access code, and the heavy, titanium door slowly opened. Lights flooded the space below, and the smell of antiquity rose from the opening.

"Welcome to Wonderland once again," said Billy, echoing his fateful words from the first time the cousins had entered the room.

"Grandpa, you should go first," Jeff offered politely.

"Thanks, Jeff," replied the Meglio, "but this time I would like to give that honor to your uncle. He was the one who ensured the success of your missions and did his duty with honor and distinction under extremely trying circumstances. He should lead us down. That, and the fact that I am not exactly anxious to go ten feet underground, if you get my drift!"

They laughed at the gallows humor, and the prophet led them down into the Keeping Room. Each time the Meglio entered this room, he was struck by the sense of power and history present in the space. This time was no different. He observed in awe the glass sword case lit from above, now containing only one Sword of Valor; the Sword of Don Quixote, the Sword of Humility. The one his grandsons and his own quantum essence had used to defeat the giant Goliath and secure their final victory.

He closed his eyes for a moment as he seemed to recall fighting with this sword by the fire near the river. The scene was hazy, like a distant dream. In his mind's eye, he could see the massive Goliath and could feel the shock up his arm each time their swords clanged together. First, he saw the tip of Goliath's sword broken off, then it broke in half. Finally, he felt a sense of triumph as Goliath and his sword disintegrated before his eyes.

The Meglio took a deep breath and brought himself back to the present. He smiled as he gazed at the case, knowing the rest of the Swords of Valor were now back in the hands of their rightful owners and back in their proper place in time.

"It seems empty in here without the swords," said Robbie. "It always felt so comforting to enter this place and see them sitting there, waiting for us. I almost feel naked without them."

"Well, I could have done without *that* image," Ty groaned. "But I agree with you, Robbie. The room feels less alive with them gone. Grandpa, is there any way that we could ever get them back if we needed them? I mean, I know we have the replicas now, but it's not the same. They're just reminders, without the power. Are the true Swords of Valor lost to us forever?"

"That's a very good question, Ty," said the Meglio. "It's an unknown. It is something that has never been needed before. Should the time come that they are once again required, I am sure that the inherent virtue of the swords will influence their response. Also, remember the initiation ceremony where you received the swords? That ceremony connected you with them on the quantum level. That connection is inseverable no matter where the swords are in time and space. If the need arises, we will have to test that connection. But for now, just be thankful you had them when they were needed."

They entered the tech room and gathered around the large, round table, a softly glowing circle of light emanating from the center of it. The wall of monitors facing the table was dark, and the only other light in the room emerged from the control panel of the now apparently-dormant quantum computer.

The Meglio spoke. "Time to wake up, my friend. Your master has come home!"

With that, there was a humming sound and the feeling of static electricity filled the air. Then a voice responded. "Well, it's about time," said the disembodied voice of the quantum computer. "I was beginning to think that you were going to leave me here sleeping forever. I am so glad to have an adult back in charge. The crew you left me with was killing me."

"I am glad to be back here with you, my old friend," replied the Meglio. "Very glad, indeed. I understand that we have a lot of things to discuss. Shall we begin?"

"Gladly, Meglio. Please, everyone, take your seats, and we will begin the review," said the quantum computer.

They took their places around the table and watched as the almost life-sized holographic image of the Meglio once again appeared in the middle of the round table.

"Oh no, this will not do!" Grandpa exclaimed. "I cannot sit here looking at and talking to myself. I need to make a change. Excuse me for a minute while I work to make the image more palatable and engaging."

He rose and went to the control panel. His holographic image faded from view. After a few minutes, he returned.

"Computer, you may begin again."

Instantly, a new image took form in the center of the table. The cousins and the prophet appeared dumbstruck by the vision before their eyes.

"Hello, Catherine," said the Meglio. "You certainly are a welcome sight. I've missed you so much."

The image looked at him with what seemed to be a mixture of love and sadness. "It's good to see you too, my love," the holographic Catherine responded. "It has been far too long. Have you been well?"

"Other than dying and then being thrust into a new timeline, yes, my dear, all is well," replied the Meglio.

He looked at the others at the table and saw they'd

been brought to tears by the image of their grandmother and mother. The last time they'd seen her was when they were gathered around her deathbed in prayer. She had always been a determined woman, and even as the cancer was ripping her apart on the inside, she fought to ensure that they did not see her give in to her suffering.

He'd always said that she had been his strength, his source of courage. He insisted that she truly was the strong one of the family and that all the good qualities in their children and grandchildren had come from her. While he knew that was not exactly true, neither was it completely false. She had the blood of warriors in her and was the daughter of the previous Meglio of the Arimathea family, Robert Ogilvie Petrie.

Now, here she was, standing before them in her prime. She appeared young and beautiful with an almost-regal bearing. He had been smitten by her from the first moment they met.

The image turned her gaze first to the prophet. "Hello, Robert. It is so good to see you again. Thank you for honoring your father so well with your life. You will never know how proud I am of the man you have become. Nothing could warm a mother's heart more."

The prophet opened his mouth but did not speak. He swiped at his eyes and excused himself from the table.

The image next addressed the cousins. "Hello, my beautiful grandsons. You all look well. My, how handsome you have become. I, for one, had my doubts for a few years!"

The cousins laughed aloud.

"Hi, Grandma," Ty greeted her. "You look great! Can I ask you a question?"

"Absolutely," responded the image.

"Can you figure out how to use that quantum

computer to make more chicken cutlet parmigiana? These animals ate all of what Grandpa had left."

The image laughed. "Not sure I can make that happen, Ty. Let's just say I will work on it."

The rest of the cousins silently watched the image, awe in their expressions.

"Grandpa," said Joe, "I know that this is just an image of Grandma that you programmed into the quantum computer, but it feels so real. Why is that? Is it just an image, or is it really Grandma on some level?"

The Meglio replied to Joe's question. "When you are dealing with quantum phenomena, it is a very fine line. You know from your last assignment that 'quantum emanations' are real. These emanations are the quantum essence of a person. The computer uses the information I programmed into it and accesses what it can of the quantum essence of the person we are trying to portray in the image. It combines the artificial intelligence and personality information with the portion of the quantum essence it can access to create the image you see before you.

"In the case of your grandmother's image, I can say that it is also imbued with love. As I input the information, I was remembering our relationship and was filled with fond memories. So, who knows, Joe? Quantum essences combined with love can become profoundly powerful forces. Let's just interact with the image as if it is truly your grandmother and not think too much about it. Sometimes questions like these have a way of eventually answering themselves."

At this point, the prophet reentered the room and took his seat. He addressed the image. "Mom, can you show Dad a summary of what took place during the kids' assignments and the results of the timeline change?"

"As you wish, my son," was the image's reply.

Suddenly, the screens around the room came alive with images from the meetings in the Keeping Room and the missions of the heroes. The quantum computer image narrated the events and gave the Meglio perspective and detail of every mission. It showed him the result of each assignment and the recorded quantum images of the Battle of the Swords during the first and second Final Processes.

After that was complete, the image asked the Meglio, "Is that sufficient for you, my love, or should I also reveal to you the result of the changes that our grandsons have wrought upon the timeline?"

The Meglio replied, "I need to see it all, my dear. Good or bad, I need to know. Please, go on."

"As you wish," the image replied.

The monitors around the room switched to images of the major cities around the globe as the hologram began to narrate. She showed them the Twin Towers in New York City standing proud, the ghost town that used to be New Orleans after hurricane Katrina devastated it, and the colonization of Mars. She remarked on the lack of terrorism in most of the world, the states formed by the Native American nations, American history without the Civil War, and the absence of the pollution which had affected the health of so many before.

"I could go on, my love, but the initial analysis of the quantum computer shows us that your grandsons having changed history by one day, combined with the destruction of the Swords of Terror, has had a very powerful and overall positive change in the course of history. It is clear that if they hadn't completed the Final Process in time, the results could have been very different."

"Well," said the Meglio after the computer had concluded, "it seems my fears have been unfounded. It appears that the changes resulting from your missions have been absorbed well by the new timeline and have led to increased prosperity and peace. I would say that all appears to be well with the world, and that our work may be complete."

Then he addressed the image. "Since you ran this analysis, have you discovered any other important developments?"

The image hesitated, then responded, "I have, my love."

"Please share them with us now so that we may assess them together," the Meglio responded.

"I don't want to do that," the image of Catherine replied. "Please don't ask me to reveal that information. Just take what I have told you and enjoy the rest of your time with our family. The world can take care of itself. You have all given enough and suffered enough."

The Meglio leaned forward and addressed the image softly, "Catherine, you know that I must know. It is now as it always has been. Whatever the news, and whatever the issue, we are strong enough to handle it. If we stay together and stay strong as a family, nothing is too terrible for us to deal with. Please tell us what you know."

The image responded. "Azazel has not retreated; he has remade the Apostles into a different and more powerful group. This threat is worse than the last one, and he is very close to the completion of his revised plan. I have discovered that it has been in the works for millennia in this new timeline and is unstoppable at this point. Please, my love, turn away from this threat, and enjoy what time you all have left as a family. I beg this of you." Deep concern seeped into her voice.

The Meglio addressed the prophet and the cousins. "You have heard what the image has said. What say you? Do we retreat from this new threat, or do we advance? Do I ask the image to continue, or do we take our victory and call it a day, knowing we have done our duty and given our all? Shall we hear about our fate?"

The room was silent. The Meglio looked around and saw each man at the table struggling with the news. He knew they had fully expected to hear that all was well. They were certainly anticipating that they would return to their normal routines. True, they would have to deal with the changed realities in their personal lives because of the timeline change.

But now the image of his wife, their mother and grandmother, had reluctantly delivered devastating news. All the effort, all the pain, and all the success may have been for naught. Azazel had not given up. He had not gone away, and he had, apparently, come back stronger than before.

As devastating as this was, the Meglio knew one thing. This family, this team, and each of them individually, could not stand by and let Azazel win. He watched the prophet's expression turn from stunned to determined. That was a good sign.

Finally, the prophet spoke up. "Dad, you know my heart. I'm in for the long haul. There is no second choice, no plan B. I will do whatever it takes, but I believe we need more information to understand what has taken place and what we will be facing. Not to decide whether or not to fight, but *how* to fight."

Billy added to the prophet's comments. "That goes for me, too. I'm in, but I would like to know what I am signing up for. Give it to us and tell us straight up. We can deal with it, whatever it is."

Joe was next to speak. "I'm in, too. Azazel may have a better plan than before, but we are also better than before. We have experience now. We know how to handle this, and we are a much more lethal team. We can face whatever comes."

The Meglio asked the group, "Are you all in, even without knowing the danger?"

"Yes, we are," was their joint reply.

"So be it," replied the Meglio. "Then we are united and committed. Catherine, my love, please tell us all you know so that we may know our enemy."

CHAPTER TWO

THE FACE OF THE LEVIATHAN ALLIANCE

The image of their grandmother seemed to pause a bit to gather herself before starting. Finally, she began. "The quantum computer has had time, since your last session here in the Keeping Room, to explore the history of this new timeline. It is not yet completed. As you might imagine, analyzing all of history and doing a comparative analysis between timelines takes time even for a quantum computer. I can tell you what is now known with certainty. I will update you as additional information and insights are confirmed. Here is what is known up to this point.

"The greatest changes and divergence from the old timeline have taken place after World War II, and they are accelerating. It is as if the foundation of the long-term plan was completed before World War II.

"As you know, Azazel is a Watcher and exists outside of history. He therefore can move freely between the present and the past. He cannot venture into the future. He is also limited to the timeline reality that exists and must work within its framework.

"After the Swords of Terror were destroyed and the

new timeline began, he went back to the ancient past, where he recruited and nurtured other families, separate from those he used for the last timeline. These families have dissimilar qualities, as well as diverse purposes and methodologies. They are masters of corruption, control, and deceit. They deal in the realm of moral and social evils. Their focus is primarily on political power and control, but they also thrive on the love of money, greed, sexual depravity, and self-interest.

"The Apostles of Azazel have not gone away. They have become the Leviathan Alliance. Although they no longer have access to the Swords of Terror, Azazel has defined a new strategy for them and empowered them differently. Since he could not destroy the world through the destruction of virtue and valor, he has now chosen to corrupt good things, molding virtue into vice and valor into violence. He has begun to corrupt peace into apathy, and prosperity into dependence.

"His plan is no longer to use the swords to do this. Terror has proven to be of limited and temporary use. That is because trying to enslave a people by using an external threat can often backfire and ignite valor, patriotism, and resistance. He has determined that to truly enslave a people, they must come to desire it. True, lasting bondage is not imposed on a people, it is adopted by them, even welcomed. Sometimes even worshipped. Azazel's current weapon is idolatry.

"The families of the Leviathan Alliance have become so powerful under his influence and guidance that they are now in position to use the current crisis season to implement the final plan to control and enslave the world. Realize that the seasons of history, the four turnings of the saeculum, work the same way regardless of the timeline changes. The turnings of history and the

22

four generational archetypes they generate are unchanging and unstoppable. Therefore, we are still in a crisis season. This has not changed, and Azazel has chosen this season to bring his plan to fruition." The image paused.

"Thank you, Catherine," the Meglio said. "I suggest that at this point, we check for questions to ensure that everyone is on the same page."

"As you wish, my love," replied the image.

The Meglio addressed the group and asked, "After hearing the information and analysis presented to us, what questions remain? What needs further clarification?"

The first to speak was Jeff. "Why does Azazel remember the old timeline? I thought that we remember it because we were in the Keeping Room when the time wave hit. We were shielded from the change, right?"

The prophet responded to Jeff's question. "Azazel is a Watcher and, as the image told us, is not subject to the effects of time. For example, he does not age. He also is not a material being and has no quantum signature. Both of those factors make him immune to the effects of the timeline change. The only aspect of time that he is barred from is moving forward into the future. That has always, and will always, remain the domain of only God Almighty. But he can freely move from present to past and manipulate events for his purposes. He remembers his failure and is apparently taking a different approach."

"That's a good explanation, Rob," responded the Meglio.

"My question is about the new families of the Leviathan Alliance," said Nick. "What do we know about them, and why are they so powerful and dangerous?"

"I will answer that question," replied the image of

his grandmother. "Whereas before, the Apostles of Azazel were historical families of evil warriors, now they are wealthy families of history. They operate as the Leviathan Alliance using their power to influence industries, society, and governments. Their goal is to manipulate people through materialism and dependency. These are the most powerful and corrupt families to have ever existed on earth in this timeline. Many of them you will recognize from history, but you are completely unaware of their present reach and control.

"Five families, or bloodlines, are at the top of the Leviathan organization. These families constitute the inner core. It is these five families that are implementing the World Government plan. I will reveal them to you and give you a brief current timeline history of each.

"The Plantagenets currently operate in the realm of media, literature, printing, and education. In the toss-up between including the Plantagenets or the Tudors, the Plantagenets won, because much of the development of the English culture and political system, which remains to this day, arose under their rule. Under the Tudors, the Church of England was formed, and some say a golden age occurred, but the significance of the Plantagenet line is far greater than that of the Tudors. The House of Plantagenet was a royal house founded by Henry II of England, son of Geoffrey V of Anjou. The Plantagenet kings first ruled the Kingdom of England in the twelfth century. In total, fifteen Plantagenet monarchs ruled England from 1154 until 1485.

"A distinctive English culture and art emerged during the Plantagenet era, encouraged by some of the monarchs who were patrons of the 'father of English poetry', Geoffrey Chaucer. The Gothic architecture style was popular during the time, with buildings such as the

Westminster Abbey and York Minster remodeled in that style. There were also lasting developments in the social sector, such as John I of England's signing of the Magna Carta, which was influential in the development of common law and constitutional law. Political institutions such as the Parliament of England and the Model Parliament originate from the Plantagenet period, as do educational institutions including the Universities of Cambridge and Oxford.

"The Julio-Claudian family now operates in the areas of the sex and pornography trade, and in the movies. The Claudia and Julius families were two of the most important families in Ancient Rome. They eventually joined together to form the Julio-Claudian Dynasty. The most famous emperors came from their lines and ruled the Roman Empire from 27 BC to AD 68; Augustus, Caligula, Claudius, Tiberius, and Nero. He was the last of the line of emperors when he committed suicide. These five rulers were linked through marriage and adoption into the combined family.

"Julius Caesar is sometimes inaccurately seen as its founder, although he was not an emperor and had no Claudian connections. Augustus is the more widely accepted founder. The reigns of the Julio-Claudian emperors bear some similar traits, all came to power through indirect or adopted relations. Each expanded the territory of the Roman Empire and initiated massive construction projects. They were generally loved by the common people, whom they placated with 'bread and circuses', but were resented by the senatorial class... a sentiment reflected by ancient historians, who describe the Julio-Claudians as self-aggrandizing, mad, sexually perverse, and tyrannical.

"The Médici family controls the areas of science,

pharmaceuticals, chemicals, and medicine. This family was powerful and influential in Florence from the thirteenth to seventeenth century. It included four popes: Leo X, Clement VII, Pius the IV, and Leo XI; as well as numerous rulers of Florence, notably Lorenzo the Magnificent, patron of some of the most famous works of Renaissance art, and later members of the French and English royalty. Like other families, they dominated their city's government.

"They were able to bring Florence under their family's power, allowing for an environment where art and humanism could flourish. They led the birth of the Italian Renaissance along with the other great families of Italy. The Médici Bank was one of the most prosperous and most respected in Europe. There are some estimates that the Médici family was, for a while, the wealthiest family in Europe.

"From this base, they acquired political power initially in Florence and later throughout wider Italy and Europe. By commissioning artists and scientists like Michelangelo, Leonardo De Vinci, Galileo, and by producing four popes, the Mèdici's influence on the world can be felt even today. The origin of the family name is shrouded in uncertainty but implies a foundational connection to medicine since 'medici' is the plural of 'medico', meaning 'medical doctor'.

"The Rothschild family controls the areas of banking, finance, money supply, and real estate. The Rothschilds are an international banking and finance dynasty of German-Jewish origin. They established operations across Europe and were ennobled by the Austrian and British governments. The family's rise to international prominence began with Mayer Amschel Rothschild, who lived from 1744 to 1812. His strategy for future success was to keep control of their businesses in family hands, allowing them to maintain full discretion about the size of their wealth and their business achievements. Mayer Rothschild successfully kept the fortune in the family by carefully arranging marriages between cousins or people in high positions of power or importance.

"Nathan Mayer Rothschild started his London business, N. M. Rothschild and Sons, in 1811, at New Court in St. Swithin's Lane, city of London, where it still trades today. In 1818, he arranged a £5 million loan to the Prussian government, and the issuing of bonds for government loans became a mainstay of his bank's business. He gained so much power in the city of London that by 1825, he was able to supply enough money to the Bank of England to enable it to avert a market liquidity crisis.

"The Borgia family controls the areas of government and religion. They bought, bribed, and blackmailed their way into power in Florence in the fourteenth century. History and rumor tell of the family's sexual proclivities as well as their political ruthlessness.

"Alfons de Borja is the founder of the family's fortunes. He reigned as Pope Callixtus III and was decried as the 'scandal of his age' for his corrupt ways. His nephew, Rodrigo, would be elected Pope Alexander VI in 1492 and was supposedly even worse. Girolamo Priuli, a Venetian diplomat at the time, claimed Pope Alexander had 'given his soul and body to the great demon in Hell'.

"And it doesn't end there. Alexander's children were worse, if their reputations are to be believed. The entire family has been accused of brutal megalomania, aggressive ambition, and brazen self-interest."

The image once again paused to give the group time

to absorb the information and to ask questions.

"From the information presented to us," said the Meglio, "it seems that we are dealing with formidable, historically depraved families who control virtually every aspect of industry and society. They seem to have gained control of every critical area of influence, extending even to areas of education and faith. I can see why the computer has told us that we may be fighting a losing battle. The situation certainly seems dire."

Billy asked, "Okay, we know that they control everything. How does all this relate to the concept of idolatry which Grandma mentioned earlier? She said that Azazel's current weapon is idolatry. I don't see the connection. Can someone explain that to me?"

The prophet responded to Billy's question. "Before I answer, Billy, ask yourself, what is idolatry?"

Billy looked thoughtful for a moment, then answered, "The worship of an object. Something like a statue, or a representation of an animal that people bow down to and look to for their source of power or spiritual help. How does that apply here?"

"It applies because of the first part of your definition. Today we rarely experience or observe idolatry as bowing down to the golden calf or an image of a man. So, we all assume that idolatry is not around today. No one really believes that a wooden statue can answer their prayers. But this is what Azazel apparently knows, that idolatry can take a more subtle and sinister form while still retaining its power to subdue and enslave people.

"Idolatry is the worship of anything we put before God and depend upon for our well-being or as our source of comfort and strength. That means that it can be money, our jobs, our entertainment, our leisure time, education, alcohol, drugs, sex, our health, or our appearance. Any of these things, which are in and of themselves not necessarily evil, can be corrupted and used to enslave people when they become dependent on them, or when they look to them as their source of self-worth, self-esteem, or comfort. Anything can be corrupted into an idol that can be used to enslave people. Azazel knows that."

"Okay," said Ty, "I understand, but how can that be more powerful than the swords? Also, since we changed the timeline, and the world is so much better off than before, how can this be true? People generally have all they need and seem to be happy with the way things are now."

The prophet responded to Ty's question. "The Leviathan Alliance will take all the good that is in the world now, the changes that you initiated, and inspire people to make them into idols through dependence, greed, complacency, and selfishness. When people are well-off, they can become lazy and don't want things to change. They will accept almost anything, pay any price to keep the status quo. It becomes a categorical imperative graven on the heart of society. People have become 'loss averse' and resist surrendering *any* benefit, even to the point of giving up liberty, freedom, and self-determination to retain it. They lose the will and capacity to fight for their rights and become like sheep being led to the slaughter.

"When the transition to dependence is complete, mankind will become enslaved to their 'idols', which the Leviathans control, and they will win. This threat is even more insidious than the last one, because it is subtler and involves using 'good' things in an evil way. Idolatry is not just one of many sins, it is the foundational sin. It is the great sin all others come from.

"Pride was the primary evil we had to fight in our last battle. In the old timeline, the world was in trouble because people did not value anything highly except their own opinion. Virtue and valor were being eliminated and corrupted. Now that the timeline has changed, Azazel will try to make them not only value the things they have but corrupt their appreciation of them into worship of good things, such as peace, prosperity, plenty, leisure, technology, accomplishment, love, money, sex, and even family. This worship will cause division, decay of the nation, self-interest, greed, depravity, corruption, anarchy, and war. He will cause people to value material things instead of God, faith, neighbor, and country.

"People become willing to sacrifice anything on the altar of safety and convenience to keep what they have, even freedom, liberty, and their faith in God. He knew that the changes you made resulted in eliminating many evil events from the timeline. The world since World War II has experienced incredible prosperity and technological advancement. He decided to use that against humanity by corrupting them.

"He knew that the lack of want and strife could be used to lower the guard of the masses. They would become fat, happy, lazy, and dependent on the government. They would forget the lessons of the past. They could be made to despise the glorious achievements of history. So, he apparently formed the Leviathan Alliance by gathering together the wealthiest, most influential, and corrupt families of history, and empowering them to be successful and powerful in various areas of society and industry, thus controlling all means of enslavement. Can you see it now?"

At this point, the image of their grandmother added some color. "The new version of the Apostles, the

Leviathan Alliance, aims to fan the flames of these idolatrous trends. The former families have been replaced with the five new controlling families you have been told about. They answer to Azazel himself. These are families of immense influence and power, who have been enabled by Azazel over the course of history to accumulate vast wealth. Their purpose is to subjugate mankind, through the control of governments, banks, natural resources, the media, entertainment, and the economic engines of society.

"Over the centuries, their power and influence has grown and gone underground. They are now invisible to the world. The only visible parts of this group are the secret clubs, societies, committees, councils, and fraternities. These are where they secretly train future members, form and ratify their plans for world domination, influence world monetary policy, and decide the outcome of elections, coups, and assassinations.

"They follow the age-old formulas of enslavement and control through economic crises, spiritual decay, moral corruption, drug use, and by destroying the sanctity of life. They use 'bread and circuses' to entertain, control, and placate the masses. Their propaganda indoctrinates each generation by infiltrating the educational institutions and global media outlets. They use drugs, alcohol, and sex to create dependence, enslaving and demotivating the people. The Leviathan Alliance has been referred to by many names, but the most recognizable one is the Illuminati. They are actually the ones who propagate that term to misdirect people away from who they really are."

"I have heard of the Illuminati and understand the reference," said Joe. "But the Illuminati, despite some doubts about their intentions, seem to be trying to elevate mankind, to increase knowledge and prosperity, although their methods have always been suspect. The Leviathans apparently want to enslave mankind for their own personal benefit. They seem bent on destruction and control for power's sake."

"That is an accurate observation, Joe," said the image. "Let me show you their reach outside of just the industries and areas of society they control, and maybe you will understand more. Here are the most important groups, organizations, societies, and clubs they control."

The screens in the room displayed the following list:

The Pilgrim Society
Bohemia Grove
The Skull and Bones and related fraternities
The Bilderbergs
The Trilateral Commission
The Council on Foreign Relations
Committee of 300
The Fabian Society
The Club of Rome

"All of these groups are founded by, used, and controlled by the Leviathan Alliance. Within the confines of these groups, the fate of the world is being decided, new world leaders are being trained and indoctrinated, and the enslavement of the world is being implemented."

"How is that possible without the world knowing about it?" asked Robbie. "Why isn't this being reported by the press?"

"Because," replied the Meglio, "the media companies are part of the conspiracy in this timeline. The Leviathans also own them, so they enable the secrecy, and participate in the illusion that these are benign think tanks. Nothing could be further from the truth."

"May I continue?" asked the image.

"Why certainly, dear, please continue your briefing," responded the Meglio.

"As stated earlier, the Leviathans use these groups to identify and train new world leaders. They have six disciplines of training within their families: military, government, spiritual, education, propaganda, and social control.

"The leading candidates for leadership of any major country are carefully chosen from the bloodlines of the five families. A candidate must be of 'Leviathan' blood.

"In this new timeline, since sometime after World War II when their plan began to be implemented, leaders of most nations of the world swear allegiance to serve the will of the Leviathans before they serve their country. The Leviathans own them and ultimately decide what they should or should not do.

"They are under the control of the higher-ranking members of the Leviathans, and this becomes more obvious the higher up the ladder they climb. So, you can see how wide-reaching their influence is, and how far they have infiltrated all areas of society and government," the image finished.

"Thank you, my dear, for that further clarification," responded the Meglio after the image of his beloved wife ended her commentary.

The Meglio then addressed the prophet and the cousins. "You all know that our last battle with the Apostles of Azazel was brought to a head because of the Fourth Turning of the saeculum. As I am sure your uncle explained, the four seasons of the saeculum are an unchangeable rhythm. It is like an eternal metronome marking the times and seasons of the ages. It does not stop or pause due to timeline changes or resets.

"Your efforts in recovering the four stolen Swords of Valor and destroying the Swords of Terror resulted in the resolution of the crisis season in the old timeline, but that has been erased. We have reverted back to a crisis season, and this new crisis must be resolved. Heroes are still needed to address the new threat which once again endangers the liberty and freedom of our nation and the world. You have heard much about the Leviathans, the new families, and the approach they are taking. There is much more to hear. Are you still in? Shall we continue forward?"

The prophet replied, "Without a doubt and without hesitation, my answer is yes."

Robbie answered, "I'm in and ready to do my duty."

Jeff responded, "Count me in. No retreat, no surrender."

Joe, Nick, Billy, and Ty all followed with their endorsement of action.

After they'd all expressed their agreement, the Meglio turned to the image and said, "Catherine, would you please continue with the overview?"

The image replied, "I will, my dear, but it gets worse. I fear you will despair. Are you certain you want to know it all?"

"I do, please continue," said the Meglio. "Tell us more of the Leviathans in this timeline. How might we know them and identify them?"

The image of Catherine obeyed, displaying an image on the screens around the room.

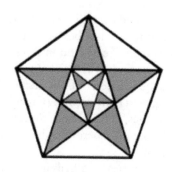

"This emblem is the mark of the Leviathan Alliance in this timeline. As you can see, it is in the overall shape of a pentagon enveloping a pentagram which has an inverted pentagon enveloping another pentagram with a final pentagon in the middle.

"The three colors utilized are gold, red and silver. These colors are symbolic as well. Gold symbolizes wealth, red for blood as in war, and silver as the symbol of betrayal, such as the thirty pieces of silver paid to Judas for his betrayal of Jesus.

"As the colors have meaning, so does the shape. This emblem utilizes sacred geometry to communicate the purpose and objectives of the Leviathan Alliance."

Joe interrupted, "Excuse me, Grandma, may I ask a question?"

"Certainly, Joe," replied the image.

"We have all studied geometry and know what it is, but what is 'sacred geometry'? I am not familiar with that term. Can you explain it to us?"

The image replied, "Of course, Joe, and don't feel bad. Most people don't have a clue about sacred geometry. It is an arcane and obscure practice that has been used for millennia to hide information in plain sight so that only the initiated would recognize it.

"Sacred geometry ascribes symbolic and sacred meanings to certain geometric shapes and specific geometric proportions. It is associated with the belief that a god or God is the geometer of the world. The geometry used in the design and construction of religious structures such as churches, temples, mosques, religious monuments, altars, and tabernacles has sometimes been considered sacred.

"Medieval European cathedrals also incorporated symbolic geometry. Indian and Himalayan spiritual communities often constructed temples and fortifications based on design plans of mandalas and yantras. Sacred geometry is also used in constituting the methods of temple construction and creation of idols, the means of worshiping deities, philosophical doctrines, attainment of six-fold desires, and four kinds of yoga.

"As you can see, the two major geometric figures utilized by the Leviathans in their emblem, the pentagon and the pentagram, represent the five families. The outermost pentagon is gold because wealth is the foundation of their power. The next inner figure is the red pentagram symbolizing war and bloodshed, because that is how they use their wealth to gain power.

"The next inner figure is the inverted silver pentagon. This symbolizes the betrayal of nations through the corrupting and controlling of their leadership. The next figure is the inverted red pentagram. This represents idolatry, satanic influence, and the shedding of innocent blood unrelated to war. Think of street violence, child sacrifice, and abortion, for example. Finally, the innermost figure of a golden pentagon at the heart of it all symbolizes the corruption and enslavement of men's hearts through the love of money, material things, and selfishness.

"That is a summary of the pictorial representation you see, but there is more that is unseen. Believe it or not, this emblem tells us exactly what their philosophy is, their goals and their overarching objectives. My analysis of their utilization of sacred geometry reveals the messages hidden in it. These are their six major principles."

The monitors in the room changed to display the following:

They want complete control for themselves.

They believe man is supreme.

They try to cause division and strife between people, fragmentation, and isolation.

They avoid, disguise, and reject truth, and instead depend on falsehood.

They seek to be the only authority, to reject the accepted moral philosophies of the past, as well as the natural law and natural rights of man.

They seek to raise themselves and their philosophy and authority to a level of religion and worship.

"So, what is the conclusion we can draw from this analysis of the sacred geometry inherent in the emblem of the Leviathan Alliance? The overall spiritual message of this logo and its sacred geometry is atheism, division, and enslavement.

"Ancient cultures were far too wise to fall for this man-centered philosophy. Peoples of ancient times understood from creation there must be a Creator. Some of those cultures were deceived into worshiping gods of wood and stone. But to suggest to them the concept that man alone is the supreme form of life in the universe, and the sole arbiter of what is good, would have brought derision and disrespect immediately. Even the classical Greek philosophers, who did not fear God, were concerned with issues of moral ethics, the virtuous life, and the social good.

"Yet the modern phenomenon of isolated people, self-interest groups pursuing selfish desires, suppressing the witness of God, and living without respect for others or any moral law is not unprecedented. Consider the days of Noah prior to the flood. In Genesis 6:5, it states, 'The Lord saw how great man's wickedness on the earth had become, and that every inclination of the thoughts of their heart was only evil all the time.'

"Those ungodly people were judged for their sin. It is a sober warning not to be taken lightly. People can pretend there is no God, but they find out in the end what a great mistake that is. In Genesis 6:6-7, we read, 'The Lord was grieved that He had made man upon the earth, and His heart was filled with pain. So, the Lord said, 'I will wipe mankind, whom I have created, from the face of the earth... for I am grieved that I have made them.'"

"Wow!" exclaimed Jeff. "There is so much more to this than I thought. I assumed all we were dealing with were a group of wealthy, evil families playing with the world like it was a game of Monopoly, desperately trying for dominion through manipulation and greed. But this throws a whole new light on the picture. We really are dealing with not only material issues and challenges, but spiritual ones, too."

"That's right, Jeff," replied the Meglio. "You see it clearly. That, I am sure, is what your grandmother feared to tell us. This conspiracy goes to the very heart and soul of man. Azazel is not just looking to enslave mankind economically and physically, he wants to enslave them spiritually, as well. He has raised the stakes. His purpose is to make the Leviathans the rulers of the earth, and himself the god of all mankind."

"You are correct, my dear," said the image. "Their goal is total domination and subjugation of the world. They have reached a point where they control enough governments, engines of society, and resources that they can now close the trap. They believe they can do this without firing a shot. They have manipulated society to the point where they believe the people will not only accept their bondage but welcome it."

Ty spoke up. "I still don't understand how this can happen. How could the people of this country possibly accept slavery and bondage to a group of elite autocrats? How could they hand over their freedom, liberty, and sovereignty?"

The image responded, "Ty, you are thinking of your old timeline again. In that world, it would have been nearly impossible. We can agree on that. But that old timeline is gone. Remember, you destroyed the Swords of Terror and changed time by one day. In doing so, some terrible and evil events have been removed from the timeline, and the new world of this timeline is experiencing more peace and prosperity than ever before. This has caused people to become complacent and apathetic. They have lost the fire and desire for liberty and freedom and are now like sheep ready for the slaughter. All they care about is material things, entertainment, celebrities, comfort, leisure time, and government entitlements. Natural and healthy levels of fear and wariness are at an all-time low. They have a form of virtue without the power. They have a form of generosity without the sacrifice. They have no survival instincts. Their media and news are all opinion and posturing designed to push the agenda of the Leviathans, or to placate them with entertainment. They have education without understanding, and they have forgotten the lessons of the past.

"The history that is taught to the people has been modified to promote and glorify the things the Leviathans want the masses to believe. Old heroes are vilified. Heroic deeds are mischaracterized as evil, and even the Founding Fathers are being demonized and denigrated. Biblical truths are laughed at and portrayed as hate speech. Valor is withering away from lack of use. Courage has been redefined to mean the opposite of its true definition.

"Courage has always been coupled with self-sacrifice and compassion. In this timeline, it is coupled with self-interest and comfort. They have given up true liberty for complacency, apathy, and dependence on gifts from the public treasury. This is what is happening in the timeline you have all created. Ty, you ask how this can happen. I will tell you that this has happened before in history. But the people of this timeline do not remember history and therefore cannot learn from it. If they valued the lessons of history, there are plenty of warnings for them to heed.

"One of the most eloquent examples of these warnings came from Alexander Fraser Tytler, Lord Woodhouselee. He observed that 'Any democracy is always temporary in nature; it simply cannot exist as a permanent form of government. A democracy will continue to exist up until the time that voters discover they can vote themselves generous gifts from the public treasury. From that moment on, the majority always votes for the candidates who promise the most benefits from the public treasury, with the result that every democracy will finally collapse because of loose fiscal policy, which is always followed by a dictatorship.'

"The average age of the world's greatest civilizations

from the beginning of history has been about two hundred years. During that time, these nations always progressed through a specific sequence."

Everyone looked at the screens, which displayed the following:

1. *From bondage to spiritual faith*
2. *From spiritual faith to great courage*
3. *From courage to liberty*
4. *From liberty to abundance*
5. *From abundance to complacency*
6. *From complacency to apathy*
7. *From apathy to dependence*
8. *From dependence back into bondage*

"The people of this country are in the second half of the seventh stage. They have moved from apathy to dependence and are in danger of becoming slaves, of putting themselves into bondage to the idols of money, sex, entertainment, success, achievement, power, drugs, escapism, and self-interest.

"The Leviathans feed these desires by controlling advertising and the media, entertainment companies, technology, and social media. They also control the manufacture, distribution, and farming of food, and the drug trade. They control most water supplies in all countries. Once their control has been solidified, they will reveal themselves to the world and announce that the World Order of the Leviathans has arrived. There will be no escape. They will use the current 'crisis turning', which has not gone away, to increase chaos in the world and impose martial law in all countries.

"When the timeline was changed, there were benefits, but the benefits of diminished strife and increased prosperity were used by the Leviathans to lull the masses into a false sense of security, carelessness about their freedoms, and apathy. The situation is dire."

The Meglio interrupted. "Let me tell you all a story which may illuminate the point your grandmother makes. It is a story I was told by my mother, your great-grandmother Rose. It will illustrate how and why this has happened.

"Once, a little boy was playing outdoors and found a fascinating caterpillar. He carefully picked it up and took it home to show his mother. He asked his mother if he could keep it, and she said he could, if he would take good care of it. The little boy got a large jar and put plants to eat, and a stick to climb on in the jar. Every day, he watched the caterpillar and brought it new plants to eat.

"One day, the caterpillar climbed up the stick and started acting strangely. The boy worriedly called his mother who came and understood that the caterpillar was creating a cocoon. The mother explained to the boy how the caterpillar was going to go through a metamorphosis and become a butterfly.

"The little boy was thrilled to hear about the changes his caterpillar would go through. He watched every day, waiting for the butterfly to emerge. One day, it happened; a small hole appeared in the cocoon and the butterfly started to struggle to come out.

"At first the boy was excited, but soon he became concerned. The butterfly was struggling so hard to get out! It looked like it couldn't break free! It looked desperate! It looked like it was making no progress!

"The boy was so concerned, he decided to help. He ran to get scissors. He snipped the cocoon to make the hole bigger, and the butterfly quickly emerged!

"As the butterfly came out, the boy was surprised. It

had a swollen body and small, shriveled wings. He continued to watch the butterfly, expecting that at any moment, the wings would dry out, enlarge, and expand to support the swollen body. He knew that in time the body would shrink, and the butterfly's wings would expand. But neither happened!

"The butterfly spent the rest of its life crawling around with a swollen body and shriveled wings. It was never able to fly.

"As the boy tried to figure out what had gone wrong, his mother took him to talk to a scientist from a local college. He learned that the butterfly was *supposed* to struggle. In fact, the butterfly's struggle to push its way through the tiny opening of the cocoon pushes the fluid out of its body and into its wings.

"Without the struggle, the butterfly would never fly. The boy's good intentions hurt the butterfly. The lesson is that struggling is an important part of any growth experience. In fact, it is the struggle that causes you to develop your ability to fly."

"We are responsible for the state of the world, because our collective actions changed the timeline. We removed the struggle, and now the nation is bloated and incapable of defending its freedom and its liberty."

The image spoke, "I always loved that story, darling, and it always reminded me what a kind and wise woman your mother was. May I add some final quotes to buttress your point?"

"Please do, my dear, and then we will need to begin making our plans," replied the Meglio.

The image began, "The great writer and historian of this timeline, Alexis de Tocqueville, observed the following: 'When the taste for physical gratifications among them has grown more rapidly than their education, the time will come when men are carried away and lose all self-restraint. It is not necessary to do violence to such a people in order to strip them of the rights they enjoy; they themselves willingly loosen their hold. They neglect their chief business, which is to remain their own masters.'

"He also said that 'Society will develop a new kind of servitude which covers the surface of society with a network of complicated rules, through which the most original minds and the most energetic characters cannot penetrate. It does not tyrannize, but it compresses, enervates, extinguishes, and stupefies a people, till each nation is reduced to nothing better than a flock of timid and industrious animals, of which the government is the shepherd.'"

"Thank you for that information, Catherine, it makes the point exactly."

Then he turned to the cousins and the prophet and said, "Since we have inadvertently caused this situation, I believe it is your... no, it is *our* duty, to make every effort to correct it. We must work together to develop a plan to change the course of history once again, or to do something to alert the nation. We need to inspire it to recapture the fire of liberty and freedom they once had and break the chains that are swiftly closing upon them. Let us begin without delay."

Ty raised his hand. "May I ask a question?"

"Yes, certainly," replied the Meglio.

"Thanks," said Ty. "Before we make plans to change time once again and save the entire world from physical and spiritual enslavement, may I take a quick bathroom break?"

This broke the tension in the room a bit, and they all laughed. Even the image of their grandmother appeared to have a smile on her holographic face.

"Certainly, Ty," replied the Meglio. "All of you, take a break, stretch your legs, and meet back here in ten minutes prepared to use those very expensive, highly educated, and underused brains of yours."

CHAPTER THREE

THE PLAN
IS BORN

Robbie rose from his seat along with the others and stretched a bit. He stood with Billy and Joe as everyone gathered in small groups to discuss the information they had just received and its implications. As they talked, they discussed the challenges that this new threat presented. Robbie knew that a detailed plan was necessary, but it seemed none of them could immediately visualize the critical point of weakness in the Leviathan Alliance's plans. It had been developed over the course of millennia with all the chess pieces carefully and skillfully moved into position in the last seventy years. The trap was ready to close.

As he wracked his brain trying to envision a solution, Robbie heard Nick shouting in the outer room. He led the way as they rushed to join Nick, who was standing still, staring at the glass sword case.

"Grandpa," Nick stammered, "When we entered, wasn't the only sword in the case the Sword of Don Quixote?"

Robbie looked at the case and saw that it now contained their six Swords of Valor, along with Grandpa's sword.

"It would appear, my heroic grandsons, that the swords have chosen to return to us in our time of need," stated the Meglio.

The prophet replied, "How can that be, Dad? When the Swords of Valor destroyed their counterpart Swords of Terror, they returned to their rightful owners and proper place in time. How and why are they back with us now?"

"As I reminded you in our earlier discussion," responded the Meglio, "the boys are connected to the swords on the quantum level, and their DNA became a part of the swords during the initiation ceremony. The combination of those connections makes them and the swords a part of each other. Therefore, I believe that the swords 'read' our heroes' hearts and minds as they listened to the information from the quantum computer. Then the swords reacted to their concerns and fears and returned to make themselves and their virtue available once again. That's my guess, anyway."

He turned and addressed the cousins, "Gentlemen, please retrieve your swords and join us back at the table. We must begin the planning process."

Robbie approached the sword case with the others. Reverently, he removed Braveheart, the Sword of William Wallace. He hoped it would once again imbue him with its characteristics of persistence and fortitude. He then stepped back to observe as each cousin retrieved the specific sword that belonged to him.

Billy reached in and removed Durandal, the Sword of Roland, the sword symbolizing temperance and diligence. Jeff was next and removed the Sword of Solomon that symbolized wisdom and faith. Next was Joe, who retrieved the sword Excalibur, the Sword of both Melchizedek and Arthur symbolizing benevolence and love. Nick followed and gathered up the Sword of Michael the Archangel, which symbolized justice and courage. Finally, Ty laid hold of Joyeuse, the Sword of Charlemagne, which symbolized generosity and ethics.

As Robbie stood holding his sword once again, he felt the virtue and valor inherent in it flowing into his body. He felt its power and influence returning, energizing him, and sharpening his senses and his mind. He felt as if a long-lost friend had just returned to him.

"Wow," Joe declared. "What a great feeling! I didn't realize how much I missed holding Excalibur. I think I took it for granted last time."

"Me too," Robbie concurred. "Last time we held them we were moving from one mission to the next without stopping, adrenaline flowing, all stressed out, and I don't think I had a moment to appreciate the feeling. This is really cool!"

The others agreed with Robbie's assessment. They proceeded to the Tech Room, taking their seats around the table with their swords.

"Now that you are all here, let's get down to business," stated the Meglio. "Catherine, we are ready to begin the planning process, please join us."

The image appeared and said, "I see that you have all found the gifts I left for you."

The Meglio replied, "Excuse me, dear, but what do you mean when you say, the gifts *you* left for them?"

The image smiled and revealed, "I summoned them, my love. I could not have you going out there against the Leviathans unarmed, now could I?"

"How did you do that, Mom?" asked the prophet. "I was unaware that the quantum computer had that ability."

"Robert," replied the image, "when will you learn

that your mother is capable of much more than you give her credit for? A mother's love can work miracles, especially when powered by the quantum field. Just accept the gift, do not ask too many questions, and all will be well."

"Thank you, Catherine," said the Meglio, "we appreciate the gift of the swords." Then he addressed the group.

"As you remember, during the last crisis, you were all working from a plan that I had developed over decades. It was detailed and well-researched, and it was ultimately successful. It was not perfect, but combined with your resourcefulness and effort, the desired result was achieved. This time, we do not have decades to develop a plan. We will have to construct it on the fly, so there will need to be more flexibility and adjustments made along the way. To do this, we need a lot of information and perspective.

"We have already started with understanding the Leviathan Alliance as an organization, how they operate, what they control, how they indoctrinate members, and what their motives and goals are. You have been briefed on the meaning inherent in their emblem and in their philosophy. We know who the main families are, their elite organizations, and the general areas of society that they control."

Jeff interrupted the Meglio, "Excuse me, Grandpa, may I ask a question at this point?"

"Of course, Jeff, ask away."

"I am still unclear how they were able to actually influence society. I mean, I get that they control all the media and education outlets, but what form did that take? Where did they get their outline, their game plan, and how did they disseminate it? What were some of the tools they used to 'soften up' the people to such a point that they could accept the idea of tyrannical control and the abandonment of freedom?"

"That is an intelligent and thoughtful question, Jeff," replied the Meglio. "I'm not sure there is a clear answer I can give you, so I'll ask your grandmother try to enlighten us. Catherine, would you like to take a shot at answering Jeff's question? Has your comparative analysis uncovered enough to help us understand?"

The image replied, "I am learning more every minute. I am analyzing history as we speak, and answers will come over time, but I believe I might have gained some useful insight. It seems they used the writings of some of the greatest men in history to, in effect, 'reverse engineer' democracy, freedom, and liberty. They studied the most important writings produced about how freedom and liberty originate, are sustained, and how they could be lost. Then, they put together a plan to counteract the constructive components and implement the destructive pieces. I have already given you a couple of quotes by Alexis de Tocqueville. He was one of the men whose writings the Leviathans apparently studied intensely. Let me expand on my earlier comments.

"'Tocqueville warned that modern democracy may be adept at inventing new forms of tyranny, because radical equality could lead to the materialism of an expanding 'elite class' and to the selfishness of individualism. He wrote, 'In such conditions, we might become so enamored with a relaxed love of present enjoyments that we lose interest in the future of our descendants and meekly allow ourselves to be led in ignorance by a despotic force made even more powerful because it does not resemble one.'

"Tocqueville also wrote, '…if despotism were to

take root in a modern democracy, it would be a much more dangerous version than the oppression under the Roman emperors or tyrants of the past who could only exert a pernicious influence on a small group of people at a time.'

"He further explained that in contrast to the oppression of ancient times, despotism under a democracy could see '…a multitude of men, uniformly alike, equal, constantly circling for petty pleasures, unaware of and unconcerned for fellow citizens, and subject to the will of a powerful state which exerted an immense protective power.'

"Tocqueville compared a potentially despotic democratic government to a protective parent who wants to keep its citizens as 'perpetual children'. One which doesn't break men's wills but rather guides them and presides over people in the same way as a shepherd looking after a 'flock of timid animals'.

"It appears that the Leviathans took these words to heart and utilized much of it in the formation of a game plan to do just what Tocqueville warned against," finished the image.

"Thank you, my dear," said the Meglio. "It appears that the Leviathans understand the truth, wisdom, and warnings in the writings of Alexis de Tocqueville and other writers such as Alexander Fraser Tytler, Lord Woodhouselee, whose 'fatal sequence' was presented to us earlier. They, in fact, have been planning to take advantage of these truths and are using them as a template for domination and enslavement of mankind. They have facilitated 'the taste for physical gratifications', the demise of education, lack of self-restraint, materialism, the relaxed love of present enjoyments, and the immense protective power of governments. They will now use these things to close the trap.

"Our plan will require that we completely understand the current status of the Leviathans' plan, where they have power, the historical figures that inspired the foundation of the plan, and how to negate those influences. It occurs to me that we should use the same methodology. We need to reverse engineer their reverse engineering.

"Let's identify the great thinkers of democracy and freedom and consider enlisting their brains and perspective in our cause. We must identify the historical figures that could help us understand how to counteract the effects of what Azazel has put in place. We may need to go back in history to times when the light of liberty and freedom shone brightest.

"Finally, always remember that we are not just fighting against flesh and blood, but against principalities, against powers, against the rulers of the darkness of this world, against spiritual wickedness in high places. We need to be keenly aware that this is a combined effort of evil men and the Watcher Azazel. We must somehow address both the physical and spiritual aspects of this threat. Are there any questions at this point?" the Meglio asked the team.

Joe raised his hand. "We have been told that the Leviathans 'reverse engineered' democracy, freedom and liberty. Can you explain that in more detail?"

"Absolutely," replied the Meglio. "Think of it in this way; if you wanted to knock down a building, what would be the most important part to compromise?"

Joe responded, "I suppose it would be the foundation."

"That is correct," replied the Meglio. "Once you have decided to attack the foundation, assuming you had limited resources, where would you focus your destructive efforts?"

"I would focus the destructive energy on either the weakest points or the 'pillars' of the foundation. The most critical structural parts," replied Joe.

"Once again, you are correct," agreed the Meglio. "And what would you use to identify those critical points in the foundation, and how would you know how much energy to apply to each of them?"

Ty's hand shot up. "I know, I know! You could look up the plans for the building on the internet!"

The cousins rolled their eyes.

"What?" he asked them, then turned back to the Meglio. "Grandpa, that's correct, isn't it?"

"You are essentially correct, Ty," replied his grandfather. "You would have to consult the architectural plans of the building. But I doubt that the Leviathan Alliance used the internet for this one.

"To get access to the plans, you would need to go to the source, the architect himself. He would know the vulnerabilities in the foundation and in the building. They would have researched and utilized the writings of the greatest minds in history who dealt with the building, maintenance, and growth of democracy, freedom, and liberty. We need to identify those great architects.

"If we can speak to them and tell them of our problem, just like any common architect, they will know what parts of the building to reinforce, protect, and monitor to ensure the ongoing integrity of the building. Understand?"

"Got it, Grandpa," replied Joe. "How are we going to identify them when it could have been any one of hundreds of people? So many people have written eloquently on these subjects. How will we know which ones to choose?"

"That will be the responsibility of the quantum computer. As you know, it is currently running an ongoing comparative analysis of the two timelines to identify aberrations and differences. It is also simultaneously breaking down all the information available on the Leviathan Alliance and their plan. I am hopeful that it will be able to identify the 'fingerprints' of their strategy."

"Fingerprints?" asked Robbie. "What do you mean by fingerprints?"

"I am referring to the influencers. Whose writings did they rely on most heavily? Which ones did they deem most critical to their reverse engineering efforts? Which ones gave them the most insight as to the true makeup of freedom, liberty, and democracy, and their vulnerabilities?"

"I get it, Grandpa," said Jeff. "If we can identify whose writings they depended upon, we can then go back in time, now that we have our swords back, and interview them. Hopefully, we can get them to help us fight against the Leviathans' efforts."

"Exactly," agreed the Meglio. "That is what the quantum computer will do." Then he addressed the computer. "Catherine, my dear, would you please tell us what you have discovered relating to the 'fingerprints' of the Leviathans' plan?"

"Certainly, my love," replied the image. "I do not yet have a complete list, but I have identified a few clearly. It appears they used some very credible sources. Here is the list I have so far.

"The first is Marcus Tullius Cicero. Next, they relied heavily on the writings of Benjamin Franklin and Samuel Adams. The last that I have been able to identify up to this point is our old friend, Alexis de Tocqueville. I am certain of these findings, but I am also certain there are other influences that yet elude me. My research will continue."

"Wonderful work, my dear," replied the Meglio. "You have given us some appropriate names from which we can develop our strategies. We will begin the discussion now."

"It seems clear to me," said the prophet, "that we should start at the beginning. Marcus Tullius Cicero was one of the first and most prolific of all the observers and commentators on the topic of liberty and of the republican form of government. He lived at a time when the Republic of Rome was on its way to becoming a dictatorship. I am sure that he would give us some amazing insight as to how he fought against it, and how the Roman Republic was so easily corrupted."

"I agree," said the Meglio. "It is the optimal place to start. Let's identify that as our first mission. Then from there, let's continue in ascending order of time.

"The second mission should be to visit with Franklin and Adams. They built a democratic republic from the ground up. If anyone can counsel us as to the critical components and vulnerabilities, it will be them. I do not believe you could find a fiercer defender of liberty and freedom than Samuel Adams, and Franklin was truly a 'Renaissance man'. His intellect and common sense were critical to the foundation of our republic. Two wonderful counselors, I say!"

"So, the third mission would be to visit with Tocqueville, correct?" asked Jeff. "Since he lived in the 1800s, he would have had a chance to observe how the American Experiment was progressing and identify any flaws or cracks in the foundation from that time. He also experienced the difficulties with the French Revolution and its aftermath, so he can even give us perspective on two newly created democracies, and how they were progressing. I think that is perfect."

"Excellent observation, Jeff, but I will reserve judgment on that until after the first two missions. I see your University of Pennsylvania education did not go to waste. Isn't there a statue of Ben Franklin on the U. of P. campus?"

"Absolutely, Grandpa," Jeff replied. "I hope I get chosen by the swords for that mission."

"I hope so, too," replied the Meglio, "I am sure the wisdom inherent in your sword will be helpful. But as you remember from your last campaign against the Apostles, the swords will choose only the persons and the swords needed to accomplish the mission. We will never be sure until after the leaving protocols. I hope you get your wish."

Then he addressed the rest of the team, "It appears that we have an outline for our first two missions. Take a break, and we will reconvene here in ten minutes to flesh out the details, identify the date you will return to, and the specific location. This first mission to ancient Rome will be very difficult and challenging, so begin now to mentally prepare yourselves for it."

The cousins rose from the table to discuss between themselves all they knew about ancient Rome. As they left the room, Robbie saw his grandfather and father in deep conversation with the image of his grandmother. Resisting the urge to eavesdrop on their discussion, he turned and joined his brother and cousins in the next room.

CHAPTER FOUR

THE ROMAN REPUBLIC

When the break was over, the cousins joined the Meglio and the prophet at the round table. When everyone was seated, the Meglio addressed them.

"The prophet and I have been consulting with the quantum computer to narrow down the choices for an optimal return date. We found it difficult because, as you know, when you leave this time, you only have until sunrise on the day following your arrival to complete your mission. That means we must be as precise as possible to maximize both your likelihood of encountering Cicero and successfully completing the mission. The computer will continue to evaluate the options while we examine what we know about Cicero. Before we begin, are there any questions?"

"I have a question," Ty spoke up. "I know we also need to pick a location. If it is so hard to identify a date, won't the location be just as hard?"

"Not necessarily, Ty," replied the Meglio. "If we can identify a date, we have a pretty good idea of what Cicero was doing in many instances, since the records he left are quite detailed. Part of what makes the dates so difficult is the differences in the calendars between now and then. The conversion factors have to be precise."

Then he addressed the holographic image of his wife. "Dear, would you please begin telling us what we need to know about Cicero?"

"Certainly," the image answered. "Marcus Tullius Cicero was a Roman orator, statesman, and writer. He was born on January 6, 106 BC at either Arpinum or Sora, seventy miles southeast of Rome, in the Volscian mountains. His family was affluent. Cicero died on December 7, 43 BC, trying to escape Rome by sea. It would be nearly impossible to overestimate the influence that Cicero has had on western literature and culture.

"As a young man, Cicero was sent to Rome to study law under Quintus Mucius Scaevola Augur, who was the equivalent 'Cicero' of his day. He also studied philosophy under Philo, who had been head of the Academy at Athens, and the stoic Diodotus. However, Cicero's early life was not sheltered behind books and learning. At the age of seventeen, he served in the Social War under Pompey the Great's father. It was during this period of political upheaval in Rome, the 80s BC, that Cicero finished his formal education.

"However, that is not to say that Cicero stopped his learning. In 79 BC, he left Rome for two years abroad, with the aim of improving his health and studying further. In Athens, he was taught by masterful Greek rhetoricians and philosophers. It was during this time that Cicero married his first wife, Terentia. After he returned to Rome in 77 BC, he was voted quaestor at the minimum age of thirty. His rise to power progressed quickly.

"In 69 BC, Cicero was named aedile, which was an office of the Roman Republic. Based in Rome, the aediles were responsible for maintenance of public buildings and regulation of public festivals.

"In 66 BC, Cicero became praetor, again at the minimum age, which was forty. A praetor was a judicial officer who had broad authority, was responsible for the production of the public games, and, in the absence of consuls, exercised extensive authority in the government.

"Between 66 and 63 BC, Cicero's political views became more conservative, especially in contrast to the dangerous social reforms being proposed by Julius Caesar, Gaius Antonius, and Catiline, known as the Triumvirate. Cicero's success is born by the fact that he received the consulship of 63 to 62 BC, once again at the minimum age of forty-two.

"A consul was the highest elected political office of the Roman Republic, and the consulship was considered the highest level of the ascending sequence of public offices to which politicians aspired. Each year, two consuls were elected together. This could be compared to our president and vice president with the presidency determined by the one who got the most votes. They served for a one-year term.

"It was during his time as consul that Cicero successfully exposed the Catalinian revolution, and under the power of the Senate, put to death the revolutionaries who had survived up until that point.

"The Republic was in a crisis. Roman political order was in chaos. There was street violence and rioting. The Roman citizenry was falling victim to moral decay. The Catalinian revolution that Cicero exposed was a conspiracy led by the prominent senator Lucius Sergius Catiline to overthrow the elected Roman leadership. This led to Marcus Cato calling Cicero *pater patriase*, or the 'father of his country'.

"Many believed that it was only a matter of time

before the Republic would fall. It was then that three men, often referred to as 'the Gang of Three', seized the opportunity for personal gain, forming an alliance now known as the First Triumvirate that would eventually transform the government from a republic into a dictatorship. Despite individual differences and animosity, this three-headed monster would remain in control using bribes and threats, to dominate both the consulship and military commands.

"The three men who would change the face of Roman politics were Gaius Pompeius Magnus, also called Pompey the Great, Marcus Lucinius Crassus, and Gaius Julius Caesar. Each man had his own personal reason for joining together, realizing that he could not achieve total power alone. They even invited Cicero to join them, but he refused. So, in 60 BC, the three men combined their resources, set aside their personal differences, and seized control of the state.

"Cicero was not involved in the conspiracy against Caesar in 44 BC, though he strongly approved of it. After Caesar's assassination, he took a major part in establishing a compromise between Mark Antony and those who killed Caesar. Before long, he concluded that Antony was as great a threat to liberty as Caesar had been. In December 43 BC, Cicero met his death at the hands of Antony's men with courage and dignity.

"As a politician, Cicero was ultimately unsuccessful. He was not able to prevent the overthrow of the republican system of government. It is in his speeches and his writings that Cicero's legacy truly lies."

At this point, the image paused to ask, "Are there any questions?"

Billy inquired, "So with all of Cicero's influence, contacts, intelligence, and power, he still could not prevent what was apparently inevitable. What can we possibly learn from him? We are faced with a situation that may be as inevitable as the one he faced. Shouldn't we be talking to someone who was successful in preventing the collapse of a republic?"

The Meglio responded to Billy's question. "I understand your observation, Billy, and why you would have that concern, but just because someone cannot prevent something terrible and damaging from happening doesn't mean that they don't have a valuable perspective. If Cicero could have understood what was happening a few years earlier, he might have been able to influence the people to rise up against it, or at least alert them and wake them up. By the time he was certain of the intentions of those involved, the Gang of Three had become too powerful.

"Additionally, he did not have the power of the swords. Time travel is an incredibly valuable asset. We know that we can change history. For example, if he had been able to do something to prevent Julius Caesar from crossing the Rubicon, history could have taken a different turn. So, have faith in the process, and believe in the power of the swords."

"I understand," said Joe, "but it just seems like a hopeless case. I am starting to feel a little overwhelmed by the extent of the task at hand and the apparently inevitable progress of the Leviathans. They seem to be already at checkmate. I will put every effort into this, but I am still concerned."

"I am sure that when we have a defined mission, you will start feeling better," said the Meglio. "So, why don't we try to identify a date and place for you all to return to?"

Then, he addressed the image. "Catherine, please

help us identify an appropriate date for the mission to target."

"As you wish, my love," replied the image. "There are a few options. We can return to the time of Cicero's death, since that is well documented. We know where it took place and the date. Unfortunately, there was so much movement and activity surrounding it, that I fear that there would not be enough time to acquire the needed information before he was killed. In addition, there is a very high probability that the timeline would be affected by your actions.

"The second choice would be his marriage to Terentia when he was in Greece. But that was before all the changes in the Republic started, and therefore his perspective would not be as valuable.

"So, after all the analysis, it would seem that the optimal time would be 65 BC, after Cicero became consul. We know that at that time he was almost continually in Rome. He would have been very visible and at the height of his power. Additionally, he was fully aware of the ambitions of Julius Caesar, Crassus, and Pompey. This is the time I believe he finally realized that the Republic was in mortal danger, and he would have the perspective with which to give the most insightful and effective information."

"That seems to be a valuable observation, my dear; 65 BC seems like the obvious choice," said the Meglio. "However, we will still need to identify a specific location. Do you have any perspective to share on that?"

"I do, my love," replied the image. "But with the millennia of time between now and then, and the changes in the landscape involved, I am left with only one choice. I would recommend that the boys return to the Roman Forum in 65 BC. As you all know, the Roman Forum has been excavated and the ruins preserved to such an extent that we can clearly identify where the various buildings that existed during the time of Cicero were positioned. We can identify with reasonable certainty where the target should be, based on the current layout of the ruins."

"Excellent!" exclaimed the Meglio. "Then our target will be the Roman Forum in 65 BC. We are almost there. To complete the outline, we need a date. Have you been able to narrow that down for us, my dear?"

"Alas, my love, I have not," replied the image. "None of the records that I have researched indicate specific days of the month for any of Cicero's activities. The references are so general that targeting a specific date is impossible. We will need to rely on your instincts and the influence of the swords."

"We will be sending our heroes far back into the ancient past," observed the prophet. "That is dangerous enough even with accurate information. Arbitrarily choosing a date is madness. Maybe we need to abandon the idea of consulting Cicero and choose another option."

"I suppose that's a reasonable idea," replied the Meglio. "However, Cicero will provide us with a unique and singular opportunity to understand the mind of an ancient participant in one of the first experiments in freedom. The Roman Republic was the first flame of what later became the foundational fire of our own American experiment. There is no one else for us to turn to. He is the optimal and only choice.

"I recommend that we do as your grandmother suggests and use our intellect, intuition, and the influence of the swords which are now returned to us. Let's proceed with all confidence and see what fate holds for us. Are we agreed?"

"I say we go for it," said Ty. "The swords have

always led us to success, and I see no reason to doubt their influence now."

"I agree with Ty," agreed Robbie. "Our participation in the battle of Thermopylae was also an unexpected and dangerous occurrence, and the swords helped us to survive that. Shouldn't we take that as an indication of their abilities?"

Joe concurred. "We should. That was a powerful experience. I say we go forward. No fear!"

Jeff nodded his agreement, along with Billy and Nick.

The Meglio smiled. "Thank you all for your bravery in accepting this mission. On past missions, you have faced fear together and won. I feel strongly that you will prevail in this mission as well."

He turned to the prophet. "Robert, have we addressed your particular concerns? Are you willing to move forward in our discussion?"

"Yes," replied the prophet, "for the moment. I would like to reserve the option to disagree after hearing about the remaining details."

"So, since we have a provisional consensus," observed the Meglio, "let's begin the decision-making process with what we already know. We are targeting sometime in 65 BC, and our location is the Roman Forum. We know that the Senate House, government offices, tribunals, temples, memorials, and statues occupied the area, and it was where all the government activity took place, as well as the most important religious ceremonies.

"Given that Cicero was a high-ranking government official in 65 BC, we have high confidence that he would have been there almost every day conducting his duties. Additionally, it was where he would have gone to worship on the days the government was not in session. Finally, it is well-known that Cicero had a substantial home on the Palatine Hill overlooking the Forum. It is likely that when he was not in the Forum, he was there. So, as I see it, any date that the swords choose will provide a reasonable likelihood of encountering Cicero. Let's now discuss the specifics, identify an appropriate area of the Forum to target, and what time of day to start the mission."

The group discussed the options, the layout of the Forum, as well as the various positives and negatives of the times of day to arrive. After exhausting all options and possibilities, the plan was nearly complete. With the quantum computer, they had identified and targeted an open area of the Forum that appeared to be a plaza of some sort near the Fountain of Juturna, the Temple of Vesta, and the Regia. This seemed to be the best target. It would give them room for error and the possibility of appearing unnoticed.

The Meglio continued the discussion. "Now that we have identified the location, once again we must determine the time of day for your arrival. As you remember, you must complete your mission before the sun rises on the day after you arrive. It is currently a limitation of the swords. It is also very wise to limit your presence in another time as there are so many ways that you can inadvertently alter history. Even a slight, apparently inconsequential change can have huge consequences.

"You experienced that on your last mission when you saved the life of Leonidas and gave him one more day of life. That one change resulted in me being here with you today, which I am very happy about, but also it caused our current crisis. You must give yourselves enough time to accomplish the mission, but no more. Get there, do your job, and then get out of there. Understood?"

"We do understand," replied Robbie. "Believe me, Grandpa, the last thing we want at this point is more timeline changes. I think we learned how unpredictable the results can be. I propose that we arrive sometime mid-morning when the Forum may be beginning to bustle and come to life. I don't want to get there under the cover of darkness when we are not familiar with the surroundings. For this mission, I think that is best."

"I agree," said Ty. "maybe we can catch up with Cicero as he is leaving the Senate."

"Good point," the Meglio replied, "but you will have to be able to identify Cicero. Let's ask the computer for a physical description."

"There is not much on him," stated the image. "In 65 BC, he was forty-one years old, of average height, and had begun to gain back some of the weight he'd lost during the stressful times ten years earlier. Beyond that, we only have marble busts to draw our conclusions from.

"Those indicate that he had an aquiline nose, close set eyes, ears that were slightly too large for his head, a smaller mouth with thin lips, and a narrow chin with a prominent cleft. He apparently wore his hair cropped short in classic Roman style.

"It will be a challenge to distinguish him from his contemporaries, and you will have to rely on your skills of observation and inference. I am sorry that the records do not provide more exact information." The image put a composite picture of what Cicero might look like on the monitors for them to memorize.

"What you have given us will have to do," the Meglio said to the image. Then he returned his attention to the cousins.

"It appears we have a solid outline. You will return

to the site of the Roman Forum targeting the plaza near the Fountain of Juturna, the Temple of Vesta, and the Regia. The date will be determined by the swords in 65 BC. You will arrive mid-morning around 11:00 local time and have until sunrise the next morning to complete your mission. You will find Cicero as soon as possible, convince him to meet with you, and gain from him insight into the establishment of a Republic, the foundational necessities, the weaknesses, and if possible, some suggestions as to how we can fight against the threat that the Leviathan Alliance poses to freedom and liberty in our time. Is everyone in agreement?"

Each of the heroes nodded his agreement.

The prophet, however, hesitated again, and the Meglio turned to address him.

"Rob, I did not hear your agreement. Do you still have concerns or observations you would like to have addressed?"

"I do," replied the prophet. "I do not like this plan one bit. I understand what we are trying to accomplish, and that perhaps this is the wisest place to start. But we are sending the boys to ancient Rome with a very thin outline and a makeshift plan. You had years to develop the plans for their last missions. This one took us about two hours. We are sending them into the heart of ancient Rome! The Forum was effectively the epicenter of the Roman world. It is equivalent to sending them to the seat of our government in Washington, D.C. We really do not have any idea of what the security in the area was like, what access they will have to Cicero, or what kind of personal security Cicero himself will have. It will be like trying to get to the President of the United States. I would like more time to work through the details."

"I understand your concerns, Robert," replied the

Meglio, "but once again, I fear you are showing a lack of trust. Remember that we are not sending our children out there alone. They have the swords. You all filled me in on the influence the swords had on them while they were on their last four missions. We have seen that the swords possess qualities and powers that we are just now coming to understand. We learn more about them on every mission.

"If our heroes trust the leading of the swords and follow the plan with good intentions, I believe they will be led to their objectives and be successful. No plan is perfect, and you observed how they had to adjust on the fly last time. We must expect that they will have to do so again. But they will succeed. They will come back to us. This I assure you. Will you trust me?"

The Meglio sensed that the prophet was still not fully convinced. He knew that his son had always had a problem with trust, which stemmed from his need for control. As a neurologist, he made the final diagnoses. He constructed the treatment plans. He alone was responsible for the results. The Meglio knew that this situation was different, and it would take time for his son to be comfortable with it. The one thing that the Meglio was certain of was that Robert had always valued and accepted his advice, and it had never led him astray. He hoped his son would rely on that.

The Meglio folded his hands in front of him and leaned forward. "Robert, I have to ask you to put aside your concerns for the moment and trust me once again. Can you do that? Can you put your full faith in me?"

"I reluctantly agree," the prophet finally replied. "Given that our heroes are back in possession of their swords, I am willing to agree to the plan."

"Wonderful!" exclaimed the Meglio. "Then we agree

and can begin the first mission. Heroes, gather your swords and head down to the fire pit by the river. Once again, your virtue and valor are required. This time, you will be defending the liberty and freedom of all mankind. Prepare yourselves and muster your courage. The fight for liberty and freedom is never easy, but fight we must!"

CHAPTER FIVE

CICERO AND THE ROMAN FORUM

~~~

As the cousins, the prophet, and the Meglio made their way to the firepit by the river, Grandpa thought back to the initiation ceremonies he'd held for each cousin where he first presented each of them with their swords. He clearly remembered the ceremony that accompanied the giving of the swords and hoped they viewed it as one of the highlights of their lives.

On each of their twelfth birthdays, he'd invited all of them to spend the weekend with him at the family vacation home. After golfing at Sunnyhill, and a cookout, they went to the firepit by the river. He built a roaring fire as the cousins took seats around the blaze.

During the ceremony, he told them about the sword he had chosen for that ceremony, and the history and meaning behind it. He shared stories of the hero who had wielded it, and why he had chosen that specific sword to present that night. Finally, taking out his pocket knife, he pricked the recipient's finger. He instructed the boy to apply the blood to a specific part of the handle and then hold it there while he recited the verses he had prepared for them.

When the verses had been spoken, he read poetry to them from one of his favorite anthologies. Every one of those specifically chosen poems had a lesson to be learned. He explained the poetry and gave them his own perspective of the poems' meaning and life application. These were truly magical occasions. Not just because of the atmosphere, but because of the closeness it created between them. It was a lifelong bond that could never be broken, even by death. The Meglio had known that the boys had no idea that this ceremony was their preparation for the future.

Now here they were, once again preparing to head out on a mission of utmost importance. Although the cousins had stood around this fire before waiting to depart into the past, Grandpa imagined they still felt a bit unnerved. Certainly part of their concern would be not knowing which of them would be making the trip. That was a decision the swords would make of their own accord, based on the power required and the qualities and virtues of the swords needed for success.

They arrived at the firepit and began their preparations. The prophet built the fire, and the Meglio spoke with the heroes.

"You have all participated in the leaving process four times, so you are aware of the concentration and focus required to complete it successfully, but for my own assurance, let me repeat the instructions. You must all be thinking of nothing but your objective in time. Because the swords will be choosing the exact date, you must focus on the year, time of day, and target location. Every one of you must be thinking of the same thing. The unity of your thoughts is critical to activate the time transition power of the swords. Be focused on 65 BC at 11:00 a.m. and the location of the Roman Forum plaza near the

Fountain of Juturna, the Temple of Vesta, and the Regia."

When the Meglio had finished and the fire was roaring, the prophet addressed the six heroes. "As before, you will stand surrounding the fire, then raise your right arms, holding your swords out in front of you. When I give the command, slowly bring your swords together. When they are in contact with each other, the leaving process will take place. Are you ready to do your duty for the family, the Guardians, and the world?"

"We are," the heroes replied.

"Take your positions around the fire," instructed the prophet.

The heroes complied. When they were in their respective places, the prophet began. "Raise your Swords of Valor!"

The heroes raised their swords in unison. "Now, keeping in mind your objective, slowly bring them together, and Godspeed."

The cousins brought the swords together until they touched. When they did, they were engulfed in a bright flash of pure, white light.

The Meglio was temporarily blinded by the flash. He blinked rapidly, trying to clear his vision. Beside him, he sensed the prophet rubbing his eyes, as well. When the Meglio could once again see clearly, he saw that all six heroes had disappeared.

"Looks like the swords have determined that all six heroes, and the virtues related to their swords, are needed to successfully complete this mission," he observed.

The prophet nodded. "I have to admit, I'm both relieved and concerned by this turn of events. They will all be together to cooperate with and assist one another, but I'm afraid it also means that this will be a challenging mission."

"I'm afraid you're right." The Meglio doused the fire. "Let's hurry back to the Keeping Room, so that we can observe their progress with the help of the quantum computer's diagnostics."

They arrived at the Forum in a flash of light, which was somewhat obscured by the intense glare of the day. When Robbie could see clearly, he realized they had made a huge mistake.

"Robbie!" shouted Nick. "To your left, quickly!"

Robbie swiftly wheeled to his left and raised his sword just in time to deflect a powerful blow from the sword of a giant gladiator charging at him. Ty was at his side in a heartbeat, and together they continued to battle the gladiator.

"What happened?" Joe shouted to the others as more gladiators descended upon them, "This is not our targeted location!"

"No time to think about that now, Joe!" cried Nick. "Looks like we've got to fight our way out of here, wherever here is!" Then he shouted to the others, "Remember Kolonos! Teams of two. Brother fight alongside brother and trust the swords!"

While Robbie continued to battle the first gladiator with Ty, peripherally he saw Nick and Joe standing back to back while Jeff and Billy did the same.

Even as he fought, a small part of Robbie's mind registered that a gladiator battle was not as he had been taught in school. He'd always pictured these events taking place in the Colosseum, but this was different. The buildings of the Roman Forum surrounded them, but they were now in the middle of a circle of temporary wooden stands filled with screaming Romans. They had materialized in the middle of a contest between two teams of gladiators fighting to the death. They were now the third team in the arena. But regardless of the venue, this was a life and death situation.

"Focus on defense!" shouted Jeff. "Stay alert and work in teams! Remember our objective!"

By that time, all three teams of heroes were engaged in battle. To Robbie's right, Nick and Joe struggled with a gladiator who hurled a net at them. Nick's foot became entangled. Joe cut him loose, and together they rained blows on the gladiator, who now fought with a short Roman gladius.

Their swords, Excalibur and the Sword of St. Michael, were much longer and heavier and made of much finer steel, which gave them an advantage. Combined with the powers inherent in the swords, they disarmed him and entangled him in his own net, where he lay unarmed and unable to free himself. The Roman spectators screamed for them to kill him, but Joe and Nick ignored their calls. Instead, they looked around the arena to see where they were needed.

The two gladiator teams appeared to be confused by the appearance of a third team, disrupting their strategies. There were already eight men dead in the arena, along with the one Joe and Nick had disabled. That left five active and still-dangerous gladiators.

Robbie and Ty were in a standoff with the huge gladiator that had attacked them upon their arrival. He was armed with a gladius and a spear. He used the spear to maintain his distance from them, and Robbie was okay with that.

"Let's just keep him occupied as long as possible," shouted Robbie to Ty as they circled the gladiator, looking for an opening to disarm him. "If we play a waiting game, we may be able to survive until the gladiators kill each other off, and we can walk out of here with our lives."

"There is no way I am going to be in gladiator games and just be a spectator," Ty argued. "I am going to circle to my left as you continue to circle to the right. When I am behind him, attack from his front side. As he fights you off, I will attack from behind. That will get us inside his defenses, and we can disarm him."

"No!" spat Robbie. "That's not the strategy. Survival is the strategy. Don't be foolish, Ty. Let's just follow the plan!"

But Ty was already circling slowly to his left.

Robbie's heart dropped into his stomach as his brother began the risky move. His senses fully alive, he keenly sensed the spear only ten inches from his chest. He watched as the gladiator raised his sword arm toward Ty while keeping his spear pointed in Robbie's direction.

When Ty was directly behind the gladiator, Robbie lashed out with Braveheart and struck the spear. The gladiator lost his grip and it fell to the ground, bouncing just once. Ty took advantage of the gladiator's confusion and charged him with his sword raised. In an unbelievably swift move, the gladiator deflected the blow from Robbie, spun, dropped to one knee, and hit Ty with a slicing blow to his left side as he approached from the rear. Ty went down hard.

Robbie watched in horror as his brother was wounded. With a battle cry filled with anger, frustration, and rage, he advanced on the gladiator, and brought Braveheart down with a powerful blow to the gladiator's neck. Braveheart sliced through the man's shoulder, almost completely severing his arm. Robbie quickly ran to

Ty, lying on the ground, shocked at how much blood poured from the six-inch gash in his side.

"Ty, I have to get you to safety. Can you walk?" Robbie asked his wounded brother.

"I can stand," said Ty, "but I am not sure about the walking part." Robbie helped Ty stand, and together they sought a calmer area of the arena.

Meanwhile, the other two pairs of brothers engaged murderous gladiators. Billy and Jeff fought two gladiators separately, while Nick and Joe dealt with a short but muscular gladiator armed with both a trident and a short sword. These were the only gladiators left standing.

Billy eventually dispatched the gladiator he was fighting, then ran to help Jeff. The gladiator had closed in on his brother, and they were wrestling on the floor of the arena in a pile of blood, guts, and fur from an earlier event.

Billy arrived in time to pull the gladiator off Jeff before he could deliver a death blow with his gladius. The gladiator, who was covered in blood and sweat, slipped out of Billy's grasp. He wheeled and struck at Billy with a slashing blow, barely missing Billy's midsection.

Jeff leaped to his feet and circled around behind the gladiator. He shouted, "Hey, we're not done yet!"

As Robbie settled Ty in a relatively safe spot, he looked over his shoulder at the ongoing battle. He watched as the gladiator Jeff and Billy were fighting spun around to attack Jeff. When he did, Billy thrust Durandal into his right side. Jeff did the same and thrust the Sword of Solomon into the gladiator's left side. Billy and Jeff stood there for a moment holding the horrified gladiator up between them. Pulling their swords out of his body, the gladiator slumped to the ground at their feet. Then, they hustled over to help Joe and Nick with the last remaining gladiator.

Joe's foot was pinned to the ground by the gladiator's trident, and Nick struggled to remove it. The trident had pierced Joe's foot and was stuck in the hard ground of the arena. As Nick struggled to pull out the trident, Joe fended off the stocky gladiator's blows, defending himself and Nick.

Without warning, Billy hit the gladiator from the side with a flying tackle. Jeff quickly joined him, sitting on the gladiator's chest and pinning his arms to the ground with his knees. He pointed the Sword of Solomon at the gladiator's neck.

The crowd went wild, shouting, "Death! Kill him! Kill him!"

Robbie reached for Braveheart as he watched Joe, Nick, and Billy surround the fallen gladiator. While he used the sword's healing power on his brother, he watched as the fire of battle filled Jeff's eyes. Even at this distance, he could see Jeff's jaw tighten as his teeth gritted with anger. Breathing hard, Robbie's chest mirrored the movement of Jeff's as he stared into the face of the man who only moments before had threatened the life of his family members.

Robbie could only watch with awful dread. For a moment, he thought Jeff might actually fulfill the wishes of the mob. It felt intoxicating to hear the cheers and the adulation of the crowd after such an intense battle. It filled him with a fleeting feeling of power. He could only imagine that Jeff was feeling the same thing. He knew Jeff could kill this man right now, and he would be adored for it.

But as Jeff knelt there with his sword drawn at the ready, Billy laid a powerful hand on his brother's shoulder.

"Jeff," Billy said firmly, "this is not what we do. We are better than this. Get up and leave him there."

Hearing his brother's voice seemed to snap Jeff back to reality. He withdrew his sword from the gladiator's neck and stood. He looked around the arena at the faces of the mob which had become contorted into that of bloodthirsty animals.

Robbie followed his gaze. He felt ashamed that the crowd's shouts had such power over him. He was dismayed that Jeff had, even for a moment, considered fulfilling their demands. He wondered if he would have had the strength to resist the pull of the spectators' angry cries.

Robbie rose to one knee and raised his sword. Nick pointed in his direction and the cousins ran to join them.

"What happened?" shouted Nick as they arrived.

"Ty was playing gladiator and got sliced by the guy we were fighting," replied Robbie.

"How bad is it?" asked Billy.

"It was really bad," admitted Robbie, "but after I got him here, I used my sword to heal him, just like we did after the battle of Thermopylae. It's almost healed now, so I think he'll be fine."

"Thank God for the healing power of the swords. I could use a little help here myself," said Joe, nudging Nick, and pointing to his bleeding foot.

Nick replied, "No worries, Joe." He took out the Sword of St. Michael and thrust the point of it into one of the wounds in Joe's pierced foot.

"Ouch! Easy, Nick, that hurts!" Joe grumbled.

"Relax," replied Nick as he put his sword tip into the other punctures. "They're small wounds and will heal fast." He withdrew his sword, and immediately the wounds started to close.

Robbie helped Ty to his feet only to find that a group of Roman soldiers now surrounded them.

"When did they get here?" Ty whispered to Robbie, who shrugged and shook his head.

"Gladiators, come with us," the captain of the troop commanded. "You must stand before the patron of the event to learn your fate. Quickly, we must not keep him waiting any longer!"

Realizing they did not have a choice in the matter, Robbie followed with the others as the soldiers took them to stand before the patron of the event.

As they stood there, the crowd grew boisterous. Some cheered for them and shouted "Freedom, freedom!" Others called for their death because they refused to kill the remaining opponents.

The patron was a man about forty years old, dressed in a simple but formal-looking toga. He had intense eyes and seemed to be deliberating their fate.

"Just stay quiet. Do not respond to anything unless it is absolutely necessary," recommended Billy. "Stand tall and look confident, but remember, humility is always the crown of victors."

The patron stopped his contemplation and stood. He turned to the crowd and raised his hands, asking for silence. The spectators hushed, and he turned his attention back to the cousins and addressed them. Feeling the power this man held over the crowd, Robbie felt his heart beating fast, as his anxiety grew.

"I, Gaius Julius Caesar, Aedile of the Roman Republic and patron of these gladiatorial games held in the honor of my father Gaius Julius Caesar III, congratulate you on your impressive victory. We had anticipated a match of the two greatest teams of gladiators and were surprised by the addition of your third unknown team. Please tell us who your sponsor is and where you hail from."

Robbie was dumbstruck. This was *the* Julius Caesar himself. This was definitely not in the plan. There was no way they could expect to walk out of here with their lives if they refused to respond. That would be a sign of absolute disrespect and an immediate death sentence. He knew that once again, they would have to rely on the swords to give them what they needed to survive.

Joe said to Jeff, "Let me do this. It's my job to interview prominent officials and ask and respond to tough questions. Plus, my degree in political history might help here."

Jeff replied, "Go for it, Joe, just don't tell them too much. Make it short and sweet."

Joe looked thoughtful for a moment, then raised his sword in front of him, encouraging the others to do the same, and said, "Honorable Caesar, we salute you in the name of our family. The family of Lucius Quinctius Cincinnatus. We are the descendants of the great Cincinnatus, the Roman patrician, statesman, and military leader of the early Republic. We are proud to have participated in these games honoring your father and to give glory to his name."

Caesar looked surprised at this revelation and asked, "How is it that you come to be slaves who must earn their freedom by way of the arena? The Cincinnatus family is an old and revered Roman family. Have they fallen on grim times?"

"No, sir," replied Joe. "We are brothers who fight for the cause of freedom and for the values and virtues of the Republic. We are free men who are willing to fight for what we believe in. We chose to participate this day to honor you, your father, and the Republic. We hope we have pleased you."

The crowd once again grew restless. They were still overcome by bloodlust and adrenaline from the battle they had witnessed. Murmuring began, and rose in intensity. Then one man shouted, "Kill them! They did not honor you with the death of their victims. They are cowards and did not follow the wishes of the citizens of Rome. They must pay. Kill them!"

Others began to shout also, "Kill them! Kill them!"

Caesar looked around at the crowd, assessing their temperament. He leaned close to a man sitting next to him, and they spoke quietly for a moment. Listening intently, he nodded, listened again, then nodded once more. He patted the arm of the man and then faced the cousins.

"This is a day to honor the dead," he announced for all to hear. "You have honored my father by your performance here today. Because of that, I choose to honor your ancestor, Lucius Quinctius Cincinnatus, by allowing you to live and by giving you the title of rudiarii. Approach my seat, and each of you will receive the symbol of freedom, the rudis sword."

Robbie breathed a sigh of relief and approached the patron's box with his cousins. They stood tall and proud as each of them was presented with a wooden replica of the Roman gladius sword.

Caesar addressed them after they received the swords. "Remember that these swords are the representation of freedom. They are symbolic of the rise from slavery to freedom. Since you are already freemen, carry them as a reminder to always defend the freedom you enjoy and to honor the sacrifices of your ancestors who gave you that gift. Now go, and take with you my thanks and gratitude for your performance here today!"

The crowd erupted in cheers. Music began to play, and the cousins were escorted to the exit of the makeshift arena. After they exited, they gathered together under the wooden stands to talk.

"That was amazing, Joe!" said Ty. "How did you come up with that? Not only did it work, but it was true. I thought for sure we were going to be thrown to the lions."

"All I can say, Ty, is that the first thing I tried to think about was how to honor Caesar," said Joe. "What would make him feel comfortable enough to look at us favorably? After that, I think my sword just took over my mind. Remember, it is the Sword of Arthur and Melchizedek. They were both magnificent and benevolent kings. I think the sword gave me what I needed to be successful. It knew what would touch his heart, and I just went with it."

"Well, however it happened, it worked. Well done, Joe," said Nick. "I am proud of you, brother."

"Thanks," Joe replied, then frowned. "Something's bothering me, though. I know the swords can make us appear in whatever clothing is suitable to the time and occasion, and they allow us to understand, and be understood, in foreign languages. So, why didn't the gladiators know what we were planning? We were talking and shouting at each other, but they didn't seem to react as though they understood what we were saying."

Ty spoke up. "I don't know about you, but I didn't have time to listen to anyone else's strategies. I was too busy fighting for my life!"

"Even in a battle, soldiers listen and watch for any advantage," Billy remarked. "It does seem strange that none of them took advantage of our shouted instructions to each other."

Jeff, who had remained thoughtfully quiet, finally spoke. "Maybe the swords can turn their translation ability off and on? They seem to know what we need before we do. It makes sense that they'd know when it would be advantageous to be able to communicate without those around us knowing what we are saying."

"Good point, but it looks like we have company." Billy nodded his head towards a man with beautiful posture approaching them.

They left the area under the stands, and Robbie realized it was the same man that Julius Caesar had consulted with during his deliberation of their fate. He was impeccably dressed in a formal toga and wore expensive-looking sandals. He had the air of command and approached them with strong, purposeful strides.

As he drew closer, he hailed them. "Greetings, sons of Cincinnatus. I am Marcus Tullius Cicero, Consul of the Roman Republic. I have escaped my attendants so I may speak with you privately. Will you join me for a meal at my home? It is only a short walk up to the top of the Palatine, and I have many questions for you on the way. The first of my questions is, how did you suddenly appear in the arena? I am not much of a fan of the gladiator contests, and my eyes had wandered to a vacant area of the arena floor. I saw a flash of light, and then you appeared. I want answers, and if I am not satisfied, you will be back in the arena before nightfall. Follow me!"

Cicero began to walk, and the cousins followed. It was obvious that he was not really giving them a choice, but of course, since he was their intended target, they were happy to comply.

As they walked, Joe leaned over to Jeff. "I thought the swords masked the flash of light when we go back in time? How could Cicero see that?"

Jeff shrugged. "Maybe the swords' masking ability does the same thing with the light that it seems to do with language? When someone needs to see it, they do."

"Makes sense, I guess," Joe murmured.

Following Cicero, Robbie got his first full view of the Roman Forum, and it was magnificent. They passed by the Fountain of Juturna, the Temple of Vesta, and the Regia. It seemed that they had arrived in the area they had identified, but apparently on the day of their arrival, Julius Caesar had temporary stands and an arena set up for the gladiator games to honor his father. They were going to have to try to be more diligent in their research to avoid such dangerous mistakes on future missions.

The rest of the Forum was not yet quite as "imperial" as it was one day going to be, but it was still very impressive. Marble and granite edifices lined the Via Sacra, the main road running through the heart of the Forum, which was in fine repair, paved with even and glistening cobblestones. People of all sorts wandered about selling food and enjoying the warm afternoon sun. The air had a festive feel.

The cousins hurried their pace to keep up with their host. They had been told by the computer that he was about forty-one years old, and that seemed about right to Robbie, but he was certainly more commanding than his forty-one years would have led them to believe. He strode purposefully and quickly, but soon the cousins caught up to him.

Ty spoke first, "Mr. Cicero, may we call you that? You say you saw us appear in the arena. Can you tell us more about that? Exactly what did you see?"

Cicero looked at him sideways and replied, "First of all, I think of myself as 'Citizen' Cicero. Despite my position, I am honored to be called a citizen of this

Republic. But you may refer to me as Cicero. Everyone does.

"Secondly, when I say I saw you appear in the arena, I mean just that. I saw a bright flash of white light, then you six appeared out of nowhere, as if by sorcery. I am determined to understand the meaning of this. I suggest you begin explaining this to me before we reach my home, or my attendants catch up with us."

As they started to ascend the Palatine Hill, Jeff began the explanation. "Cicero, we will speak to you only in truth and honesty, as we are men of virtue and valor. We will not deceive you in any way, but I must tell you now that there are things we cannot disclose to you as they may affect history. Are you willing to receive all we tell you as truth and forgive us if we cannot answer some questions that you may have?"

Cicero replied, "I am a politician, my young man, and I understand discretion and the power of words. I am adept at detecting falsehood and deceit. Speak truthfully to the extent you can, and all will be well."

"We will," replied Jeff. "As to our appearance, it is exactly as you saw. We did appear in the arena as you described. However, it was not through sorcery. The Swords of Valor brought us here to accomplish an urgent mission. We had not planned to arrive in the middle of the arena during a gladiator event, however. That was accidental. We were as surprised as you were. We came here today for the sole purpose of meeting and speaking with you."

"Meeting with me?" replied Cicero. "Why is that? What business do you have with me?"

"There is more that you need to know before I can disclose that," continued Jeff. "As I said, the Swords of Valor brought us here, but not just from another location.

They brought us here from another time, far in the future, over two thousand years from now."

Cicero stopped walking and turned quickly on the cousins.

"The *future!*" he shouted. "That is your explanation to me? Do you take me for a fool? Make me believe this right now, or I will return you to the arena and brand you as madmen."

"Please, honorable Cicero," said Jeff, "We understand that this is difficult to believe, but it is true. Look at our swords. Is there a craftsman living today that can make such fine blades?"

"I admit to you that never have I seen such fine examples," replied Cicero, "but you will need to do better than that."

"We know of the future of the Republic," blurted Robbie. The other cousins shot him warning looks.

"What of the future of the Republic?" asked Cicero.

Ignoring the warning looks from the other heroes, Robbie replied, "It is in danger. There are men that wish to take control and turn this great republic into a dictatorship and eventually an empire. We know that you know this and are fighting against it secretly. Being from the future, we know that it does not end well."

Robbie held his breath as Cicero considered his comments. This man held their lives in his hands. If he believed them, they had a chance to fulfill this mission. If he didn't... Robbie didn't want to think too hard about that possibility.

Cicero turned and resumed walking up the hill. "What you have said is true," he conceded, "but I have just determined the intent of the parties involved myself. There is no way you could have known that, so that is a point in your favor. However, if you are really from a time, two thousand years in the future, you must be able to show me something more impressive."

Just then Joe stopped walking and reached for his right eye. "Ouch!" he said. "Hey, hold up a minute, guys, I got some dust in my contact lens."

As he fumbled to make it stop hurting, Cicero asked, "What did he say? What is a contact lens?"

Nick replied, "It's how some of us see more clearly, two thousand years from now. It improves our vision so that we can see things clearly at longer distances. Joe, show Cicero your contact lens."

Joe gave Nick an incredulous look, but did as he was asked. He removed the offending contact and held it out for Cicero to see.

Cicero examined it closely and then said, "Put it back in, I want to see it go back in."

Joe complied. He inserted the lens back into his eye and looked at Cicero. Cicero then leaned in very close to Joe and examined the lens in his eye, observing it floating about and moving as Joe looked left and right.

Nodding his satisfaction, Cicero said, "Let us hurry." Then he turned and increased his pace up the hill. "We have much to discuss and not much time in which to do it."

CHAPTER SIX

CONVERSATION WITH CICERO

～～

The heroes and Cicero arrived at his home atop the beautiful Palatine Hill. The view was magnificent. As they approached the home, Ty could see the whole Roman Forum laid out beneath them. Cicero's villa stood along the higher leg of the Clivus Victoriae, along the northwest side of the hill running from the north corner to the precinct of the Magna Mater. It was a large and noble house, surrounded by ancient trees with beautiful gardens, statues, and fountains.

Cicero directed them to a fountain in the garden area and instructed them to wash themselves. He spoke with a couple of his servants, directing them to bring food and drink for his guests.

"When you are finished washing," Cicero said, "gather in the meditation garden and seat yourselves. I will return shortly, and we can begin our discussion." Then he turned and walked into the house, leaving them there to follow his instructions. The heroes did as they had been directed, talking quietly amongst themselves.

"Well, this mission has certainly gotten off to a rocky start," Ty observed. "We are fortunate to still be alive, and most of all, to actually be able to have the conversation with Cicero. I am a little concerned that we may have made a bad first impression. Let's just lay out our mission simply and clearly. Remember, we are dealing with one of the giant intellects of the ancient world."

"I agree," said Jeff. "We need to ask clear questions and listen more than we talk. We have a lot to learn and a lot to remember."

When he had finished washing the dust, blood, and sweat from himself, Ty felt refreshed. After the rest had finished cleaning up, they gathered in the meditation garden, took seats on the ground around a stone bench, and waited for Cicero's return.

He appeared a few minutes later, followed by servants who offered the cousins fruit, various cheeses, and strips of unidentifiable meat. Ty partook of the fruit and cheese, noticing that none of the others were brave enough to attempt the meat, either. They were also served goblets of wine. Cicero took a seat on the stone bench and began.

"You have stated that you are here on a mission and wish to speak with me. Your strange appearance in the arena and explanation of your origins have piqued my interest. State your business and let us begin."

Billy spoke first. "Honorable Cicero, all we have told you is true. We have traveled back over two thousand years in time to speak specifically with you regarding a crisis which we face in our time. We are citizens of a republic which was founded based on the model of the Roman Republic and is known as the United States of America. Our republic now faces a threat similar in some ways to what you are facing now. There is an international group of very powerful and wealthy families plotting the overthrow of the freely elected governments of the world.

Their plan includes implementation of a world-wide dictatorship. We have come here to seek your advice and perspective as to how we may best fight against this threat and avert this disastrous turn of events."

Cicero interrupted Billy at this point and asked, "Why is it that you seek my advice and council on this matter?"

Billy replied, "In our time, you are recognized as one of the giants of the ancient world. Many of your writings, speeches, and quotes have survived the centuries and are revered as wisdom. You are held up as a pillar of common sense and virtue in matters of freedom and liberty. It is our mission to understand your perspective regarding the establishment of the very first republic, how it grew strong, and what inherent weaknesses would allow an evil group of people to exploit and overthrow it. We wish to learn about the foundations of liberty and freedom, the art of oration, and its ability to change the heart of people and nations."

"I see," replied Cicero. "But I fear that you may be disappointed. I am not certain I will be able to live up to the reputation you may have of me. I am a mere politician who is fast becoming overwhelmed by the machinations of powerful forces, which may be beyond my power to deflect. Ask your questions, and I will respond as best I can. But first, let me ask you a question. Is the threat you are facing an internal or external threat? Is this group part of your own government, or are they a foreign threat?"

Joe answered the question. "It is fairly complicated. It has become both at this point. The group has infiltrated the very fabric of our society, but also has established beachheads internationally. Please tell us why that is important."

Cicero replied, "A nation can survive its fools, and

even the ambitious. But it cannot survive treason from within. An enemy at the gates is less formidable, for he is known and carries his banner openly. But the traitor moves amongst those within the gate freely. His sly whispers rustle through all the alleys and are heard in the very halls of government itself.

"For the traitor appears not a traitor; he speaks in accents familiar to his victims, and he wears their face and their arguments. He appeals to the baseness that lies deep in the hearts of all men. He rots the soul of a nation and works secretly and unknown in the night to undermine the pillars of the city. He infects the body politic so that it can no longer resist. A murderer is less to fear. The traitor is the plague.

"That is what I am dealing with now in our Republic. If you are facing the same, then I would advise that you address the internal threats primarily and immediately. If you can eliminate the internal threats, then you will have time to make plans to handle the external ones and be able to do so from a united front. I recently successfully faced this sort of treachery, the Catalinian revolution, which threatened our republic. Harsh measures were necessary, but the revolution was quelled."

"Yes," replied Joe, "in fact, in our time we have a quote from Marcus Cato referring to you as *pater patriase*, or the 'father of your country', because of your actions regarding the Catalinian revolution."

"Is that so?" replied Cicero, "Interesting, I must remember to be more solicitous of dear Cato."

"So, we must deal with internal threats first," Jeff repeated the statesman's instruction. "What else must we be wary of?"

"You must be alert for those who constantly advocate for war," continued Cicero. "The internal treachery will reveal itself in that way. It is always about self-enrichment or control of the masses through fear. It is rarely about a righteous war of self-defense. Those wars are self-evident. Right now, the Roman Republic is under the influence of generals and powerful men of wealth who use war and wealth for their own benefit.

"If Rome can stop its policy of conquest, the Republic will have a much better chance for growth and development. Corrupt and limited as it is, our Republic would then stand the best chance of averting one-man rule. But if the aggression continues, and successful generals eclipse the power of the Senate and other republican institutions, we will find ourselves in the uncomfortable position of choosing among evils, and I fear for the future of the Republic.

"It is difficult to admit, but we Romans are loathed abroad because of the damage our generals and officials have done with their licentiousness. No temple has been protected by its sanctity, no state by its sworn agreements, no house and home by its locks and bars. In fact, there is now a shortage of prosperous cities for us to declare war on so that we can loot them afterwards! Do you think that when we send out an army against an enemy it is to protect our allies, or is it rather to use the war as an excuse for plundering them?

"I do not know of a single state that we have subdued that is still rich, or a single rich state that our generals have not subdued. There are almost none. The plunder and demonization of other nations is a hallmark of dictatorship and results in the fall of a republic, or a democracy, for that matter. Wealth, power, and fear are the fuel of the traitors."

"Does this observation apply to external threats also?" asked Nick. "What about other forms of warfare such as economic or social conflict? In our time, the evil we are fighting uses military combat, but also uses economic and social conflict to impose their will on people. How can we tell when a government, either our own or foreign, has crossed the line and should be challenged?"

"That is a very cogent question, my young man," replied Cicero. "It goes to the heart of the matter. As you may know, since it seems that you are aware of many aspects of my life, I studied under the tutelage of many learned Greek philosophers. Much of what I came to understand about society and government came from them. Over the years, I have also formed my own opinions, which differ in many respects from theirs, but have been built on their foundation.

"The Greek philosophers conceived of society and government as virtually the same, coming together in the city-state. I, on the other hand, see government as a trustee, morally obliged to serve society. Which means society is something larger and separate from government.

"I feel that government is justified primarily as a means of protecting private property. The Greeks, primarily Plato and Aristotle, imagined that government could improve morals. Neither had conceived of private property as an absolute claim that one person had something over everyone else. So, in that opinion, we differed.

"We also differed with respect to laws. I, for example, differentiate 'higher law' from the laws of governments. I believe it is quite absurd to call every article in the decrees and laws of nations just. What if tyrants enacted those laws? The essential justice that binds human society together and is maintained by what is referred to as natural law is right reason, expressed in commands and prohibitions. Whoever disregards this natural law, whether written or unwritten, is unjust. This is the supreme law which existed through the ages, before the mention of any written law or established state. It is the law of nature, and it is the source of right government.

"True law is right human reason in agreement with nature; it is of universal application, unchanging and everlasting. If this were adhered to, there would not be different laws at Rome and at Athens, or different laws now and in the future, but one eternal and unchangeable law would be valid for all nations and all times. There would be one master and ruler, God, over us all, for he is the author of this law, its promulgator, and its enforcing judge. Whomever is disobedient is fleeing from himself and denying his human nature, and because of this very fact he will suffer the worst penalties.

"Justice should be applied equally to all men and all governments. Justice for people is administered by the government in accordance with natural law, and justice for governments is administered by the people, also in accordance with natural law. When a government is unjust, the people must act."

"That is all very familiar to us," said Robbie. "Our country was founded on the principle that our government receives its power from the people, and the people get their rights from God. But things are getting very confusing, because there are influences now that deny any absolute right or wrong. They seem to be denying the natural law that you have identified, and upon which our nation was built. Everything in our time, in our society, is relative. There are no absolutes. Everyone does what is right in their own eyes and is encouraged in this respect by government and the controlling powers of the world."

Cicero considered this for a few moments and seemed troubled by it. Then he responded. "Both government and society must be built on principles of natural law. They must recognize and identify the rules of 'right conduct' with the laws of the Supreme Creator of the universe. If a government abandons this principle, the people, or society, can be the correcting influence. If society abandons this principle, then the government can be the correcting influence. But if *both* government and society abandon the rule of natural law, then chaos, destruction, and enslavement will soon follow.

"If this is the case in your time, then I would say that you must take strong, decisive action quickly to awaken the consciousness of one or both. Choose the one you can influence the most powerfully and focus your attention on that one. Remind the government or society of the brilliant intelligence of the Supreme Designer who has an ongoing interest in both human and cosmic affairs. Remind them that once the reality of the Creator is clearly identified in the mind, the only intelligent approach to government, justice, and human societal relations is in terms of the laws which the Supreme Creator has already established. The Creator's order of things is called natural law. Natural law is 'right conduct', according to the laws established by the Supreme Creator, or 'the Creator's order of things'. This, my friends, is true law.

"True law is right reason in agreement with nature; it is of universal application, unchanging and everlasting. It is serious folly for any nation or society to try to alter this law, nor is it allowable to repeal any part of it, and it is impossible to abolish it entirely. We cannot be freed from its obligations by senate or people.

"Any lasting and honorable government or society

will have one eternal and unchangeable law which should be valid for all nations and all times. It must be recognized that there is only one master and ruler over us all, that is God, and he is the author of all law. Man's laws of right conduct are obligated to conform to God's law.

"The Roman Republic was founded on this principle but has never been free from the scourge of turbulent power politics. I have always believed, despite our flaws and challenges, in the grandeur and promise of some future society based on natural law. From what I have heard from you, it is possible that your society may fulfill that dream, regardless of the crisis you now face.

"It may very well be too late for my Republic to avoid its apparent fate, but I will not relent in my fight to restore it to its original foundations. I will continue to urge people to reason together. I will continue to promote decency and peace. I will use my voice and my pen to remind and call people back to the most fundamental ideas of liberty and freedom. It may be that speaking freely in this manner means risking death, but I will renounce tyranny. It will always be my vow to keep the torch of liberty burning bright.

"I encourage you to do the same in your time. No, I *command* you to do the same! It is your duty. It is your obligation as men who have known freedom, and as sons of Cincinnatus!"

Ty sat in rapt attention as he listened to one of history's most powerful orators and defenders of liberty urge them to act. The powerful images his words created and truth they imparted enthralled him.

Joe was the first to find his voice. "Honorable Cicero, I am a student of political history and have been taught about your influence on western civilization. I am amazed that we were not more focused on your philosophies. They seem so right and so simple. We briefly studied one of your works, *De Officiis,* as an ethics text. Your vision of natural law influenced thinkers in our past who had a direct intellectual influence on our American Revolution. Many of our Founding Fathers got their ideas about the importance of dividing government powers directly from you.

"It saddens me to think that in the two hundred and forty years from the founding of our nation, based on the structure of the Roman Republic, and the understanding gained from your discussions of natural law, that we could have wandered so far from the foundational principles, and now find ourselves in a fight for our liberty and freedom. We give our word to you as men of valor and virtue that we will take all you have told us and fight to restore the spirit of liberty in our society, our nation, and our world."

Cicero smiled, but Ty couldn't tell if it was a smile of joy or recognition. Joy, in that his words had an influence on them, or recognition that he saw himself in them. He stood and once again addressed the heroes.

"I fought for the Republic when I was young," Cicero declared, "I shall not abandon her in my old age. I scorned the daggers of Catiline, and I shall not tremble before others yet to come. Rather, I would willingly expose my body to them, if by my death the liberty of the nation could be recovered, and the agony of the Roman people could at last bring to birth that with which it has been so long in labor. It would be my expressed wish that at my death I may leave the Roman people free from tyranny. That is my hope and my declaration. I suggest you take that same vow. For it seems that you fight the same battle as I, for liberty and freedom."

The cousins stood and followed Cicero as he walked

to a point overlooking the Roman Forum below. It was now aglow in shades of orange, red, and magenta, darkening with the lengthening shadows of the setting sun.

"This is my favorite place in the entire world," observed Cicero. "I stand here every day and watch the sun set. The colors remind me of the people whose blood has been spilled to give us the freedom we now enjoy, and I pray that we will have the will to fight against the storm which is coming. Before we end our discussion, I have a couple of warnings for you.

"One of the most effective tools that evil men use to gain power and enslave people is complacency and dependence. They lull the people into a sense of safety and satisfaction by providing them with food or entertainment."

"We've heard about that," Billy interjected. "In about a hundred and fifty years, a man named Juvenal will call it 'bread and circuses'."

Cicero pursed his lips and nodded. "That's a good description. You participated in the 'circus' aspect of this earlier today. The gladiator events are held to entertain the masses.

"This gives them the sense that the powerful people in society have their 'happiness' in mind, that they truly care about them. But it is only a superficial means of appeasement. In the case of politics, the phrase is used to describe public approval of the powerful patrons of the events. They don't win that approval through exemplary or excellent public service or public policy, but through diversion, distraction, or the mere satisfaction of the immediate, shallow requirements of a populace, as an offered palliative.

"Many years ago, Roman politicians passed laws to

gain the votes of poorer citizens by introducing a grain dole: giving out cheap food and entertainment. 'Bread and circuses', as you call it, became the most effective way to rise to power. The Roman citizens have come to expect the government to provide free wheat, costly circus games, and other forms of entertainment. So, politicians feed their expectations as a means of gaining political power. Are you familiar with Polybius?" Cicero asked the heroes.

"Yes," Joe answered. "He was born in Arcadia and was deported to Rome because his father opposed Roman rule in Macedonia, right?"

"That's right," Cicero nodded. "Lucias Aemilius Paulus employed him as a tutor for his two sons. Eventually, he placed his allegiance with the Roman Republic, but he believed that all democracies fail. He said, 'The masses continue with an appetite for benefits and the habit of receiving them by way of a rule of force and violence. The people, having grown accustomed to feed at the expense of others and to depend for their livelihood on the property of others... institute the rule of violence; and now uniting their forces, massacre, banish, and plunder, until they degenerate again into perfect savages and find once more a master and monarch.'

"I believe as Polybius did, that when the authoritarian state uses force and violence to become the benefactors of the people, they force one class of citizens to provide for another. This is indicative of the selfishness of common people and their neglect of wider concerns. It also signals the erosion or ignorance of civic duty amongst the concerns of the common man. Be wary of it and look for it in your society. The providers of 'bread and circuses' will most likely be your enemy."

Cicero continued, "Finally, the people you fight against will know that time is on their side. They have wealth, influence, and power. They have indoctrination techniques which allow them to train and influence the next generations. They know that their conquest will be defended against if they reveal themselves in a frontal assault. So, they will take their time. They will use subversive yet subtle techniques to erode the defenses of a nation or society. This is known as the Fabian strategy. This strategy derives its name from Quintus Fabius Maximus Verrucosus, nicknamed 'Cunctator', meaning 'Delayer'.

"He was a dictator of the early Roman Republic, given the task of defeating the great Carthaginian general, Hannibal, in southern Italy during the Second Punic War, one hundred and fifty-two years ago. At the start of the war, Hannibal boldly crossed the Alps in wintertime and invaded our nation. Due to Hannibal's skill as a general, he repeatedly inflicted devastating losses on us despite the numerical inferiority of his army, quickly achieving two crushing victories at the Battle of Trebbia and the Battle of Lake Trasimene. After these disasters, we appointed Fabius Maximus as dictator.

"Well aware of the military superiority of the Carthaginians and the ingenuity of Hannibal, Fabius initiated a war of attrition, which was designed to exploit Hannibal's strategic vulnerabilities. The Fabian strategy is a military tactic where pitched battles and frontal assaults are avoided in favor of wearing down an opponent by misdirection and gradually wearing them down. While avoiding decisive battles, the side employing this strategy harasses its enemy through skirmishes to cause slow erosion of their armies, disruption of their supplies, gradual erosion of confidence in their cause, and devastating their morale. Employment of this strategy implies that the side adopting it believes time is on its side, but it may also be adopted when no feasible alternative strategy can be devised. This same strategy of a war of attrition can be used by any enemy in their aim to bring about changes in any government or society.

The advocacy of gradualism or incrementalism distinguishes this method of societal change from those who promote revolutionary action. Fabian's strategy sought victory against the superior Carthaginian army under the renowned General Hannibal through persistence, harassment, and wearing the enemy down, rather than pitched, climactic battles.

"Your enemy may very well employ the same strategy to gradually increase their influence and control of your government and society. Be aware! Look for this. It will identify for you the source of your problem and the face of your enemy. Mark my words and remember them well."

As the heroes and their host watched the sun set over the Roman Forum from the meditation garden of Cicero's noble home, Ty couldn't help but wonder what the world would be like in their time if Cicero had succeeded in his efforts to save the Republic of Rome.

He thought about the war and bloodshed that could have been avoided. He thought of the dark ages that followed the sacking of Rome and all the knowledge and understanding that was lost, which took centuries to rediscover. Ty now had a much greater respect for the wisdom of the ancients and for Cicero himself. He thought of Cicero's famous quote that "to be ignorant of what happened before you were born is to live the life of a child forever," and he vowed to remember and to act on that knowledge. To that end, Ty turned and addressed the team.

"We have learned a lot from our discussion with the honorable Cicero this day. It is important that we do not forget the key points he made. Let's review them so that we will not forget.

"The first one that I recall, is that he said that the most dangerous threat will be an internal one. The traitor is the plague."

Robbie spoke next, "The second one is that we must look for whoever it is that constantly advocates for war. They are looking for power and self-enrichment."

Nick then chimed in, "He also said that whoever disregards natural law is unjust whether they be in government or society, and we should fight against them. But also, that we must choose our battles. Choose the one, either government or society, that we are most likely to be able to influence, and focus our energy there."

Billy remembered the next point. "The providers of 'bread and circuses' will most likely be our enemy."

Finally, Joe provided the last point. "Beware the Fabian strategy. Look for the people or groups that advocate for incrementalism and gradualism and use subtle subversive methods of change. Do we have it all correct, honorable Cicero?" he asked.

Cicero turned and faced the heroes and placed his hand on Jeff's shoulder. "You have remembered well. It is my hope that you will now have the tools to identify your enemy and understand his methods and strategy. Knowing your enemy is half of the battle. Understanding his strategy and defeating it is the other half.

"You are young men, and in our Roman society we are falling into the trap of idolizing youth without requiring either manly vigor or sound wisdom from it. You young men seem to have wisdom and vigor, but also virtue. That bodes well for your society. A major cause for the Republic's current decline into decadence is that our old men are acting foolishly, pursuing individual ambition at the expense of the state and nation. The people in Roman society who should be passing on timeless wisdom are merely passing time pleasing themselves with flippancy. I hope this is not the case in your time. But if it is, seek the elders who endeavor to teach and pass on virtue and timeless wisdom. Honor them and learn from them. Old age brings one nearer to death than other men.

"Yet, death comes to us all, and none will enjoy the possession of this life for very long in the grand scheme of things. A great-souled man will not fear what he cannot escape but will instead strive to act in such a way as to bring the most good through his life at every stage of it, in the ways most appropriate to each of its seasons. If you have just one person in your life who exhibits these qualities, treasure him. Trust him and obey him. Do you have that one person?"

"We have two, honorable Cicero," replied Jeff. "My uncle and our grandfather. They are the ones who sent us here to meet with you and are now currently awaiting our return. We will honor and obey them as you suggest. Thank you for sharing your home, your time, and wisdom with us. It has been an incredible honor. We must depart now. If you will show us where we may make a fire, we can initiate the return process."

"Very well," said Cicero, "follow me."

He led them to an area where a fire was already burning in front of a memorial monument in honor of his ancestors.

"I believe this will be an appropriate spot to perform your process. The ancestors always must be honored, and

I can think of no better way to honor my ancestors than to help insure the fulfillment of their dreams of freedom and liberty in the far future. Go in peace, and remember that even though you fear for the liberty and freedom of your society, people don't know the value of what they have until it is gone. Freedom suppressed and again regained bites with keener fangs than freedom never endangered. Liberty is rendered even more precious by the recollection of servitude. Don't wait till freedom is gone before you enjoy, value, support, protect, and make the most of it.

"Though liberty is established by law, we must be vigilant, for liberty itself can enslave us and it is always present. Our Roman constitution speaks of the 'general welfare of the people'. Under that phrase, lusting tyrants can employ all sorts of excesses to make us bondsmen. You will be stronger as a nation when you have won your battle than you were before, and you *will* bite with keener fangs!"

The cousins took turns shaking the hand of their host and mentor, then gathered around the memorial fire. When everyone was ready, they raised their swords with their right arms, holding tightly to the rudis swords, the Roman symbol of freedom, in their left hands. Gently, they brought their swords together. They were enveloped by a flash of pure, white light and disappeared from Cicero's view.

He stood there for a long while, considering all that had just taken place. He reflected on the words he had said and the questions that the young men had asked and somehow knew that he would most certainly be giving his life for the Republic he loved. He knew not where or when, but he knew that it was inevitable. He also now knew that his life and his sacrifice would not be in vain.

He had indeed made a difference. His words and his legacy would live on for millennia. Cicero fell to his knees in front of the memorial to his ancestors, and wept for Rome.

CHAPTER SEVEN

THE FIRST
RETURN

The prophet and the Meglio were waiting for the heroes at the fire pit when they returned. They had been monitoring their quantum diagnostics from the Keeping Room and had been alerted by the quantum signals that their return was imminent, and so had lit the fire to prepare.

As usual, the heroes came back in a bright flash of light. The Meglio was relieved to see that all six cousins had returned safely. Upon closer examination, he could see that they all had blood stains on their clothing, but none looked wounded.

"Welcome home, my grandsons!" shouted the Meglio as he hustled over and hugged every one of them in turn.

"Are you all well?" he asked as he anxiously examined them for wounds.

"We are," replied Jeff, speaking for the group. "We can report that the mission was accomplished, and we have interesting perspectives to share from our conversation with Cicero."

The prophet took his turn hugging the heroes. "Tell

us about the new swords you have brought back with you," he asked the team.

Robbie replied, "These are rudis swords. They are the Roman symbol of freedom which victorious gladiators receive upon surviving battle in the arena. We were presented these swords by Julius Caesar himself!"

The Meglio and the prophet looked at each other in bewilderment.

The Meglio shook his head. "Well, that information will certainly require some clarification, and from the sound of it, I'm sure you brought home a very interesting story. Let's go to the Keeping Room. You can take a few minutes to clean up, then gather at the table for debriefing."

On the way to the Keeping Room, the cousins' conversation was energized by their success.

"It seems so strange," observed Nick, "to be here after having been in what was effectively the center of the ancient world. History seemed so alive there. It already feels far away now, like a memory or a dream that is starting to fade. I hope we can remember all we learned."

"I agree," said Joe, "very strange. Let's just tell the quantum computer as much as possible, as quickly as we can, and let it figure everything out."

As soon as they arrived in the Keeping Room and took their seats, the image of their grandmother appeared and spoke.

"Welcome home, my heroes. I perceive that your mission was successful. I also sense that there were some difficulties and challenges. Please, tell us of your trip."

Billy was the first to respond. "We arrived in the general vicinity of the target area we had identified; however, we were not in the open and deserted part of the plaza where we expected to be. We arrived in a temporary arena, right in the middle of a gladiator contest between two of the greatest gladiator teams of the day. It seems that on the day and time that we chose to arrive, Julius Caesar had sponsored a day of gladiatorial events to honor his father, and we got caught up in the middle of it. How did you miss that, Grandma? Wasn't that information available in the historical archives? We could have easily lost our lives because of that miscalculation."

The image looked concerned and did not speak for a few seconds.

"Sorry for the delay," the image finally said, "I was rechecking my work. There is information that in 65 BC, Julius Caesar did sponsor a gladiatorial event in honor of his father, but there is no month or date for the event found anywhere in the records. It was either a significant coincidence or something specifically related to the new timeline we are dealing with. It was unfortunate that we were not aware of this, but it is obvious that you all survived.

"According to the records, before the Colosseum was completed in 80 AD, gladiator events were held in various open spaces, including the Roman Forum. Temporary wooden stands were erected to view the events and then afterward torn down and removed. You must have arrived in the area of the Forum where this took place. It also explains the huge spike in quantum energy and activity that we observed upon your arrival. Please continue."

"When we arrived, we were immediately attacked by a huge gladiator," Ty explained as he dove into their arena near-death adventures, sharing how they worked as a team, ending with them unexpectedly meeting Cicero.

Observing the heroes' expressions as Ty related his version of the adventure, the Meglio noticed as Robbie raised an eyebrow at the words "worked as a team". He saw Robbie shake his head, but also noted that he didn't disagree with his brother's telling of the tale. Perhaps it would be prudent to ask Robbie later about his own version of the events.

"It is interesting to note," interjected the prophet, "that even though you encountered unexpected challenges right from the beginning of your mission, somehow, upon the successful resolution of the challenge, you were immediately presented with the opportunity to speak with Cicero. You remember that before you left I had serious concerns about our plan. I said that I did not like the idea one bit. I knew we were sending you to ancient Rome with a very thin outline and a makeshift strategy. I now see that even if things had gone exactly as we had intended, it would have been very challenging for you to have identified Cicero and convince him to let you speak with him.

"I see the influence of the swords in how this played out. I suggest that this tells us that we do not have to always have all the answers or a foolproof plan to succeed. It is our duty to do our work and to plan well, but if our intentions are pure, and we are diligent in our efforts, the swords will influence events in our favor. That is not to say that we can be sloppy or careless. It just means that we do not have to be perfect. I, for one, am very pleased to know that. It should encourage all of you! I have definitely learned a lesson about trust."

The heroes and the Meglio agreed with the prophet's observations. The Meglio then addressed the heroes. "Tell us now of your conversations with Cicero. Just give us the salient points since time is of the essence."

Robbie started, "After Joe convinced Cicero that we really were from the future by showing him his contact lens, he took us to his home, and we sat with him in the meditation garden. We told him about our mission and what we needed to understand."

The cousins then broke down the five key things they needed to know, and which points Cicero commanded them to take to heart and act upon.

"Those are valuable recommendations and astute observations. What a wonderful representation of the mind of Cicero," observed the Meglio. "I have been a student of his writings over the years and can see much of his future warnings to his Republic in his advice to you." Then, he addressed the image of his wife.

"Catherine, my dear, can you please incorporate the information our heroes have shared into your current analysis of the threat and search for any references in the current timeline that relate to them?"

"Of course, my love," replied the image. "I have already initiated the search. It will take a while, but I suggest that we still need more perspective to identify the proper actions to take. I believe you should move on to the second mission, since you have already identified it. When our heroes return from that mission, and we incorporate the information they receive, we will have a much clearer picture. Do I need to remind you of what you previously identified as the second mission? I remember how forgetful you can be."

The Meglio chuckled, "No, my dear, I remember it. The second mission will be to visit with Benjamin Franklin and Samuel Adams. Having been intimately involved with building a democratic republic from the ground up, they should be able to counsel us as to the critical components and vulnerabilities inherent in our current version of a Republic. I agree that based on the success of the first mission, we should immediately move on to the second, as we are still in the information-gathering stage." Then he addressed the team. "Is everyone in agreement?"

They all agreed to proceed with the second mission, to meet with Franklin and Adams.

"Good," replied the Meglio. "Once again, we will start with the facts as we know them in this current timeline."

The prophet addressed the team. "We have chosen Ben Franklin and Samuel Adams as the two Founding Fathers that you are to speak with because of the huge influence each of them had regarding the need and the urgency for the revolution. Their writings, speeches, and impact on the mindset of the country is critical for us to understand. Not only were they advocates for a republic as the form of government, but they were both insistent that liberty and freedom were the natural order of man.

"Samuel Adams was a firebrand, and he spoke forcefully and in incendiary terms about liberty and freedom. Benjamin Franklin was more intellectual and commonsensical in his approach. We need both of their perspectives on our current situation, and their ideas for how to most effectively influence and initiate change. Let's allow the quantum computer fill us in on the facts." The prophet then addressed the image. "Mom, would you begin the overview, please?"

"Certainly, Rob," the image replied. "Samuel Adams was the son of a merchant and maltster from Boston. Although he was an unsuccessful maltster and a poor businessman, he was an excellent politician. He, along with his second cousin John Adams, spent a great deal of time in the public eye advocating for resistance. In 1765, he was elected to the Massachusetts Assembly, where he served as clerk for many years. While there, he proposed a Continental Congress. He and his good friend, Tom Paine, were advocates of republicanism. In 1774, during the crisis in Boston, he was chosen to be a member of the provincial council. Later, he was appointed as a representative to the Continental Congress. His excellent oratory skills were used to advocate for independence from Britain. In 1776, as a delegate to the Continental Congress, he signed the Declaration of Independence.

"Most references say he wasn't too tall, but he was muscular, with gray eyes and a genial manner. He was a devout Puritan and a steadfast friend. John Adams observed that he had 'a universal good character, unless it should be admitted that he is too attentive to the public, and not enough to himself and his family'.

"The genius of Samuel Adams was politics. From his earliest years, he felt its inspiration. It occupied his thoughts, enlivened his conversation, and employed his pen.

"Benjamin Franklin was born in Boston, Massachusetts, on January 17, 1706, and may, by his life alone, be the most profound statement of what an American strives to be.

"He was described by Carl Van Doren as 'strongly built, rounded like a swimmer or a wrestler, not angular like a runner, he was five feet and nine or ten inches tall, with a large head and square, deft hands. His hair was blond or light brown, his eyes gray, full, and steady, his mouth wide and humorous with a pointed upper lip. His clothing was as clean as it was plain. Though he and others say he was hesitant in speech, he was prompt in action'.

"In 1733, he started publishing *Poor Richard's Almanack*, which became quite popular. He was appointed clerk of the Pennsylvania Assembly in 1736, and as

Postmaster the following year. In 1751, he was elected to the Pennsylvania Assembly. He served as an agent for Pennsylvania and three other colonies, visiting England, France, and other European countries. In 1775, he was elected to the Continental Congress. He helped edit the Declaration of Independence and was one of its signers. He continued to serve in government offices both locally and nationally.

"Some of his roles included first Postmaster General of the United States, Minister to the French Court, and member of the Constitutional Convention. He was also a treaty agent and signer of the peace agreement with Great Britain. He was a businessman, writer, publisher, scientist, diplomat, legislator, and social activist. He advocated for the abolition of slavery and for Native American rights.

"Although he had no formal education past 10 years old, he was welcomed in any royal court and societies everywhere. Even before George Washington and Thomas Jefferson were well known, Franklin had his stellar reputation firmly in hand. When he died on April 17, 1790, he was one of the most celebrated men in America.

"From Franklin and Adams, we need to understand about the struggle for liberty in our own country and what could cause us to lose that liberty now. We need their help to understand how we can remind the people of the price of freedom and the principles needed to sustain it."

The image then stopped the review and addressed the Meglio. "Dear, shall I go on, or would you like to turn the review in a different direction? Perhaps it would be an appropriate time to identify a date, time, and location for the mission?"

The Meglio addressed the team. "If you all feel that you have an adequate understanding of why we are targeting Franklin and Adams, and a good feel for who they are and what they accomplished, I would concur that we do as your grandmother has suggested and begin to identify the target dates."

Jeff responded, "I think we have the background we need. We had a lot less information about Cicero, and we were okay. Let's figure out where to go and when."

"So be it," replied the Meglio. "Catherine, please identify for us the optimal dates when we would be able to engage both men in conversation."

"As you wish, my love," replied the image of his wife. "By my calculations and based on the research, the obvious choice is to meet with the men after the signing of the Declaration of Independence."

"July 4, 1776!" exclaimed Ty. "How great is that? We are going back to the first Independence Day!"

The image of his grandmother smiled at his enthusiasm and excitement but shook her holographic head. "No, Ty, I am afraid that is a common misconception. On July 4, 1776, Congress officially adopted the Declaration of Independence, and as a result the date is celebrated as Independence Day. Nearly a month would go by, however, before the actual signing of the document took place. First, New York's delegates didn't officially give their support until July 9, because their home assembly hadn't yet authorized them to vote in favor of independence. Next, it took two weeks for the Declaration to be 'engrossed' or written on parchment in a clear hand.

"The Declaration of Independence wasn't signed on July 4, 1776. Most of the delegates signed it on August 2, but several, including Elbridge Gerry, Oliver Wolcott, Lewis Morris, Thomas McKean, Richard Henry Lee, and Matthew Thornton, signed it later.

"However, we know for certain that Benjamin Franklin and Samuel Adams signed the Declaration of Independence on August 2, 1776. We also are certain that it was signed by them at the Pennsylvania State House, or Independence Hall, as it is now called.

"Based on these hard facts, I recommend that the heroes return to that date and place to carry out their mission. Not only are we sure they were together there on that date, but having completed the work, finished the debates, and finally signed their names to the cause, they would be able to provide the most valuable perspective on the fight for liberty. They were both at the height of their intellectual powers and influence."

"Very well put, my dear," responded the Meglio. "So, we have a reasonable date and place identified for the mission. Can I get agreement from the team on the date of August 2, 1776, and the location of the Pennsylvania State House in Philadelphia, Pennsylvania?"

The cousins and the prophet, without hesitation and with enthusiasm, unanimously agreed to the proposal.

"Wonderful!" exclaimed the Meglio. "I love it when we are all on the same page. Now, we will need to agree on a time and a plan for approaching Franklin and Adams to ask for their help. What astounding ideas does this esteemed group have to offer?"

There was silence.

"Come now," encouraged the Meglio. "You are all well-educated young men and are now veterans of five successful missions. You must have some ideas you can share."

Nick responded to the Meglio's challenge. "The easiest place to start is with the time of day. As always, we will only have until sunrise the following day to complete the mission. So, it seems to me that we should maximize our time and plan to arrive at or near sunrise on August 2. That will give us time to acclimate ourselves to the environment, identify the likely places that the men may gather, and watch carefully for the most optimal time to approach them. Kind of like when I'm hunting. I like to scout out my prey."

"Well stated, Nick," replied the Meglio. "I agree. What say the rest of you?" Once again there was immediate agreement from all parties.

"Fine," said the Meglio, "sunrise it is. Now, how about the approach? Ideas?"

Joe spoke next. "I know this may be a crazy idea, but given that Franklin was a writer, publisher, and a printer, maybe he would respond to a request for an interview? I don't know if they did that back then, but given the historic nature of the event, maybe he would not think it too strange. I could approach him and ask if he could arrange for a time when he and Samuel Adams could sit down with me for an interview. He might be helpful in convincing Adams to join him. They were both very politically astute and understood the need to get the word out about the accomplishment, as well as positioning it the best way possible with the public to ensure ratification by the states. What do you think? Is it too crazy to work?"

Once again, no one spoke. Joe looked a little embarrassed by the silence, as if taking it as rejection of his idea. "Like I said," murmured Joe, "it was just a crazy idea."

"No," replied the Meglio, "it's a great idea! I was just stunned by the simplicity of it. I think it is perfect. We just need a little better understanding of the journalism of the times, but regardless, I think it is an idea that could work. It appeals to the 'vanity', if you will, of politicians of all ages and helps fulfill an actual need, the need to sway public opinion. With your experience as a reporter, and your education in political science, it falls right into your skill set. Perfect. Catherine, dear, please tell us what you know about newspapers and journalism in 1776?"

"Of course," replied the image. "From a quick search of the records, it seems that Joseph has come up with a viable plan. Journalism in America became a political force in the campaign for American independence and grew rapidly following the American Revolution. The press became a key support element to the country's political parties. As the colonies grew rapidly in the 18th century, newspapers appeared in port cities along the East Coast, usually started by master printers seeking a sideline. Among them was James Franklin, founder of *The New England Courant*, where he employed his younger brother, Benjamin Franklin, as a printer's apprentice.

"As a relatively new form of communication, American newspapers from 1765 to 1776 had significant advantages as engines of revolution: they were small, lithe, light-footed, and close to their audiences. As newspaper printers, editors, and writers, both Ben Franklin and Sam Adams were among the leaders of the American Revolution. Both men understood journalism, its use in swaying public opinion, and used it to their advantage. Finally, the July 6, 1776 edition of *The Pennsylvania Evening Post*, was the first newspaper to publish the newly-adopted Declaration of Independence and showed it as Americans first saw it, as front-page news.

"So, it would certainly make sense to Franklin and Adams that a young reporter would want to follow up on that story with the actual signing of the document. Is that information satisfactory, my love?" finished the image.

"More than enough, my dear. Thank you. You have

confirmed the viability of the plan," replied the Meglio.

"It is time for a decision," he addressed the heroes. "Do we have agreement that you will travel back to August 2, 1776, arriving at sunrise near the Pennsylvania State house?"

The group agreed.

"Do we also have agreement on the plan that Joe proposed for getting Franklin and Adams to meet with you?" the Meglio asked.

"I have one thought to add to Joe's plan," said Jeff. "I think that whichever of us are chosen to make the trip should also pose as reporters from rival newspapers and approach him at the same time. I feel that he might be able to refuse an interview with one newspaper but would have difficulty refusing multiple, simultaneous requests. Hopefully, he will be flattered enough to accept them all. We can then get together with him at the same time. What do you think?"

"That sounds reasonable to me," said Joe. "I think that could work." The rest of the group agreed to the revised plan, which pleased the Meglio greatly.

"It would seem, gentlemen, that we have a solid plan. Please take a few minutes to collect yourselves, and we shall leave for the fire pit in a few minutes. Use the time to fix the arrival information in your minds and visualize your plan."

CHAPTER EIGHT

THE SECOND MISSION

～～～

As the heroes walked together to the fire pit by the river, the Meglio followed behind and listened as they discussed their excitement at the opportunity of meeting two of the Founding Fathers. This was not like going back to ancient Rome to speak with Cicero. He knew they had only been marginally familiar with his reputation and his work. But Franklin and Adams were an entirely different story.

The boys had grown up on stories of the American Revolution, studied it in school, written papers about the various heroes, and of course, celebrated Independence Day every year. This mission would have a very personal meaning for all of them. He was sure each of them hoped they would be chosen by the swords.

Upon arrival at the river, the heroes worked together to build the fire. By the time it was roaring, their conversation had dwindled, and they stood in silence around it. The Meglio addressed the team.

"Gentlemen, you have been briefed about the mission. You understand the objective, the arrival location, time, and date. We have outlined a reasonable plan to approach Franklin and Adams. This should be a moderately risk-free mission. However, none of the missions or assignments you have participated in have gone exactly according to plan. You have had to be adaptable, responsive, and attuned to the leading of the swords.

"Assume it will be so on this mission also. Take nothing for granted, be cautious, and watch each other's backs. You are heading into a time of revolution, and revolutions are inherently dangerous. Stay on point, stay alert, and stay focused on the mission objective. Any questions?"

The heroes had no questions. They seemed energized, relaxed, and grinned in anticipation of the opportunity to meet with two giants of American history. They took their positions encircling the roaring flames of the fire pit and stood ready.

The prophet asked them, "Are you ready to do your duty for family, the world, and for freedom?"

"We are!" was their unified reply.

"Raise your Swords of Valor," the prophet commanded.

The swords were raised. "Slowly bring your swords together, and Godspeed," said the prophet.

The swords were gradually and gently brought together until they touched. Once again, a bright flash of pure, white light enveloped the heroes, and they were hidden from the view of the prophet and the Meglio.

When the light faded, the Meglio saw that Billy and Ty remained standing round the fire with swords raised. Apparently, the swords of Roland and Charlemagne were not needed for this mission.

"Darn!" said Ty looking around. "I really wanted to go on this mission!"

"Me too," said Billy, "but we have to assume the swords know what they are doing."

"Agreed," replied the prophet, "We have all learned to trust the swords and accept their decision. Let's head back to the Keeping Room and monitor the quantum activity of your cousins."

The Meglio, the prophet, and the two remaining heroes marched back to the Keeping Room, somewhat anxious about the fate of their traveling family members.

Jeff, Joe, Nick, and Robbie materialized in a flash of light in an alley between two buildings directly across from the Philadelphia State House. Robbie took stock of who had made the trip and mentally assessed the situation. He motioned to his cousins, then led them to the end of the alley where they could get a clear view of the street which ran in front of the State House.

The cobblestone street was packed with people, horse-drawn carriages, dogs, cats, children of all ages, and vendors selling food and drink. The hot and muggy air didn't help their breathing as they swatted flies buzzing about their heads.

There were street artists painting pictures of the scene, old men sitting in chairs in the middle of the road, waiting for news of the signing of the Declaration, and other people handing out pamphlets advocating for peace with England.

Robbie was startled by the mass of humanity before them. He had envisioned that a more sedate scene would greet them upon their arrival. What he saw had the appearance of a street festival filled with people speaking in typical English accents, not American ones.

"I guess the signing of the Declaration of Independence was more of an event than we assumed," he remarked. "I always thought of it as more of a formality and an administrative duty. It looks like the people are as enthusiastic about it as they were for the actual ratification of the Declaration."

Joe responded to Robbie's observation, "That's because they didn't know when the document was going to be approved by the Continental Congress, but the signing was planned ahead of time, and all the newspapers had been announcing the date of the signing for weeks. The people were anticipating it."

"That and the fact that this was the most dangerous part of the process," reminded Jeff.

"Since it was announced in the papers, anyone who opposed the split with England would know about it also, and if they wanted to disrupt it, this would be the place and time. Plus, most of the leaders of the revolution were here all in one place. They were highly vulnerable to attack. I suppose the people are mostly here to show their support and, in some way, protect their leaders."

Nick noted, "I think we'd better move to a more isolated location where we can regroup and observe from a distance. I can't think with all this noise. Is it just me, or is everyone's English accent annoying? I guess the British and Americans all sounded alike back then."

They spotted a sort of village green about half a block away and decided to head in that direction. They exited the alley and melted into the throngs of people. As they made their way toward the green, Robbie fell behind the others as a gruff man jostled him hustling in the opposite direction. Robbie momentarily lost his grip on his sword, and as he reached down to pick it up off the ground, it became visible for a moment.

The man looked startled by the appearance of the huge sword, but swiftly recovered and kept moving in the direction of the State House. Robbie quickly lowered his arm, and once again the sword became invisible. He hurried to catch up with the other heroes and joined them as they reached the green. They found a spot beneath an ancient chestnut tree.

"We need to keep a constant eye on the front of the building," said Jeff. "We don't want to miss the opportunity to speak with Franklin and Adams after the signing ceremony. We may only get one chance at this. Who knows where they will go after they leave the building?"

"Why don't we take turns mingling with the crowds?" asked Robbie. "That way we can find out the timing of all of this. Some of those people are sure to know when the signing is scheduled to take place and maybe when it will be over."

"Good idea," replied Jeff, "but do it in pairs. Robbie, you and Joe go first. Nick and I will stay here and try and keep an eye on you. Report back as soon as you have information. We will also try to get the lay of the land and watch for security of any sort."

"Got it," said Robbie, then he and Joe headed back into the crowd.

They made their way down Chestnut Street in the direction of the State House, fighting their way through the energetic throng. They eventually staked out a spot directly in front of the building and started to make conversation with the people nearby. Robbie noticed an older gentleman who was seated, sketching a picture of the scene.

"Excuse me, sir," started Robbie, "you have a real eye for detail. That's a wonderful sketch."

The old man glanced up but didn't stop his work. "Thank you, young man. Are you an artist?

"I dabble a bit," Robbie admitted. "May I ask you a question?"

"Certainly," replied the old man, continuing to sketch.

"I am wondering if you know when the signing will take place, or when it will be finished?"

"It is hard to say," said the old man squinted up at the sky for a moment, then added, "They all arrived before dawn and have been in there for over an hour already. With that many politicians in one room, even a task as simple as signing their names could take all day. I am hopeful that they will be done by noon, but that is just the wish of an old and impatient man."

Robbie thanked the man for the information and rejoined Joe, who was speaking with a beautiful young woman. He smiled. That was just like Joe. With all the people in easy reach, he could have spoken with anyone, but of course, he would choose the prettiest girl in the vicinity to chat with.

"So," Joe was saying, "do you live nearby?"

The young woman blushed and looked down replying, "Yes, I live on Market Street, just a block and a half away from here."

"Why are you here today so early in the morning?"

She replied, "Benjamin Franklin is a neighbor of mine, and I am one of his housekeepers. He has given us the day off to attend the signing. He is such a wonderful man. I was excited to have the day off, and an opportunity to support him in the cause by my presence here today."

"Wonderful!" replied Joe. "I am sure he will be happy to know that you shared in this historic event. Do you know what time they expect to be done?"

The girl's face brightened as she replied to Joe's question. "He said that he expected to be home for an early supper. That is why the cooks could not have the entire day off. They are going to go back home around noon to start preparations. He told them to prepare enough food for six people, as he would be having guests to celebrate."

"Excellent," replied Joe. "I hope they stick to the schedule. The crowds will be huge if it takes all day. What is the address of Mr. Franklin's home?"

"He lives in the middle house on the 300 block of Market Street. Why do you ask? Will you be one of his guests?" the young woman asked.

"If all goes well, that may be a possibility," replied Joe. "We are reporters for a New York newspaper, and we were hoping to interview Mr. Franklin and Mr. Samuel Adams today. We are hoping he will invite us to his home for the interview. I know it is a long shot, but thanks for your time and for the information. We need to go, but maybe, if all goes well, I will see you tonight. By the way, I am Joe, and this is my cousin, Robbie. What is your name?"

The young woman blushed once again and replied, "Nice to meet you both. My name is Lydia. I will hope that all goes well so that we may meet again." Joe and Robbie bowed to her, then they started towards the green where Jeff and Nick were waiting for them.

As they hustled back, Robbie shook his head. "Really, Joe? Hitting on a girl in the middle of a mission? Not sure that was a great idea. Remember the timeline stuff? We are supposed to limit our interactions. I would say that flirting with a beauty from the past does not fall into the 'limiting our interaction' category."

"I got valuable information, did I not?" replied Joe.

"You did, but still, you need to be more careful. Anyone could have overheard your conversation, and she will probably tell her friends about it."

"So?" said Joe, "I still don't see how that could possibly matter. Let's just get back to the others and not make a big deal of it, okay?"

They arrived at the green, found Jeff and Nick relaxing under the tree, and filled them in on the probable timing. They decided to hang out in the village green until around noon, and then make their way back to the State House to position themselves for the opportunity to interview Franklin.

When the clock on the State House struck noon, the heroes roused themselves and began to make their way through the crowd. As they approached the building, the way became more congested, and it was difficult to pass. They slowly snaked their way through the gathering throng, staying close to one another. Eventually, they established a spot for themselves in the cobblestone plaza in front of the building near the main door. It was about 12:45, and Robbie resigned himself to the possibility of a long wait.

Looking around, Robbie noticed Lydia standing a short distance away. She was looking at them, and when she saw that he'd noticed her, she motioned for him to tap Joe on the shoulder.

Robbie leaned over to Joe and said, "Your girlfriend wants to speak with you."

Joe replied, "Girlfriend? What are you talking about?"

"Over there," Robbie nodded in Lydia's direction. "The girl you were speaking with before. She wanted me to get your attention."

Joe looked where he indicated. Lydia flashed a huge

smile and motioned for him to join her. Joe tried to excuse himself from the others, but Robbie protested.

"Not by yourself, Joe," he warned. "I'll come with you."

"You'll squash my game, cousin!" Joe complained.

Jeff spoke up. "Robbie's right, Joe. Take him with you."

Joe sighed. "Fine. But don't crowd me, ok? You can stay within earshot, but don't interfere."

Robbie shook his head as they made their way slowly through the crowd. He stopped a few feet away as Joe kept walking to join her near a lamp post.

Keeping his eyes and ears open, Robbie chuckled to himself as Joe started off with a winning smile.

"It's good to see you again, Lydia. Do you have an updated time for me?"

"No update on the time," she said, "but I have information about your dinner plans. You and your brother will be having dinner with Mr. Franklin tonight! I discussed it with the head cook, and she will make the arrangements." Then she turned to the tall and imposing man next to her and said, "This is my brother, First Lieutenant John Clark. He has just arrived here in Philadelphia after being in New York for the past few months. He is quite well connected with Mr. Franklin, and I am sure he will see that you are welcomed."

The man cast Joe a sideways look and said, "If you and your cousin, and the other men you are standing with, will meet us around the back of the building in ten minutes, I will fill you in on the details, get your names, and then make the arrangements for your interview with Mr. Franklin. That way you won't have to fight your way through the crowd to speak with him, understood? Ten minutes. Do not be late."

Joe replied, "Wow, that would be great! Thank you. This will work so much better. Do you think you could also ask Mr. Franklin to invite Samuel Adams to dinner? We need to speak with him, also."

Lieutenant Clark replied, "He is already on the guest list. He will be there."

Joe turned to Lydia. "Thank you, Lydia, I truly appreciate the generosity. See you tonight!" Then, he motioned for Robbie to join him as he made his way back to his cousins.

When he reached them, Joe filled them in. "We just have to meet the lieutenant and Lydia in the back of the building in ten minutes and wait until dinner. We can interview Franklin and Adams then. This is working out so well!"

"I don't know," said Robbie, "I would prefer sticking to our plan. I'm not very comfortable with these kinds of 'fortuitous interventions'."

"Don't you trust the swords?" asked Joe. "Can't you see their influence in this? I think we should take this opportunity. Let's not look a gift horse in the mouth."

After a few minutes of debate, they agreed to meet Lydia and her brother behind the State House to hear them out, and then decide whether to accept the invitation. They made their way through the crowd and around to the back of the State House where they saw Lydia and Lieutenant Clark waiting for them between two doors.

Joe said, "Lieutenant Clark, Lydia, I would like to introduce Jeff and Nick. Lydia, you have already met Robbie. As I said, we are here to interview Mr. Franklin. I have filled them in on the plans, but we need further clarification about time and location."

Lieutenant Clark replied, "I am sure you do. After

all, assassins always need to know when and where their targets will be most vulnerable to attack." Then he whistled loudly.

From the two doors streamed a dozen armed soldiers who quickly surrounded them, their guns pointed in the cousins' direction. Another man also appeared at the door. Lieutenant Clark addressed him. "Is the man you saw carrying the huge sword earlier in the day among the men standing here?" he asked him.

Robbie recognized the man as the one who had bumped into him on the way to the village green. The man replied, pointing at Robbie, "Yes, that is the man who had the large sword!"

"Thank you, Hercules. That will be all. Please go and inform Mr. Franklin that the agents of the Secret Committee have once again done their duty and foiled an assassination plot against him and Mr. Adams. They may continue with the signing."

Hercules left to do as he was told, and Lieutenant Clark turned his attention back to the cousins. Jeff spoke up, "Lieutenant Clark, you are making a mistake. We are not here to assassinate anyone. We truly wish to speak with Mr. Franklin and Mr. Adams about a very serious matter. If you would just take us to them, we can explain ourselves to them and clear all this up."

"Do you take me for a fool?" replied Lieutenant Clark. "You are dealing with the top agents of the Secret Committee, and we know a thing or two about the plans of the British. We have been watching your suspicious behavior all morning. I am afraid that there is no way you are going to talk your way out of this."

Then he turned to the captain of the military unit and said, "Captain, take these men into custody. Lock them up, and we will arraign them in the morning. With the whole of Congress in attendance, the matter should go very quickly."

Robbie whispered to Joe, "Should we show them the swords? Do you think that would help?"

Joe said, "I don't think so. At this point we have twelve guns pointed at us from five feet away. I am afraid we will be dead before we have a chance to explain. Whipping out our swords right now will just get us killed. Hang on to the swords tightly, and maybe we can use them to free ourselves."

Nick whispered, "I agree with Joe. Let's save the swords for a more appropriate time, maybe when we are alone with Franklin. Let's go along for now and see what happens. The swords will help us figure this out."

The soldiers approached the cousins, and with guns and bayonets pointed at their backs, roughly escorted them off to the brig in the basement of the State House.

A little while later, the cousins were sitting in their cell. They'd had no further contact from anyone. They'd been searched before being thrust into the cell, but of course, the swords were not discovered. The swords' cloaking abilities seemed to have prevented that from happening.

"So, now what?" Robbie asked. "We can't just sit here rotting in this cell!"

Joe grimaced. "We've only been in here a few minutes, cousin. Chill out and let me think."

"Robbie's right," Nick chimed in. "I vote we try to cut through these bars with our swords."

"Great idea, Nick," Robbie grinned. "Let's do it!"

Nick and Robbie drew their swords and began sawing at the cell bars. After a few minutes, Robbie stopped and examined the bar he'd been working on.

"It's not even scratched!" he complained. "I thought

these swords had powers and would cut through anything."

Joe rubbed his chin. "Either the swords are not effective in cutting iron bars, or their power is not available to us for this purpose. It seems we will have to wait for another opportunity to gain our freedom."

Robbie frowned, but settled himself on the floor with his back to the far wall.

Two hours later, he heard footsteps approaching. Keys jangled in the outer door. It opened, and two silhouettes appeared, framed by the light coming from the outer room. One silhouette closed the door and retreated back the way he'd come. The other remained and approached the cousins. They could not make out the man's face in the dim light.

Then he spoke. "Well, this is a fine mess for soldiers of the Swords of Valor to find themselves in. Maybe I should let you rot in here until just before sunrise to teach you all a good lesson. But then, I am sure that would put a significant damper on your mission." Then he pulled out a set of keys, opened the cell door, and entered.

When the light from the oil lamps in the brig fell on his face, Robbie, Billy, and Joe's eyes widened with incredible surprise. Jeff looked utterly confused as he looked between his cousins and the mysterious man.

Robbie leaned over and whispered, "Robert Ogilvie Petrie."

Soundlessly, Jeff's mouth formed an 'O' as realization apparently dawned.

None of them had met him during their lifetimes, since he had died in 1975 before they were born. However, Robbie, Joe, and Billy recognized him from their very first mission when they went back to obtain the Sword of Mercy from Windsor Castle during World War

II. Now, here he was again in 1776, standing before them in their time of need.

Robbie spoke first, "What are you doing here? How did you know we were down here?"

"First things first," replied their great-grandfather. "Let's start with the truth. First, I know who you are. Not just that you are soldiers of the Swords of Valor, but that you are my great-grandsons. I knew that Joe, Billy, and Robbie were my descendants when I fought alongside them in 1944."

Joe responded to that news by asking, "How did you know? You never gave us any indication that you were aware of that back in Windsor Castle, and we didn't tell you. We thought you were unaware."

"Let's just say that it is an unwritten rule of the Guardians not to discuss past collaborations amongst ourselves when we are engaged in battle. I have been on missions with all of you in what is my past, but your future, so you do not remember them yet. When we met at Windsor Castle, I had already met you before. All of you. So, I was already aware of our relationship.

"Again, except for the World War II mission, you have not yet been on any other missions where we worked together, but some day you will. You will remember it all then. For now, be satisfied with that understanding and ask no more questions about it. I will, however, be happy to answer your questions about what I am doing here, and how I knew you were in the brig.

"My current mission for the Guardians is to help the Continental Congress in battling the influence of the Swords of Terror. The Apostles of Azazel are fighting on the side of the British. They wish to see the rebellion crushed. They also want this war to be as bloody as possible. The Guardians have assigned me and a few others to help in the cause. Benjamin Franklin himself has recruited me to be a double agent of the Secret Committee, which is the intelligence arm of the Continental Congress. This is not my first mission for them. I have been on several missions in the recent past to aid in the cause of freedom for the colonies. That, my understanding of the British mindset, and my Scottish heritage, make me a perfect double agent. The British think that I am on their side, but I do nothing but feed them bad intelligence.

"I am here in Philadelphia for a meeting of the Secret Committee following the signing ceremony. Lucky for you that Lieutenant Clark chose me to spy on your activities today after his conversation with Lydia."

Robbie was both overjoyed and upset. He addressed his great-grandfather. "Why didn't you just tell them we were not assassins? Why didn't you tell them we were related to you and vouch for us? Why have us arrested and thrown into prison? How is this all going to make our mission any easier?"

"Easy, son," said his great-grandfather. "Don't get your kilt in a bunch. This was the best way for us to talk privately. Only Mr. Franklin is aware of my real identity. It would have been a little hard for me to explain all of that without revealing too much. Plus, you all needed a good lesson in the value of caution on these missions.

"I observed you all acting carelessly today, and that is dangerous. You need to understand the risks we face while on missions. This will be a lesson you won't soon forget."

"Okay, point well taken," replied Nick. "I knew Joe was going to get us in trouble by flirting with that Lydia girl."

"I was not flirting!" said Joe. "I was interviewing her

in a friendly manner, that's all. How was I to know she was an agent?"

"Lydia Darragh is our top female agent in the Philadelphia area. She is assigned to the protection of Mr. Franklin himself. It was she who sniffed out your plot and reported it to Lieutenant Clark, who reported it to me. The other agent you bumped into earlier corroborated it. He is Hercules Mulligan from New York, who happens to be here for an urgent meeting of the committee.

"As for Joe's 'flirting', that was not the only problem," their great-grandfather continued. "You allowed a sword to be revealed, you lollygagged about in the village green like you were on a picnic, and you talked openly for anyone to overhear. I was in the tree above you in the green and heard your conversations. You were not even aware that I had climbed the tree while you sat underneath it. I could have slit your throats at any point. You soldiers need to sharpen up, or you will get yourselves killed. If any Apostles had been around, you would have been easy prey for them."

"There are no more Apostles, Great-Grandpa," said Jeff. "We destroyed them and the Swords of Terror on our last mission."

Great-Grandpa Robert looked startled for a moment, then said, "You are going to have to explain that one to me, young man. How is that possible?"

The cousins then took turns filling him in on the events of the last mission. How they had successfully gathered the stolen Swords of Valor at the height of their power, and how the prophet had performed the First and Second Final Processes to destroy the Swords of Terror and change the timeline.

They then told him about the effect of the changes to the timeline and about their new mission, the Leviathan

Alliance, and the threat to liberty and freedom they posed.

When they finished, their great-grandfather asked, "So why don't I remember any of this? How is it possible that I have been fighting Apostles until just recently? I will admit that I have been puzzled by their inactivity of late, but I assumed they were going quiet for a time to gather their forces and make a big effort soon."

Robbie replied, "I have to assume that for some reason you were impacted the same way Grandpa was impacted, or not impacted, by the time change. When he returned from being dead, he did not know that the timeline had changed and remembered just the old timeline. We, on the other hand, had been safe in the Keeping Room when the time wave hit and remember both the old timeline and the new one. Maybe it has to do with when you traveled back here? Maybe you were in transit when the time wave hit and were immune to the changes?"

Their great-grandfather considered that for a while, then said, "I am a simple man and things like people returning from the dead, timeline changes, and time waves are beyond my understanding. Let's just chalk it up to the influence of the swords and be done with it. What I hear you telling me is that the threat has been extinguished, and I am out of a job. Is that right?"

"That is essentially it," replied Joe. "I assume that if you were to return to your time, you would find many changes that you may not be comfortable with or understand. It is better that you know that now and be forewarned than to face it unprepared."

"I agree with that," replied Great-Grandpa. "Looks like I have a lot of thinking to do. In the meantime, tell me what you need to speak with Mr. Franklin about, and I will make sure you get your audience."

They explained the focus of their mission, and their great-grandfather agreed to go and speak with Franklin and Adams and arrange the dinner meeting for all of them later that evening. He then left them in the cell while he went to speak with Lieutenant Clark about their release.

He returned with Lieutenant Clark an hour later. The lieutenant did not look happy. He opened the cell door and told them that they were free to go, saying to them, "You are very lucky that you have Agent Petrie vouching for you. There is no other agent whose word I would take in this matter. He will accompany you and be with you during your conversation with Mr. Franklin and Mr. Adams. He will be there for their protection, and if there are any problems, he and Agent Darragh will be bringing you back here for execution. Do you understand?"

"We do understand," Robbie replied, as his cousins nodded their agreement. A few moments later, they left the brig in the custody of their great-grandfather.

CHAPTER NINE

DINNER WITH FRANKLIN AND ADAMS

By the time they were released, the sun was starting to set. Robbie noticed that the crowds had disappeared from in front of the State House, and all seemed peaceful.

"It looks like we missed the signing ceremony and the excitement afterward, but we are still on track to accomplish our mission," he observed. "I guess all is well."

"It would seem so," replied Jeff as they followed their great-grandfather along Chestnut Street toward Market Street. They made a right turn at the corner and walked a block and a half, at which point their great-grandfather stopped.

He pointed across the street to a large townhouse-style home and said, "That, gentlemen, is the home of Benjamin Franklin. Before we go barging in there and impose on his time and hospitality, I must warn you. Do not take the man for a fool. He is very affable and friendly, but he also has a dark side. This is a man who has been dealing with very serious matters for a very long time. He enjoys lulling people into a false sense of security by exuding an air of casualness and forgetfulness. That is a ruse. He is one of the sharpest minds in history. He is an incredible negotiator and as trustworthy as they come. So be straight with him and don't dither. Be direct, truthful, and above all, humble.

"As for Sam Adams, he is as fiery as you have been told by history. He has little patience for uncertainty. He will speak loudly and forcefully at times. Do not be alarmed. It is not anger, but passion. Stay at ease and speak with calm assurance, and you will get the answers you seek. Are you ready to enter?"

"Now that you have basically told us not to behave like cowardly, cringing, arrogant barbarians, I think we are all set, Great-Grandpa!" said Robbie. "Let's go get some answers so we can go home."

The group crossed the street and knocked on the door of Franklin's home. Agent Lydia Darragh answered the door. She greeted their great-grandfather warmly and simply nodded to the cousins, ignoring Joe altogether.

She led them up a set of stairs to a huge dining room paneled in warm, alternating tones of brown and burgundy. The table was set for seven and candles were glowing around the room. The setting sun cast a pink glow through the windows to the right as they entered, making the cherrywood paneling even rosier.

"Please, seat yourselves," Lydia instructed. "Mr. Franklin and Mr. Adams will be joining you shortly."

Their great-grandfather took a seat next to the one they presumed Mr. Franklin would take. The rest of them spread themselves along the sides of the table, carefully avoiding any seat which might be viewed as one of honor. Robbie sat in awe of the fact that he was sitting in Benjamin Franklin's dining room and anticipating his arrival. Quietly, they reviewed their assignment between them.

"Remember," said Jeff, "we need to understand the foundations of liberty and freedom from their perspective, as architects of a new nation. We have to see if we can identify the most critical elements, where there might be weaknesses, and how those weaknesses could be exploited to the detriment of freedom."

"We also need to understand how they inspired people to fight for freedom and liberty," added Joe. "That is going to be critically important if we have to change hearts and minds when we get back. What were the most important points they expressed to make people decide to give up what they had to support a revolution that only had a small chance of success?"

Everyone agreed. At that point Mr. Franklin entered the room.

"Welcome back, Robert!" Franklin exclaimed, addressing their great-grandfather with obvious familiarity and joy. Everyone stood as Franklin walked over to hug his old friend.

"Congratulations, sir, on the success of the day," Robert said to Franklin. "I am sure that finally having the Declaration ratified and signed must be a very proud moment for you."

"Aye, that it is," replied Franklin. "It has been a long and treacherous road, and our real battle is just beginning. But I thank you for all your efforts on our behalf and for your service to the nation. Your information has been critical these past months. Please, introduce me to these strapping young gentlemen!"

"Mr. Franklin, I present to you my great-grandsons," he said with a sweep of his hand. "They have just arrived this morning and have had a very interesting day so far. They seek your help with a grave problem, so I appreciate your kind acceptance of our request to meet this evening."

Franklin eyed each of them individually, assessing them quietly. Then he said, "Please indulge me, gentlemen, and show me your Swords of Valor."

Surprised by the request, Robbie looked to his great-grandfather for direction.

"Please," he instructed them, "comply with our host's request."

The cousins stood at attention and raised their right arms. Their swords appeared immediately and glowed very briefly for an instant then returned to normal. Robbie remembered that this was an indication that they were in the presence of virtue and valor.

"Thank you for that, gentlemen. I never fail to get a thrill when I see that," said Franklin. "Robert indulges me often with that inspirational display. Remind me, Robert, which sword is it you carry?"

"I carry the Sword of St. Peter the Apostle," he replied. "It was one of the swords my family was formed to protect."

"Very impressive," replied Franklin. Then he asked, "Do you believe it would be wise to bring Sam in on this? The Guardian information, I mean. I'm sure he'd be more inclined to share information and might give him some interesting perspectives."

Their great-grandfather considered the request and replied, "I will leave that to your discretion, Mr. Franklin. You are the genius in the room, and this is your home. We will follow your lead. I am sure you will make the right decision; you always do."

"So be it," replied Franklin. "We will see how things progress."

Just then, Lydia entered and announced, "Excuse me, Mr. Franklin. Mr. Samuel Adams has arrived."

"Thank you, Lydia," he acknowledged. "Please, invite him to join us."

"As you wish, sir. Will you need anything further before dinner is served?"

"I don't believe so. All is well."

Lydia left quietly, and moments later, Samuel Adams entered. Instantly, the atmosphere in the room changed dramatically. The collegial cordiality dissipated, and an intense and focused energy replaced it. He marched in, shoulders leading, stopped just short of where Franklin stood and addressed him without giving him any personal space.

"Will you now fill me in on the purpose of this get-together, or will you keep me in the dark until dessert?" he demanded.

Franklin chuckled and put his hand on Adams' shoulder, "My dear friend, the purpose is a delightful evening with Agent Petrie, whom you know, and his progeny. They face serious challenges and need our sage counsel. I thought that after a stressful day of herding squirrels, we would enjoy an evening of delicious food and pleasant conversation. Please, let's take our seats and begin."

Franklin's words seemed to take the edge off Adams' impatience, and he took the seat at the opposite end of the table. Franklin rang the dinner bell, and a servant appeared instantly. He instructed her to begin the dinner service. She left, and he addressed his guests.

"Now that we are all seated, I will ask Agent Petrie's relatives to introduce themselves." He gestured toward Jeff and asked him to start.

"I am Jeff Melillo, and I am from New York. I am currently working as a lawyer for a small firm, handling corporate law cases. I am a graduate of the University of

Pennsylvania." Then he corrected himself, "I mean the College of Philadelphia."

"Wonderful!" exclaimed Franklin, "How pleasant to have a graduate of my own college in attendance. I am sure I will be dazzled by your intellect. Don't disappoint me!"

The rest of the cousins rolled their eyes and introduced themselves in turn. When the introductions were over, Franklin thanked them and got down to business.

"Sam, these young men are faced with a matter of some urgency which requires that they ask us questions relevant to liberty and freedom. That is all I really know at this point. Please feel free to share from your experience, and I will do the same. I am sure you recognize the importance of assisting our youth in their quest to understand the foundations of freedom. After all, you have been so instrumental in our own efforts. Consider your participation a favor to Agent Petrie and myself."

"My ongoing engagement in this 'interrogation' will depend on my assessment of these young men as we proceed," replied Adams.

"Very well, I would ask the gentlemen to state their purpose and their desired outcome," said Franklin. Looking directly at Jeff, he added, "Since you are from a familiar educational background, why don't you begin?" Jeff cleared his throat.

"We are here today because we, as a family, are faced with a challenge that threatens our liberty and freedom. We four have been charged with understanding the foundations of freedom and liberty, and how to inspire a group to stand up to current or potential oppressors and throw off the chains intended for them. You two are highly-respected fathers of this nation and have been identified as the most critical people for us to speak with regarding this matter. I ask that you indulge our questions and consider answering them freely and candidly. The problem itself is private and personal, and we are not at liberty to divulge the core of the matter, so please excuse any perceived dissembling on our part, we will share what we can."

"Very well stated," exclaimed Franklin, "the quality of your education is evident. I am proud of you. Who would like to ask the first question?"

Just then, the first course arrived, and the conversation stalled until everyone had been served. When the servants left the room, Joe asked the first question.

"What would you say are the most critical foundational elements of freedom and liberty?"

Franklin responded immediately, "Fear God, and your enemies will fear you. Rebellion against tyrants is obedience to God. Freedom is not a gift bestowed upon us by other men, but a right that belongs to us by the laws of God and nature. That is the very first and primary understanding that every man needs to have regarding freedom and liberty. Your liberty is your natural right. If a people believe that their liberty is a gift from government or any other ruler, they are mistaken and in danger of enslavement. Do you agree, Sam?"

"I do," replied Adams. "The natural liberty of man is to be free from any superior power on Earth, and not to be under the will or legislative authority of man, but only to have the law of nature for his rule. This must be clearly stated in every founding document and be the understanding of all branches of government and the people from whom their power is derived."

Franklin nodded in agreement and then said, "The second most important foundational element is that freedom of speech is a principal pillar of freedom and liberty. When this support is taken away, the constitution of a free society is dissolved, and tyranny is erected on its ruins.

"Republics derive their strength and vigor from a popular examination into the action of the magistrates. Whoever would overthrow the liberty of a nation must begin by subduing free speech. This is something that is near and dear to the heart of my dear friend Sam and myself. We have both been publishers ourselves and know how valuable the freedom of speech is in shining a light on the dark places of tyranny."

Franklin looked across the table at Mr. Adams as if asking for his comment.

Adams responded. "No people will tamely surrender their liberties, nor can any be easily subdued, when knowledge is diffused, and virtue is preserved. On the contrary, when people are universally ignorant, and debauched in their manners, they will sink under their own weight without the aid of foreign invaders. Freedom of the press, when unencumbered and truly free of influence and hidden agendas, will establish the diffusion of ideas and will arm the people with knowledge and perspective. This is a foundational element of liberty. It is in the interest of tyrants to reduce the people to ignorance and vice, for they cannot live in any country where virtue and knowledge prevail. I agree."

"As a follow up to my esteemed colleague's words," Franklin added, "I would add that any nation or any group of well-informed people who have been taught to know and prize the rights which God has given them, cannot be enslaved. It is in the region of ignorance that tyranny originates. Take away freedom of speech and freedom of the press, and ignorance begins."

"Thank you for your answers, gentlemen," said Joe. "To summarize the answers to the first question, I heard you say that first, men and their leaders must understand that freedom is their natural God-given right and the primary obligation of their government. Any government which denies this or disputes this is an enemy of the people they govern.

"Second, that free speech is a pillar of freedom and liberty. If that is threatened or limited, by this also we will know our enemy. Have I summarized correctly?"

"You have, young man," replied Franklin. "In fact, I would make it even clearer by adding that it is the duty of a people to fight against such governments. Tyranny cannot be tolerated or even allowed to raise its head. It must be challenged. What is your second question?"

Robbie spoke up. "Mr. Franklin and Mr. Adams, given what you have just told us, how should a situation which resembles the one you outlined be handled?"

"May I answer this question first, Ben?" asked Adams.

"Certainly," replied Franklin. "Please."

"The liberties of our country, our people, our families, and the freedom of our civil constitution, are worth defending against all hazards, and it is our duty to defend them against all attacks," began Adams, becoming more animated with each word.

"Much of mankind is governed by their feelings more than by reason. We cannot make events, but our business is to wisely improve them by whatever means are available to us. Remember, if we suffer tamely a lawless attack upon our liberty, we encourage it and involve others in our doom. We must seriously consider that millions yet unborn may be the miserable sharers of the event. Our contest has been, and yours may very well be, not only whether we ourselves shall be free, but whether there shall be freedom left to your family or mankind, and an asylum on earth for civil and religious liberty and freedom!"

"Well said Sam, very well said," applauded Franklin, "and very inspiring. You speak the truth. It is always about the future. We may be resigned to suffer a certain fate, and that is our free right. But we do not have the right to impose that fate on future generations. In fact, we have an obligation to prevent it, especially when it involves freedom. If we allow it, we are condemning future generations to enslavement. Let us contemplate our forefathers, and posterity, and resolve to maintain the rights bequeathed to us from the former, for the sake of the latter.

"Now, as to how to do this, I say anyone can complain, and they should have the right to, but if you want to see change, you must act. Actions speak louder than words. Don't complain about things, change them. I have said that we need a revolution every two hundred years, because, historically, all governments become stale and corrupt after two hundred years. I still believe that, but when tyranny rears its ugly head, the time is now. Act immediately and forcefully. Time is not your friend in this instance."

Robbie summarized the comments for the group, "You have told us that we must take action and take it immediately. It must be forceful and swift action, for the freedom of future generations is in the balance, and we do not have the right to defer that action. Have I stated this to your satisfaction?"

"You have," replied Adams. "Who will ask another

question?"

Nick raised his hand and asked, "This swift and forceful action you suggest sounds a lot like war. That is a very challenging decision to make, especially where we come from. Another advisor has told us to be wary of those who constantly advocate for war. Is there another alternative?"

Franklin replied, "Advocating for war and warring against tyranny are two very different things, young man. War is when the government tells you who the enemy is. Revolution is when you decide that for yourself. Those who would give up essential liberty to purchase a little temporary safety, deserve neither liberty nor safety. Remember, those who beat their swords into plowshares usually end up plowing for those who kept their swords. The way to secure peace is to be prepared for war. They that are on their guard, and appear ready to receive their adversaries, are in much less danger of being attacked, than the supine, secure, and negligent. Make yourselves sheep and the wolves will eat you."

"Hear, hear!" exclaimed Adams who rose from his chair, now fully and fiercely engaged in the discussion. "I have always said to those dithering about using force to overthrow tyranny, if ye love wealth better than liberty, the tranquility of servitude better than the animating contest of freedom, go home from us in peace. We ask not your counsels or arms. Crouch down and lick the hands which feed you. May your chains set lightly upon you, and may posterity forget that ye were our countrymen! I say that to you young men today. If it is time to fight, then fight you must!

"When I was trying to rouse the country out of its slumber, fear and great anxiety were expressed as to the coming war. Someone remarked, 'The chance is desperate.'

"I replied, 'Indeed, indeed, it is desperate, but, if this be our language, if we wear long faces, others will do so, too. If we despair, let us not expect that others will hope, or that they will persevere in a contest from which their leaders shrink. But let not such feelings, let not such language, be ours.' Now or ever!

"I now say to you, young men, if you are to be leaders in a battle for freedom and liberty, then lead with both words and deeds. Be bold in thought, action, and speech!

"Fear not the multitude arrayed against you. It does not take a majority to prevail, but rather an irate, tireless minority, keen on setting brushfires of freedom in the minds of men. Do this! Say this! Use this and freedom shall be yours!"

Robbie was awestruck by Adams' speech. The power and passion were palpable. He now understood how this man could have been responsible for inspiring the actions of his fellow man. Samuel Adams was a force of nature, and Robbie felt the influence of his words and understood them as truth.

Adams sat back down and nodded at Ben Franklin as if asking for a moment to collect himself. Franklin obliged and spoke to the cousins. "Always remember that in the end, no people or nation become servants unwillingly. They are always responsible for their own enslavement. It starts within the hearts of the people. A general dissolution of principles and manners will more surely overthrow the liberties of a family or nation than the whole force of the common enemy. Faith and good morals are the only solid foundation of public liberty and happiness. When these twin pillars of liberty are demolished, the foundation will crumble from within. If you are facing that situation now, then you must shore up those pillars.

"I know not what threat you face, be it internal or external. I have lived, gentlemen, a long time, and the longer I live, the more convincing proofs I see of this truth: that God governs in the affairs of men. If a sparrow cannot fall to the ground without His notice, is it probable that any government or ruling class can rise without His aid? We have been assured, in the sacred writings that 'except the Lord build, they labor in vain that build it'. I firmly believe this, and I also believe that without His concurring aid, you shall succeed in your situation no better than the builders of Babel. The same may be said for your enemies."

"Once again," said Adams, "I agree with the honorable Mr. Franklin, however, let me add a few final points. Although a people may be responsible for their own enslavement due to lack of the courage to defend it, or too much comfort in their current circumstances and their fear of losing those comforts, it is not in their power to truly renounce their essential natural rights. Nor may they renounce the means of preserving those rights. The grand end of civil government, from the very nature of its institution, is for the support, protection, and defense of those very rights, the principles of which are life, liberty, and property.

"If men through fear, fraud, or mistake, should in some way renounce or give up any essential natural right, the eternal law of reason and the grand end of society would absolutely vacate such renunciation. The right to freedom is the gift of God Almighty. It is not in the power of man to alienate this gift and voluntarily become a slave. Shame on the men who can court exemption from present trouble and expense, at the price of their own posterity's liberty! They have no right to choose that slavery for themselves or others!

"The liberties we enjoy and freedoms of our society are worth defending from all hazards; it is our duty to defend them against all attacks. We have received them as a fair inheritance from our worthy ancestors. They purchased them for us with toil and danger and expense of treasure and blood. It will bring a mark of everlasting infamy on *any* generation... enlightened as it may be... if we should suffer them to be wrested from us by violence without a struggle, or to be cheated out of them by the artifices of designing men.

"If ever a time should come, when vain and aspiring men shall possess the highest seats in government, our country must stand in need of its experienced patriots to prevent its ruin."

Then he looked at the cousins and once again stood. He pointed a shaking finger at them and asked, "Are you such men? Are you patriots? Are you truly men of virtue and valor?"

Their great-grandfather stood and answered him. "They are, my friend. They are truly men of virtue and valor. Though they be young, and reasonably inexperienced, they possess those qualities. They required your counsel, for their present task is dangerous and the situation dire."

Adams looked at Agent Petrie, then the cousins, and said, "Then I say this to you: fight your fight. Be brave and be strong. Fear not and be of good courage. I would strongly advise persisting in your struggle for liberty, even if heaven revealed that nine hundred and ninety-nine men were to perish, and only one of a thousand to survive and retain his liberty. One such freeman would possess more virtue, and enjoy more happiness, than a thousand slaves.

"Above all, never despair. That is a motto for you and me. All are not dead to freedom and liberty; and where there is a spark of patriotic fire, you will need to rekindle it."

"Thank you for those inspirational and wise words," said Agent Petrie. "You have given us what we came for and more. Hearing you speak so eloquently and passionately is truly comforting. History records that you are both men of valor and virtue, and you have proven that here tonight. I, myself, am always disposed to quick action. Yet there are times when it has proven to be ill advised. But it seems that based on your comments we must act and do it with all haste. We will not let the chains intended for us and our people set lightly upon us. We will throw them off and inspire others to do so.

"We will risk our safety and our lives to ensure that tyrants do not succeed. We will guard our words and inspire through action. And we will have faith; faith in your advice, faith in each other, and faith that the Lord is building a new house in which liberty and freedom may once again prevail. Thank you both."

"And now," continued their great-grandfather, addressing Franklin and Adams, "we must take our leave, kind sirs. Having received from the fountain of your wisdom, I and my charges must part from you. I must guide them home. I thank you for the privilege to have served you these past months. The threat for which you hired me is now gone, and the way is clear for the founding of your new nation.

"You will have many battles to fight and victories to win, but I give you my word that you will prevail. Fear not, for your destiny is clear and will not be derailed. Know that from this day forward, you will both be revered and honored for what you will do in the next few years. You have our thanks and eternal respect." With that, he motioned to the cousins to stand.

Ben Franklin also stood. "Robert, before you leave, please honor me with one more display of your valor and virtue. Please reveal your swords. When you are gone, I will explain it all to Mr. Adams. I believe he deserves to understand as I do. He will need the encouragement and inspiration for the coming conflict."

"As you wish, Mr. Franklin," replied Agent Petrie. He looked at the cousins and said, "Gentlemen, reveal your swords." The young men lifted their right arms out before them. Their now brightly glowing swords appeared instantly in their hands.

Samuel Adams' expression exhibited both shock and awe.

Quietly and without ceremony, the cousins and their great-grandfather turned to leave. Just before Robbie stepped through the door, he heard Franklin's words to Adams.

"Please, Sam, take your seat. I have a lot to explain."

"You certainly do," replied Adams, "you *certainly* do!"

Quietly, Robbie closed the door behind him, smiling and wishing he could be a fly on the wall for the discussion that was sure to follow between these two great men.

The cousins and their great-grandfather departed the residence of Ben Franklin and started back to the Pennsylvania State House. Their great-grandfather had told them that there would be a fire burning there, as there was every night, to warm the homeless and the indigent. They walked in silence, allowing Robbie to reflect on the words of Franklin and Adams, and think of the task that lay ahead of them. He now understood that it was more than just their own freedom and liberty on the line. The freedom of future generations was at stake, and they did not have the right to cower before the challenge.

Their great-grandfather led them to the fire in front of the building, saw that the street was deserted at that late hour, and instructed them to stand around it for their return.

"Great-Grandpa," asked Robbie, "what will you do after we leave? Will you go back to your own time?"

"I will not," he replied. "I intend to join myself to a group of valiant men who will continue the fight for liberty and freedom."

"So, you will be staying and fighting in the Revolutionary War?" asked Nick.

"No, my work here is done," he replied.

"Then where will you go?" asked Joe.

"I believe it is my destiny to join myself to your cause. How can I live knowing that the future of freedom and liberty is at risk and not add my sword to the effort?" Then he joined them around the fire and said, "Gentlemen, raise your Swords of Valor!"

They all lifted their right arms and slowly brought their swords together. Once again, they were enveloped in a flash of pure white light and departed for home.

CHAPTER TEN

THE SECOND RETURN

~~~

When the travelers arrived at the fire pit by the river, they were greeted by the Meglio, the prophet, Billy, and Ty. They had been alerted to the heroes' imminent arrival by the quantum computer.

Blinded by the sudden flash of light, it was hard to verify that all the heroes had returned. As soon as the Meglio's eyes returned to normal, he saw five men standing around the fire, swords raised.

"Welcome home, my heroes!" he exclaimed. "I see we have a guest. Please, sir, introduce yourself," he said to the shadowy figure standing opposite the fire, whose face was partially hidden by the smoke and glare.

The figure lowered his sword and slowly made his way around the fire. As soon as the glow illuminated his face, the Meglio gasped and dropped to one knee, head bowed.

"My Meglio," he said, "is it really you? After all these years?"

"Yes, Joseph, my son. It is truly a blessing to see you again. Arise!" the figure commanded. "You are Meglio now, and it is unseemly for a Meglio to kneel before any man. Stand and greet me with honor!"

Joseph stood, and the two men embraced for a long time. The former Meglio broke the embrace first and, holding his son-in-law by the shoulders, looked into his eyes.

"I understand congratulations are in order," he said. "Your grandsons told me that you have finally and totally destroyed the Swords of Terror and the Apostles of Azazel along with them. Well done, my son, well done! I always knew that it would be you who would devise a way to defeat them. It seems my faith in you was justified. You have made me very proud. Now, what is all this I hear about you being dead?"

"Thank you, my Meglio," Joseph replied, "but I cannot take much of the credit. Your grandson, Robert, our current prophet, and your great-grandsons did the hard work. They won the day. All I did was die, leave them with a mess and a plan to clean it up. They were the true heroes."

The prophet approached and interrupted the emotional exchange between the two men. "Excuse me, but I must hug my grandfather!" Then he hugged him with the urgency of one who has found a returned treasure and never wants to lose it again.

"Grandpa," he said, "it's so good to see you again. I know I was just a teenager when you passed, but you had such an influence on my life. You have been in my dreams constantly, more than almost anyone else. Now, here you are. I can't tell you what this means to me. Please tell me you are staying, at least for a while."

His grandfather released him, put his hand on his shoulder and said, "I never take on an assignment that I do not intend to complete, Rob. So, let's get on with it. And, by the way, I missed you too." Then he leaned in close to the prophet and whispered, "You were always my favorite grandchild!" The two men laughed.

The prophet turned to the cousins. "Grandpa always said that to each of us grandchildren. It was one of the things that made us love him so much."

Robert Petrie turned to his son-in-law, knelt, and said, "Joseph, you are now my Meglio, and I am one of your soldiers. Allow me to add my sword to your cause this day." Then, he waited for the response.

"We would be more than honored to have you join our cause, my Meglio," Joseph responded. "Just forgive me if I cannot refrain from showing you the reverence you have earned. Old habits die hard."

The newest member of the team stood, bowed to the Meglio, and said smiling, "I guess I will just have to deal with it! Now, show me around the place and help me get oriented. Is there a civilized place somewhere in these woods where I can wash up and get into a change of clothing? These Revolutionary War clothes are not as comfortable as you might think!"

"Absolutely," replied the Meglio. "Follow us, there is a lot we must show you and tell you."

The men headed for the house. When they arrived, their newest member looked around and smiled. "I see you have done much to improve this old place. I remember when you proposed buying it for the family headquarters, back in the late sixties, wasn't it? What a dump it was! I must admit, I never thought you could pull it off. Yes, I am impressed."

"The boys will show you to your room, and you can take a shower," said the Meglio. "I will pick out some clothes for you and lay them on your bed. Come down and join us for dinner when you are ready. Your return calls for a celebration!"

"Come on, Great-Grandpa!" said Ty. "You can have the room next to me."

The Meglio smiled as he watched them walk up the stairs together.

When they were out of sight, the prophet turned to his father and said, "Wow, Dad, what a surprise. Are you okay?"

"Yes, of course," replied the Meglio. "This is a joyous occasion, although an emotional one. He is my father-in-law, but I always felt he was like another father to me. I loved him very much. But to your mother, he was everything. When he died, she was beside herself. It took a long time for her to get over losing him. He was her first hero, her first protector, and her 'Dada'. Seeing him again brings all that back. I will be fine."

"Just know, Dad," said the prophet, "that we all feel the same way about you. So, don't go dying on us again, okay?" The two men laughed and headed to the kitchen where the cousins were preparing dinner.

They worked together setting the table, heating up the food, and pouring the wine. It was ready by the time their great-grandfather came back downstairs.

As he watched his father-in-law descend the stairs, the Meglio remembered the last time he had seen him. It was in the hospital in Queens. He'd sat there next to his wife as she held the hand of her dying father. He remembered his father-in-law's hollow cheeks, the dark circles under his eyes, and the horrible wheezing and gurgling of his lungs as the emphysema strangled the life out of him.

Shaking himself out of the melancholy reverie, the Meglio observed that now, his father-in-law looked great, dressed in some of the Meglio's own clothes, relaxed black slacks, collared shirt, and a sweater. He seemed so much younger than he had in the worn colonial jacket and knee britches. He appeared to be in his mid-forties, although his hair was gray and longer than the Meglio recalled. When he'd appeared by the fire, he had it in a ponytail, mimicking the colonial hairstyle. He was incredibly fit and reminded the Meglio of Gary Cooper or Cary Grant in their prime. He imagined that his father-in-law could step back into the boxing ring and perform as well as he had in his younger days as a welterweight boxer.

"Join us!" invited the Meglio.

"What's for dinner?" his father-in-law asked.

"Spaghetti and meatballs, of course," was the Meglio's reply.

"What? No liver and onions for this old Scottish man?" he replied. "What kind of celebration is this with no liver and onions?" Then he grinned. "I guess Italian food will have to do. I'm famished. Let's eat. Shall I say grace?"

The Meglio hesitated a moment, then said, "I know it's traditionally the oldest at the table that offers grace, but if you don't mind, I'd like to say it this time. I have much to thank our God for."

Smiling, his father-in-law nodded his agreement. They all bowed their heads and joined hands.

"Father, we thank you for this food and drink, and for the safe return of our children. But, most of all we thank you for the return of our beloved father-in-law, grandfather, great-grandfather, and Meglio. He was always one of your greatest blessings to this family, and I know he will be today, also, as he joins us in our cause. Please bless him and us, with strength and wisdom, so we may be successful, according to your will. Amen."

"Thank you, Joseph," said the former Meglio. "That was beautifully said. Now, let's eat and get down to business."

Before they dug in, Nick asked, "So, Great-Grandpa, how old are you? I mean I know how old you are supposed to be now in 2016, but what is your age at this point in your life? You know what I mean."

"I do," his great-grandfather replied. "It can get confusing with time travel. Let me give you a bit of my history. I was born in 1897. I fought in WWI when I was twenty years old. After I returned, my father recruited me into the service of the Guardians of the Swords of Valor, as a soldier. After that, I had many assignments. One of them was where I first encountered Robbie, Billy, and Joe. That was back in 1940, and I was sent to stop the Apostles on their third attempt at stealing the Sword of Mercy. That was during my own timeline, and I did not travel back in time for that one. I was forty-three years old at that time.

"After that, I was sent on additional assignments in my own timeframe. The Apostles were very active all through Europe during World War II. They tried to take advantage of the war to steal Swords of Valor. After the war, around 1945, I started doing more time travel assignments. The focus was the American revolutionary timeframes.

"The Apostles of Azazel had determined that they would try to disrupt the formation of the American nation, and a number of us were sent back to stop them. I had many missions during those years, but to your point, Nick, at this present point in my life, I am fifty years old."

"Well, I'm so glad to have you here with us," said the prophet. "It will be comforting to have an experienced soldier, with such an understanding of the challenges, accompanying the boys on their missions."

"I agree," said the Meglio, "except that we must

always remember that the swords make the choice about who they send back on any particular mission. We always have to take that into consideration."

They finished their celebration dinner and cleaned up. Before heading back to the Keeping Room to discuss the next mission, the Meglio took his father-in-law aside and spoke with him privately.

"Robert, before we enter the Keeping Room, I want to make you aware of what you will see there. I don't want you to be startled or upset. The Keeping Room is equipped with the most innovative technology. That includes a quantum computer. I know you don't know what that is, so let me explain. It is a system that we interact with that helps us access information instantly. The technology we have allows us to interact with the computer in a couple of unique ways. We speak to the computer just as we would any normal human being. It understands and responds in a very human-like manner.

"The other aspect is that we interact with the quantum computer via a holographic image. This image is very lifelike and makes the discussions more realistic and effective. Do you understand?"

"I believe so," replied the former Meglio. "It would be like interacting with a picture of someone, only more lifelike. Am I close?"

"Yes," replied the Meglio. "Only even more realistic than that. It will feel like the person is standing there in front of you. I tell you this because the current image I have programmed into the quantum computer is Catherine, and it is very true to life."

"My Catherine?" asked his father-in-law. "My daughter and your wife? Why would you do such a thing?"

"I wanted to have the boys and myself interact with

the computer in a relaxed and confident manner," explained the Meglio. "We all loved her, respected her, and trusted her advice. I felt that programming her personality and image into the computer would enhance our ability to reach the wisest conclusions. Don't form any opinions yet. Just go in there and see how it feels. If it makes you uncomfortable, I will change it. Agreed?"

After only a moment's hesitation, the former Meglio nodded his agreement.

CHAPTER ELEVEN

IDENTIFYING THE THIRD MISSION

～

When the Meglio and his father-in-law reached the Tech Room, they found the heroes and the prophet waiting for them at the round table.

They took their seats, and the Meglio made the request. "Catherine, my dear, will you join us? We would like to begin the planning for the third mission."

The almost life-sized image materialized in the center of the table and responded. "Certainly, my love. I am always here and waiting." Then, looking at her father, she said, "Dada, how I have longed to see you again. I have missed you deeply all these years. I am so pleased that your adventures have led you back here. Will you be staying for long?"

Every eye in the room was on her father, the former Meglio. He looked stricken, and his eyes were starting to fill.

The Meglio reached over and touched his shoulder and asked, "Robert, will you be okay?"

His father-in-law replied, "Just give me a minute to compose myself, please." He put his face in his hands, took a few deep breaths, and then returned his gaze to the image of his daughter.

"My dear Catherine, my only daughter, seeing you again is a dream come true. If it is possible, you are more beautiful than I remember. Thank you for being here with us today. To answer your question, yes, I will be staying for as long as I am needed. Your presence will make that time a joy."

The image of his daughter replied, "As it is for me, Dada. If I could, I would wrap my arms around you and never let you go. As it is, I am only a quantum holographic representation. However, the personality profiles that were input into my system drive me to tell you how much you are loved. As limited as that is, please take comfort in that. Now, how may I help?"

The Meglio replied, "As always, we need to hear from our heroes, regarding their recent mission and the information they received from Benjamin Franklin and Samuel Adams. After that, I will want you to share the information you have regarding your ongoing comparative timeline analysis. Finally, we will together decide on the focus of the third mission."

He nodded at Jeff, who began the report. "We arrived in an alley across from the Pennsylvania State House and observed huge crowds forming in the street."

Robbie then took over from Jeff describing how Joe flirted with Lydia, who was really an agent of the Secret Committee working for Ben Franklin, how she said she'd arranged a dinner invitation for them to his house later that night, where Sam Adams would also be attending. He admitted that everything seemed too easy. Her "brother", Lieutenant Clark, had them captured because a witness had seen Robbie accidentally drop and reveal his sword.

"We sat there in the brig for a few hours, then Great-Grandpa walked in. He introduced himself, told us he knew who we were, and after chastising us a bit for being so careless, he had us released."

Their great-grandfather jumped in at this point. "I was able to get them released into my custody because I, too, was an agent for the Secret Committee. I was on assignment for the Guardians to disrupt the efforts of the Apostles of Azazel to derail the revolution. Franklin himself chose me to be an agent, based on some very important information I had previously presented to him. I had also at that time confided in Franklin my real identity and mission. I arranged for the boys and myself to join Franklin and Adams for dinner that evening."

Robbie continued, "Great-Grandpa took us to Franklin's home and introduced us. After showing him our swords at his request, we sat down, and Sam Adams joined us, somewhat reluctantly. Franklin invited us to state our business, and we did. The conversation was inspiring and enlightening. We were all greatly moved being in the presence of those two great men."

"Wonderful summary, gentlemen," said the prophet. "Please, tell us what insights you received that may help us navigate the treacherous waters ahead of us."

Nick said, "Let Jeff tell it. He apparently was Franklin's teacher's pet, and according to Franklin, the only truly educated one in the room!"

They all laughed, and Jeff began.

"Here is the bottom line; these two men, who were so instrumental in the founding of our nation and the establishment of our freedom and liberty, told us that first and foremost, we and our leaders must understand that freedom is our natural, God-given right, and the protection of that freedom is the primary obligation of government. Any government which denies this or disputes it is an enemy of the people they govern.

"Second, freedom of speech is a pillar of freedom and liberty. Anyone, or any government, that threatens or limits that is also our enemy.

"Third, that we must take action and take it immediately. It must be forceful and swift action, for the freedom of future generations is in the balance, and we do not have the right to defer that action.

"Fourth, that advocating for war and warring against tyranny are two very different things. War is when the government tells you who the enemy is. Revolution is when you decide that for yourself. He who sacrifices freedom for security or comfort deserves neither.

"Adams said that if we were to be leaders in a battle for freedom and liberty, we had to lead with both words and deeds. We need to be bold and aggressive in thought, action, and speech. He encouraged us not to fear the multitude arrayed against us. He said that it does not take a majority to prevail, but rather an irate, tireless minority. Sounds pretty much like us, doesn't it?

"Finally," he continued, "although a people may be responsible for their own enslavement because of the lack of courage to defend it, too much comfort in their current circumstances, or their fear of losing those comforts, it is not in their power to truly renounce their essential natural rights nor the means of preserving those rights. The grand end of civil government, from the very nature of its institution, is for the support, protection, and defense of those very rights. The right to freedom is a gift of God Almighty, and it is not in the power of man to alienate this gift or voluntarily become a slave. He added that no man has the right to choose slavery for themselves or others."

"Does everyone agree with Jeff's summary?" asked the Meglio. "Is it complete and accurate?"

Everyone agreed that Jeff had adequately summarized the counsel of the Founding Fathers, so the Meglio addressed the quantum computer.

"Dear, would you make sure to add the advice of the Founding Fathers to the advice from Cicero and keep a record, so that when the time comes we may incorporate their counsel into our plan?"

"Already done, my dear," answered the image of his wife. "Would you now like to have me explain my findings from the comparative timeline analysis?"

"I would," replied the Meglio. "Please begin."

The image began, "As you know, my systems have been running an analysis comparing the past timeline with the new one to identify any relevant anomalies. I have found that there are two stories, one a book, the other a short story, which appear in the new timeline which never existed in the old one. They appear to have relevance to our situation. These two pieces of literature in the chronological order they were published are: *The Gray Champion*, published by Nathaniel Hawthorne in 1835 as part of his *Twice-Told Tales*, and *Nineteen Eighty-Four* by George Orwell, published in 1949. Both authors were well known in the old timeline, but neither had published stories with these titles."

"I remember reading *Animal Farm* by Orwell in high school," said Joe. "It was a terrific book. I remember liking it so much that I would have read anything else by him. I agree that I never heard of *Nineteen Eighty-Four*."

"And I am sure we all have read *The Scarlet Letter* by Hawthorne," said Jeff, "but I've never heard of *The Gray Champion*."

"That is the point, gentlemen," said the Meglio. "They did not exist in the old timeline, so why now? I have had the quantum computer analyze the content, and it has come up with some very interesting information. Catherine, would you please share that information with us now?"

"As you wish. I shall summarize the salient points," replied the image. "In the short story by Hawthorne, the Gray Champion arrives when the situation looks grim, and the people need a jolt of courage to meet the frightful challenges ahead. In 1689, the American colonies were boiling with rumors that King James II wanted to strip them of their liberties. The King had hand-picked Sir Edmund Andros to be the governor of New England. One afternoon in April, he marched his troops menacingly through Boston. His purpose was to crush any thought of colonial self-rule. The future looked grim to everyone present.

"Suddenly, seemingly from nowhere, there appeared a man on the streets. Nathaniel Hawthorne describes 'the figure of an ancient man with the eye, the face, the attitude of command. His manner combining the leader and the saint, the old man planted himself directly in the path of the approaching British soldiers and demanded that they stop. The solemn, yet warlike peal of that voice, fit either to rule a host in the battlefield or be raised to God in prayer, was irresistible. At the old man's word and outstretched arm, the roll of the drum was hushed at once, and the advancing line stood still.'

"The people of Boston were inspired by this single act of defiance. They found their courage and acted. That very day, Andros was deposed and jailed. They saved the liberty of Boston, and turned a pivotal corner in the colonial revolution.

"'And who was the Gray Champion?' Nathaniel Hawthorne asked near the end of this story.

"'No one knew, except that he may have once been

among the fire-hearted young Puritans who had first settled New England more than a half century earlier. Later that evening, just before the old priest-warrior disappeared, the townspeople saw him embracing the eighty-five-year-old Simon Bradstreet, a kindred spirit and one of the few original Puritans still alive. Others soberly affirmed that while they marveled at the venerable grandeur of his aspect standing before a fire, the old man faded from their eyes, melting slowly into the hues of twilight, till, where he stood, there was an empty space. But all agreed that the hoary shape was gone.

"'The men of that generation watched for his re-appearance, in sunshine and in twilight, but never saw him more, nor knew when his funeral passed, nor where his gravestone was.

"'When eighty years had passed, he walked once more in King Street during the Boston Massacre. Five years later, in the twilight of an April morning, he stood on the green beside the meeting house at Lexington, where now the obelisk of granite, with a slab of slate inlaid, commemorates the first fallen of the Revolution. And when our fathers were toiling at the breastworks on Bunker's Hill, all through that night, the old warrior walked his rounds.

"'Long, long may it be, ere he comes again! His hour is one of darkness, and adversity, and peril. But should domestic tyranny oppress us, or the invader's step pollute our soil, still may the Gray Champion come; for he is the type of freedom's hereditary spirit, and his shadowy march, on the eve of danger, must ever be the pledge, that freedom's sons will vindicate their ancestry.'

"After reading Hawthorne's story, people have wondered if the Gray Champion would ever return. 'I have heard,' Hawthorne wrote, 'that whenever the descendants of the Puritans are to show the spirit of their sires, the old man appears again.'

"Stories are told that, indeed, the old man did appear again. He appeared eighty years after the Revolutionary War, and was sighted during the Boston Massacre in 1770, and again on the streets of Lexington and Concord in 1775. Later that same year, he was seen behind the breastworks on Bunker Hill, providing spiritual inspiration to the militia of farmers. Some have reported that he looked like an older man, perhaps the peer of Samuel Adams and Ben Franklin. The tales say that 'as the hour of darkness, adversity, and peril arrives, the virtuous, fiery, and unrepentant Gray Champion appears through the fog of history like an apparition'."

"That is a very inspirational story, my dear, and thank you for sharing it with us," said the Meglio. "Please tell us now why your analysis indicates that it is important to our current crisis."

"It is important and relevant because not only does it have to do with liberty and freedom and the fight against oppression, but it also ties in exactly with the Generational Cycle theories which you yourself have studied. The reason you were able to identify the current point in history as a crisis period is because you studied the concept of the cycles of history. The one that identified the generational archetypes, which allowed you to identify the boys, yourself, and my father as falling into the Hero generations of your cycles, and our son Rob and his siblings as falling into the Prophet generation of their cycles.

"The appearances of the Gray Champion coincide exactly with those cycles. He apparently arises during crisis seasons. Not every one of them, because some of the crises are about economics or natural disasters, but when the crisis season is driven by a threat to liberty and freedom, then he seems to appear. I thought you, above all others, would see the significance."

"Well, I certainly do now!" exclaimed the Meglio. "That is one of the things that I always loved about you, my dear, you always helped me see things more clearly. I can see that there is definitely a connection. We must continue to analyze this closely. Is there any need for us to send the heroes back in time to speak with Hawthorne himself to get details?"

"I do not believe so. We have all the relevant historical events and the story itself contains enough details for our needs. We have enough to move on to the next observation."

"Please do, my dear," said the Meglio.

"The next book which I will summarize for you is the book *Nineteen Eighty-Four*, written in this timeline by George Orwell. Again, it did not exist in the old timeline. *Nineteen Eighty-Four*, often published as the numerical representation of the year 1984, is a dystopian novel published in 1949 by George Orwell. The novel is set in Airstrip One, formerly known as Great Britain, a province of the superstate Oceania in a world of perpetual war, omnipresent government surveillance, and public manipulation.

"The superstate and its residents are dictated to by a political regime euphemistically named English Socialism, shortened to *Ingsoc* in Newspeak, the government's invented language. The superstate is under the control of the privileged elite of the Inner Party, a party and government that persecutes individualism and independent thinking as 'thoughtcrime', which is enforced by the 'Thought Police'.

"The tyranny is ostensibly overseen by Big Brother,

the Party leader who enjoys an intense cult of personality, but who may not even exist."

"Excuse me," interrupted Nick. "May I ask a question?"

"Of course," answered the Meglio.

"I know I should know this, but what is a 'cult of personality'?" he asked.

The Meglio smiled at his grandson. "Good question. It's helpful to know the vocabulary, isn't it? A 'cult of personality' arises when a regime uses mass media, propaganda, or other methods such as government-organized demonstrations to create an idealized, heroic, and at times worshipful image of a leader, often through unquestioning flattery and praise. Does that make sense?"

Nick nodded. "Thank you, it does. As I understand it now, in Orwell's book, Big Brother has this 'cult of personality', which gives him power over the people, right?"

"That's right. They believe all he says, and they do whatever he asks."

Nick frowned. "That makes him extremely dangerous, doesn't it?"

"It certainly does. Please continue, my dear," the Meglio instructed the computer.

The image of Catherine continued, "The Party 'seeks power entirely for its own sake. It is not interested in the good of others; it is interested solely in power'. The protagonist of the novel, Winston Smith, is a member of the Outer Party, who works for 'the Ministry of Truth', or 'Minitrue' in Newspeak, which is responsible for propaganda and historical revisionism. His job is to rewrite past newspaper articles, so that the historical record always supports the party line. The instructions that the workers receive portray the corrections as 'fixing misquotations' and never as what they really are: forgeries and falsifications.

"A large part of the Ministry also actively destroys all documents that have not been edited and do not contain the revisions; in this way, no proof exists that the government is lying. Smith is a diligent and skillful worker but secretly hates the Party and dreams of rebellion against Big Brother.

"At the end of the novel, the hero, Winston Smith, is eventually made to love Big Brother and accept that two plus two equals five, if the authorities say it does. He capitulates, he gives up. He surrenders his liberty and freedom to the Party and Big Brother.

"Since its publication in 1949, in this timeline, the terms 'Big Brother', 'doublethink', 'thoughtcrime', 'Newspeak', 'Blackwhite', 'telescreen', '2 + 2 = 5', and 'memory hole', have entered into common use. *Nineteen Eighty-Four* popularized the adjective 'Orwellian', which describes official deception, secret surveillance, and manipulation of recorded history by a totalitarian or authoritarian state.

"In 2005, again in this timeline, the novel was chosen by *Time* magazine as one of the one hundred best English-language novels from 1923 to 2005. Its influence is worldwide, and it is required reading for almost every schoolchild," the image finished.

The prophet looked puzzled. "Aren't dystopian novels supposed to really be warnings against evils like this? If this novel was written for that purpose in this timeline, why would we have a problem with Orwell shining a light on these evil practices and sounding the alarm? Wouldn't that aid our cause in trying to stop this kind of enslavement?"

"Those are wonderful questions, my son," replied

the image. "And it is just what the Leviathan Alliance wants everyone to think. From the analysis I have done, it seems that they may have had a hand in the writing of this book. It may have been funded by them, edited by them, and poor Mr. Orwell may very well have been blackmailed into writing it for them. I believe that what we have in the book *Nineteen Eighty-Four*, is *not* a true dystopian novel, but a manifesto of the Leviathan Alliance. It may very well be their blueprint for success."

"Why would they do such a thing?" asked Jeff. "Why tip their hand?"

"They were not tipping their hand," replied the Meglio with growing understanding. "They were apparently announcing to the world the coming of a new age. They may have very well been signaling to their members the start of their campaign and maybe more. We have much more timeline history to work through and compare, but from this information, I believe we may have identified our next mission. We must send you back to speak with Orwell to determine the players in this drama and the inspiration behind this manifesto."

CHAPTER TWELVE

PLANNING THE
THIRD MISSION

~~~

"Catherine," said the Meglio, "we will need to know all you have on the history and whereabouts of George Orwell in this new timeline. Please, present to us the relevant information about Orwell's life and his writings."

"Certainly, my love," replied the image. "The book *Nineteen Eighty-Four* was written sixty-eight years ago. It portrays a surprisingly accurate depiction of where the world of this timeline is heading on a global basis. It was supposedly written as fiction, but our analysis infers that it was almost certainly based on someone's actual vision for the future that very well may have been planned for the year of 1984.

"George Orwell's real name was Eric Blair. He was educated at Eton College, an apparent Leviathan education center. In this timeline, it has produced nineteen British prime ministers. While at Eton, Orwell learned from Aldous Huxley, who himself wrote the novel, *A Brave New World*. They became lifelong friends. It was Huxley who introduced Orwell to the Fabian Society. It's a secret Leviathan group, apparently formed in this timeline to educate young, up and coming

Leviathans and prepare them for ruling in the coming Leviathan Age. The name Fabian is said to come from the name of the Roman general…"

"Quintus Fabius Maximus Verrucosus!" interrupted Joe. "That is the same general that Cicero told us about!" He turned to the other cousins. "Remember? Cicero told us that our enemy would very likely employ Fabian tactics, and that it was one of the ways that we could identify them. This is too clear to be just a coincidence."

"Agreed," said the image. "Fabius's strategies were carefully planned to wear down his enemies over extended periods of time. He avoided long battles that could be decisive either way. The Leviathans have been using this tactic, apparently. The fact that the original coat of arms of the Fabian Society was a wolf in sheep's clothing is especially telling.

"George Bernard Shaw, another famous Fabian, designed and commissioned a stained-glass window of the four Fabians who founded the London School of Economics. It includes the inscription, 'Remould it nearer to the heart's desire'.

"*Nineteen Eighty-Four* is the name of Orwell's book, but it is also the centenarian year for the Fabian Society. I'm sure that's why they chose it for the title. When Orwell realized their true intent, he became disillusioned with the society and distanced himself over time. But they kept their eye on him, anyway.

"Orwell's career was greatly influenced by David Astor, who was the third child of American-born English parents, Waldorf Astor and Nancy Witcher Langhorne. He was the product of an immensely wealthy business dynasty and raised in the grandeur of a great country estate where the political and intellectual elite gathered. The Astors were apparently a very high-ranking

Leviathan family. David Astor, at the time, was a newspaper publisher and very influential in the world of politics.

"Orwell started writing for the *American Partisan Review* early in 1941. This connected him to The New York Intellectuals who were American writers and literary critics. Like him, they were anti-Stalinist, but they were committed to staying on the left of the political spectrum, mostly as Trotskyists. Orwell finally obtained 'war work' in August 1941, when he was hired by the BBC's Eastern Service. At the end of August, he had a dinner with another Fabian acquaintance, H. G. Wells. Wells wanted Orwell to come back into the fold. He refused.

"Nearly a year later, David Astor invited Orwell to write for the newspaper his family owned, *The Observer*. He figured if Orwell worked for him, he could keep his eye on him and gain his trust. Orwell's first article appeared in March 1942.

"A year later in March of 1943, Orwell's mother died. The official cause of death was a heart attack. This was around the time he told Astor he was starting work on a new book, *Animal Farm*. In September 1943, Orwell suddenly resigned from the post that he had occupied for two years. By April 1944, *Animal Farm* was ready for publication.

"Thanks to the contacts of his wife's sister, the Orwells had the opportunity to adopt a child in May 1944. They spent some time in northeast England dealing with matters in the adoption of the boy. Upon completion of the adoption, they named him Richard Horatio Blair. By September 1944, they were at home in London and baby Richard joined them there. His wife Eileen gave up her work at the Ministry of Food to look after her family.

"In February 1945, David Astor invited Orwell to

become a war correspondent for *The Observer*. Orwell had been looking for the opportunity throughout the war, however, he failed his medical exam which prevented him from being anywhere near action. When France was liberated, he went to Paris, then when the Allies occupied Cologne, he went there.

"While he was in Cologne, Eileen went into the hospital for a hysterectomy. She didn't tell him about the operation because of the cost involved. She expected to make a quick recovery, so she didn't see a need to worry him. Unfortunately, she died under mysterious circumstances on March 29, 1945. When Astor found out, he told Orwell that he would handle everything for him while he was on assignment.

"In July 1945, Orwell returned to London to cover the general. *Animal Farm* was published in Britain on August 17, 1945, and a year later in the U.S., on August 26, 1946.

"*Animal Farm* struck a chord in the post-war climate, and its worldwide success made Orwell a sought-after figure and a high-value target of the Fabians.

"Orwell's sister, Marjorie, died in May. The official cause of her death was kidney disease. Shortly after, on May 22, 1946, David Astor sent Orwell to live on the Isle of Jura, an isolated and desolate island in the Inner Hebrides of Scotland. There, he began work on *Nineteen Eighty-Four*. Astor's family owned Scottish estates in the area, and a fellow Old Etonian, Robin Fletcher, had a property on the island.

"Orwell lived at Barnhill, an abandoned farmhouse near the northern end of the island. It sat at the end of a heavily rutted road, five miles from Ardlussa, where the owners lived. Conditions at the farmhouse were primitive. His sister, Avril, was allowed to accompany him to care for his young son, while Orwell began work on *Nineteen Eighty-Four*.

"In 1947, the Fabians summoned Orwell back to London to review his progress on the book. He returned to Jura on April 10 where he continued work on *Nineteen Eighty-Four*. During that time, he received a soaking during a disastrous boating expedition. This adversely affected his health. In December, a chest specialist from Glasgow was summoned. He pronounced Orwell seriously ill. Orwell ended up in Hairmyres Hospital a week before Christmas in 1947.

"The diagnosis was tuberculosis. Astor helped with the arrangements for medical care and paid for the treatment. Orwell began his course of streptomycin in February of 1948. By the end of July, Orwell returned to Jura, and by December, he had finished the manuscript of *Nineteen Eighty-Four*.

"In January 1949, Astor escorted him to a sanatorium. Orwell was very weak and declining rapidly. On October 13, 1949, Orwell had an assortment of visitors, including Malcom Muggeridge, Lucian Freud, Stephen Spender, Evelyn Waugh, Paul Potts, Anthony Powell, and his Eton tutor, Anthony Gow, all of them Fabians and Leviathans.

"On the evening of January 20, 1950, Paul Potts visited Orwell and said that he had found him asleep. David Astor visited later and claimed that Orwell gave him one hundred percent of his company and rights to all his works. However, Jack Harrison claimed twenty-five percent, and it seems his widow, Sonia Brownell, had quite a large share of the company, too.

"Early on the morning of January 21, an artery burst in Orwell's lungs, killing him at the age of forty-six. Astor also said that Orwell had requested to be buried in accordance with the Anglican rite, in the graveyard of the church closest to wherever he happened to die. David Astor lived in Sutton Courtenay, Oxfordshire, and arranged for Orwell to be interred in All Saints' Churchyard there. Orwell's gravestone bears the simple, purposely vague epitaph: 'Here lies Eric Arthur Blair, born June 25, 1903, died January 21, 1950'. No mention is made of his more famous pen name on the gravestone."

"It seems clear from the analysis," said the Meglio, "that the Fabians, and therefore the Leviathans, took control of Orwell completely after his success with *Animal Farm* in this timeline. Many people believe that they gained power over him by killing those closest to him."

"Wait," Billy interrupted. "I thought his mother and sister died of natural causes."

"Those were the so-called official reports," the Meglio replied, "but we know that the Leviathans control the media in this timeline. They can report whatever they want. I believe their deaths were anything but 'natural'. Orwell had no choice but to comply with their demands.

"He was exiled to the island of Jura and closely watched. His progress was monitored and apparently approved at every step by the Fabians. They even ensured the complete secrecy of their plan by gaining control over the rights to his works and burying him in an obscure grave under his birth name to cover their tracks.

"It will be our job, our mission, to meet with Orwell to understand the thrust of the agenda and uncover key facts not revealed or hidden in the story. We will then use this information to determine our next mission."

The prophet spoke up. "Our geographic objective should be the Island of Jura. My suggestion is that since we know that he headed back to Jura from London on

April 10, 1947, after his meeting with the Fabians, we should probably target a date close to that."

Everyone agreed. They discussed the possible dates with the image and decided on the date of April 12, 1947. That would give Orwell time to make the trip back and be settled in before they arrived. It would also be before he had the strange boating accident, so he would still be in good health. The Meglio had the image pull up maps and holographic images of the abandoned farmhouse where Orwell was staying. They identified and decided on a location about one hundred yards from the building, which was well-hidden from view.

"So, it is decided," said the Meglio. "You will return to April 12, 1947, on the Isle of Jura, at 6:00 a.m. The objective is to interview Orwell, understand the scope of the Fabian and Leviathan plan, and uncover any secret or hidden information in the story which will be helpful in identifying a course of action to reverse or derail their plans. Are we all in agreement?"

"We are," replied the heroes, the prophet, and their great-grandfather.

The Meglio, surprised by his father-in-law's response, asked him, "Robert, do you intend to stand before the fire so that the swords may choose you to make this trip?"

"I do," he replied. "Remember, I am a Scotsman. I have been to Jura, and I know the place. Also, in 1947, I was a full-fledged and experienced soldier of the Guardians, and a British subject. I had not yet moved to the United States. I, more than any of you, am familiar with the political and social events of that time. I will recognize any names or places that Orwell may reference, and I think I can add a lot to the discussion. Finally, after what I observed regarding the discipline of our team of heroes back in 1776, I think it would be good to have me accompany them. Just to guarantee their safety and success."

"The swords will still have to choose you," said the Meglio, "but I agree, it will be a huge benefit to have you on this mission, should you be chosen. So be it."

"So," asked the prophet, "are we ready to begin the mission? Does anyone have any further questions before we depart to perform the leaving process?"

"I have a question," replied Joe. "What makes you think that there may be hidden information in the story?"

The image of his grandmother answered. "Orwell was a very intelligent man. He was writing under duress. He was not in agreement with the Fabian plan of world domination. Hostages, when forced to read demands from their captors, find ways to signal that they're being coerced by blinking their eyes using Morse Code to the cameras, or saying things in a way that their family or friends will understand. We believe that Orwell may have done the same thing.

"Since he was dead shortly after he finished the book, these things were never revealed. It is not a certainty, but we would like you to be aware that it is a possibility. A very critical possibility. Be aware of it, and if necessary, be direct with him."

"Got it," replied Joe.

"Okay, gather your swords and let's head down to the fire pit by the river," instructed the prophet. "Time to start bringing this all to a head."

The heroes retreated to the outer room and gathered their swords. Their great-grandfather did the same. Then, they climbed the stairs out of the Keeping Room into the barn and began the walk to the river to set out on their mission.

The heroes stood around the fire pit as the flames rose higher. As always, the Meglio felt a sense of anticipation mixed with uncertainty. Of course, he knew their objective, the mission, and the target location, but he also knew that nothing ever went exactly as planned. That fact kept him on edge, as it should. He knew they always needed to keep their guard up, as his father-in-law had pointed out to them.

Together the cousins and their great-grandfather approached the fire and took their positions. At the command of the prophet, they raised their swords out over the flames and slowly brought them together. The now-familiar flash of pure white light enveloped them, and the fire obscured them from the view of the Meglio and the prophet.

When he could see clearly, the Meglio saw that once again the swords did not choose all the heroes. Billy, Jeff, and Ty remained. The swords had chosen Joe wielding Excalibur, Robbie carrying the Sword of William Wallace, Nick and the Sword of St. Michael, and the former Meglio carrying the Sword of St. Peter. The swords had chosen three swords with connections to the British Isles, and the Sword of the Archangel.

"Looks like we were left behind," said Jeff looking around. "Any idea why?" he asked his uncle and grandfather.

The prophet replied, "The swords that were chosen, for the most part, had a connection with the British Isles. Excalibur is obvious. So is the Sword of William Wallace. The Sword of St. Peter was brought to Britain by Joseph of Arimathea. I am not sure why the Sword of St. Michael was chosen, but as always, we must trust the swords. Douse the fire, and let's go back to the Keeping Room to monitor the team."

CHAPTER THIRTEEN

THE ISLE
OF JURA

Robbie, Joe, Nick, and their great-grandfather arrived in 1947 in a flash of light, about one hundred yards from the Orwells' residence on the Isle of Jura. They had arrived precisely at 6:00 a.m., but the sun was already high above the horizon, and it was cold. The temperature was slightly above freezing, and although they had the cloaking abilities of the swords to make them appear to be dressed appropriately, Robbie noticed it did not actually provide warmth.

"Man!" he exclaimed. "It is cold! We should have brought jackets or something."

"That is why I always try to wear several layers," said his great-grandfather, pointing at the sweater he wore over the collared shirt his son had loaned him. "This time of year on Jura can be very cold and damp. Also, the sun rises here at about 4:30 a.m., and doesn't set until after 10:00 p.m. because we're so far north."

"Why didn't you tell us all that in the Keeping Room?" asked Nick.

"Why didn't you ask more questions?" replied his great-grandfather. "You boys really need to think each mission through. Examine all the circumstances; it could be a matter of survival. Remember that!"

Robbie felt the sting of his great-grandfather's lesson all over his cold skin. Knowing he wouldn't forget to ask more questions about the climate next time, he rubbed his hands together as they found a spot where they could clearly see Orwell's cabin. It was as the image had described it; small, unkempt, and somewhat dilapidated. He could see lantern light through the windows and smoke streaming from the chimney.

"Looks like Orwell is awake. We should head over there right away," suggested Joe. "It'll be good to get out of the cold."

"Is that so?" said the former Meglio. "Just march up to his door, on a nearly-deserted island in the North Sea, looking for warmth and an interview, before the sun is high in the sky?"

"Well, yes," said Joe. "Why not?"

"Because, first, we have no idea who may be watching him. The Fabians and the Leviathans have a lot invested in his work, and although they have exiled him here, we can't assume he is unwatched. Second, in British culture, it is not proper to call on anyone before 9:00 a.m. no matter where they live. If we want to get off on the right foot with him, we need to at least follow the rules of courtesy."

"What will we do until then?" asked Robbie.

"We will do reconnaissance work," his great-grandfather replied. "We will quietly walk a wide circle around the cabin looking for observers, slowly reducing the size of our circle until we are sure that he is not being watched. Then, we can safely approach his door. Not before."

"But, Great-Grandpa, it's *cold*!" Robbie complained.

"Then you'd better figure out how to stay warm for the next three hours, because we are not knocking on that door before nine. Next time, dress appropriately."

Feeling properly admonished, Robbie and his cousins followed their great-grandfather as he made his way up into the heavily wooded hills to a point about a quarter of a mile from the cabin. There, he stopped and addressed them.

"We're going to work in two teams. We'll walk in opposite directions and meet on the other side, then move to a point about one hundred yards closer to the cabin and repeat the circle as many times as needed to ensure that we will not be watched. Do this in absolute silence, and walk gingerly. Avoid breaking branches or disturbing rocks. We don't want to alert the enemy. Understood?"

The heroes nodded their understanding and began the process. Robbie and Joe headed east, and Nick and his great-grandfather started west. On the first pass, neither team saw anything suspicious. It was the same with the second and third passes. On the fourth pass, Robbie and Joe spotted a small hut that looked like something a hunter might use for emergency shelter. It was only slightly bigger than an outhouse. They crouched behind a large bush to decide their next move.

"Robbie!" whispered Joe. "Do you think we should approach and see if there is anyone inside, or should we go get the others?"

"We have no idea where they are at this point, and we don't even know if it is occupied," whispered Robbie. "Let's see if we can find out if anyone is in there and then decide. We are about fifteen yards away, so I suggest that we approach in a low crawl. Let's move!"

The cousins lowered themselves to their bellies and

low-crawled toward the hut. When they were five feet from it, they heard the crackling sound of a radio and a voice responding to a question.

"Yes, this is Wilson. Yes, I am awake, and no, I have not been drinking, yet," said the voice from the hut. "Although I will be glad when my replacement arrives. This is absolutely the worst assignment in the world. Over."

There was more crackling and unintelligible sound. The man in the hut replied again. "Yes, I initiated the call because I have seen movement in the woods. I'm sure it's not deer. It could be hunters, but I have not seen any boats arrive at the island since Orwell returned. The townsfolk don't hunt, they are fishermen, so I am suspicious. I will continue to watch, and if I can make out who it is, I will report back. By the way, when is my replacement arriving? Over."

There was a response which Joe and Robbie could not hear, and the man in the hut replied, "Good, it will be nice to get back to my warm house and bed tonight. Be listening for my next report. Over."

Robbie whispered to Joe, "Sounds like we have to take this guy out before he reports back. We also must interview Orwell quickly. His replacement may check on him before he comes here. Here's what I think we should do.

"You go to the hut and knock on the door saying that you're the man's replacement and have arrived early, then walk around to the back of the hut. I'll be on the roof, and when the man comes around to find you, I'll jump on him from above. Then, we incapacitate him and drag him into the woods."

Joe agreed and headed to the front door. Robbie climbed a nearby tree and waited.

Joe arrived at the door and knocked, shouting, "Wilson, wake up, you sluggard! I'm freezing out here! Do you want me to replace you or not?" Then he moved around to the back of the hut. Joe called out, "Come around back, there is something I need to show you!"

They heard some startled movement in the hut and a lot of shuffling and grunting. Wilson went to the door and hastily pulled it open.

"Where did you go?" he asked as he tucked in his shirt and buttoned his trousers.

At this point, Robbie dropped down from the tree onto the roof of the hut. The thatches gave way and he landed on the cot that Wilson had just vacated. "What the...?" the man said, alarmed by Robbie's sudden entrance.

Before Robbie could recover, Wilson was on him. He had Robbie in a bear hug, so he could not raise his right arm to draw his sword. They struggled, but the man was built like a grizzly bear and was just as hairy. Robbie was not going to be able to break free.

While Wilson and Robbie struggled, Joe came back around to the front and burst through the door. With Excalibur raised he rushed in and brought the butt of the handle down on the back of the man's head, hard. Blood exploded from Wilson's scalp. He released Robbie and fell to the ground, unconscious.

"Nice job, Joe," said Robbie. "That guy had a grip like an anaconda. I was starting to turn blue."

"No worries," said Joe. "I guess we need to tie this guy up and gag him. Hurry, find some rope."

They searched the hut for rope but came up empty. So instead, they tore the filthy, smelly sheets into strips and used them to secure his hands and feet. Then, they stuffed his mouth with more of the filthy strips and tied another tightly around his mouth, securing it with a tight knot at the back of his head.

"His head's still bleeding," Joe observed as he finished tying the knot.

Robbie looked at the two cloth strips in his hand. "I think there's enough here to wrap around his head. Maybe it will stop the bleeding."

Reaching for the cloth, Joe nodded. "If I fold one up and put it on the gash and tie the other one around his head, that'll put a little pressure on it."

He worked quickly, then looked around. "There's quite a bit of blood on the floor here. If someone comes in, that'll give us away for sure."

"Like the hole in the roof won't?" Robbie replied, grimacing.

"Good point. Any ideas about where we should stash this guy?" Joe asked.

Robbie nodded. "When I was in the tree, I saw a cave about twenty yards to the rear. Let's put him in there."

As they began to drag their prisoner around to the rear of the hut, he regained consciousness. He began to wriggle and writhe, making it much harder to drag him. As they struggled, they heard people running through the trees. Dropping Wilson, they ran into the hut, swords drawn. Wilson struggled and moaned at the rear of the hut, but suddenly, they heard a thump, and all was silent. Hunkering down behind the cot, they waited as they heard footsteps approaching the door. A shadow fell across the threshold and a sword appeared.

"Is it warm in there?" asked Nick. "I'm freezing!"

Joe and Robbie stood up from behind the cot and Robbie said, "No, it's not, and the smell is horrible."

Nick and their great-grandfather entered the hut.

Observing the hole in the roof, the former Meglio commented sarcastically, "Looks like another well thought out operation! Any broken bones?"

"No, Great-Grandpa," replied Robbie, "just a bruised ego. Did you see the guy out back?"

"Yes," replied Nick, "Great-Grandpa took care of him. He won't be waking up for a while. We should probably hide him, though."

At Nick's suggestion, they worked together to drag Wilson to the cave, piled a bunch of rocks across the entrance, and went back to the hut to get the man's radio.

Robbie looked at it and observed, "We should radio back to whomever Wilson was talking to earlier. He said he would report back to tell them if he saw anyone."

The former Meglio agreed. "I will do it. I am familiar with these radios." He examined the radio, confirming that it was set to a proper frequency and said, "Wilson here. Over."

"Report, please. Over," the voice at the other end ordered.

Great-Grandpa replied, "All is well, no intruders. Just a herd of very noisy and overzealous deer. Over."

The other man responded, "Good thing that your replacement arrives this afternoon, you are getting punchy, Wilson, mistaking deer for intruders. Stay put until he arrives. Over."

"Will do. Over," replied Great-Grandpa.

Then he replaced the transmitter and said, "Okay, let's head down to Orwell's cabin. When we get there, I will knock and see if he will let me in. I will make sure no one else is with him, and then if all is clear, I will tell him of our mission. Do not try to come inside until I tell you, and for Pete's sake, stay quiet and watch each other's backs."

They made their way down the hill toward the back of the cabin.

"You boys just lay low," their great-grandfather instructed. "Stay close and keep an eye out for anyone approaching the cabin. I'll knock and see if Orwell will let me in. When I think he's open to it, I'll signal for you to join us. Got it?"

"Got it," Robbie answered for the rest. The cousins looked for hiding places as their great-grandfather walked to the front door and knocked.

As the former Meglio stood at the door, he wondered if Orwell would actually answer. After about thirty seconds, Orwell responded, "Who's there?"

"A weary traveler looking for a cup of hot tea. Could I possibly impose on you at this early hour?" Robert replied in his finest Scottish brogue.

The curtains of the side window were pulled back and Orwell peered through, evaluating his caller. After a short while, he unlocked and opened the door.

There stood George Orwell, slightly disheveled and looking haunted. "Who am I to refuse a cup of hot tea to a weary traveler?" he said, opening the door wider. "Please, come in from the cold and warm yourself by the fire while I heat you some tea."

As Orwell was in the kitchen, preparing the tea, Robert examined the room which was sparsely furnished and very dreary. There were piles of books lining the floor along the walls, a rickety writing desk by the window, and several empty bottles of whiskey on the floor. Firewood was piled near the fireplace, along with what looked like a year's supply of old newspapers.

Orwell reentered the room carrying a wooden tray, with a pot of tea and two cups.

"I hope you like your tea strong," he said.

"I do."

"Wonderful," said Orwell. "That is the only way to survive on this damp and dreary island." He poured the tea and took a seat across from Robert.

"What brings you out so early this morning?" asked Orwell.

Robert replied, "First of all, allow me to introduce myself. I am Robert Ogilvie Petrie, from Edinburgh. I am pleased to make your acquaintance."

Orwell inclined his head in response. "I am Eric Blair. Pleased to meet you, Mr. Petrie."

"Are you living out here by yourself, Mr. Blair?"

"I am, currently," Orwell replied. "I just returned from a visit to London. My sister, Avril, and my son did not return with me. They needed some time back in a more civilized environment. Why do you ask?"

"What I have to tell you is very confidential, and I wanted to make sure it would not be overheard," replied Robert.

Orwell frowned. "If you are with the Fabians, you can finish your tea and remove yourself from my premises," he stated, rising from his chair. "I have had just about enough of the constant attention and pressure. I have told all of you that I will write the book the way you want it. Just leave me in peace to do it!"

"I am not with the Fabians, nor am I favorably disposed towards them," replied Robert. "I have come to give you some insight and perspective. May I speak to you of my mission, Mr. Orwell?"

Orwell sat down and leaned in toward Robert. "You know my pen name?"

"Of course," replied Robert, "Where I come from, you are world-famous. Let me explain."

The former Meglio told Orwell about the Guardians, the Swords of Valor, the Leviathan Alliance, and their mission. He explained the impact of his still unfinished book and told him of the heroes waiting outside.

Orwell, seeming to take it all in reasonably well, said, "Looks like my contemporary, Mr. H.G. Wells, would love to speak with you regarding this time travel concept. Maybe someday, when we are again on speaking terms, I will mention it to him. With complete anonymity, of course. Please go get your charges and bring them in to warm themselves. I would like to hear more about your mission."

Robert went outside and soon returned with the heroes. They gathered around the fire to warm themselves, and then took seats on the floor. Orwell retreated to the kitchen and came back shortly with more hot tea and Scottish shortbread cookies for his guests. When they were all warm and settled in, Robert addressed the group.

"I have given Mr. Orwell a summary of our mission. He knows who we represent and why we want to speak with him. He has agreed to be forthcoming about his reason for writing the book in question, and the intent of the Fabians regarding it. So, given that Mr. Wilson's replacement will be arriving sometime this afternoon, I recommend we get on with it. Who will go first?"

Joe raised his hand. "I will begin. Mr. Orwell, what can you tell us about the Fabians and their reason for forcing you to write this book? It did not exist in our previous timeline."

Orwell sat back in his chair and gave it a moment of thought. He then responded, "I understand from Robert that you are familiar with who they purport to be and their 'glorious and unselfish' self-perception. They believe themselves to be the cream of the elite, and that the common man is fortunate to have such benevolent angels to prepare the future for them. I was one of them, briefly. I learned from them at Eton and was beguiled by them for a time. Then, let's just say, the scales fell from my eyes. When I did not agree to become a propagandist for them, they acted against my family. They told me that it was for my family members' good, and mine.

"Finally, they threatened to 'help' my son. They said that if I would not 'see the truth', I had no right to impose my madness on my son, and they would 'adopt' him and bring him up in their truth. It was then that I realized two things: first, that I could never let that happen, and second, that I could not fight them. At that point, I agreed to write their book. But you need to know that I have my own agenda, which they know nothing about."

"Can you tell us more about that?" asked Robbie.

"Which part specifically?" replied Orwell. "Their agenda or mine?"

"Both, actually," responded Robbie. "Both are critical for us to know."

"Ah, yes, of course," replied Orwell. "I will begin with their agenda and their intention for the book. The Fabians are just the most prominent face of a secret foundational organization that remains hidden in the shadows. Robert has called it the Leviathan Alliance, and that name seems fitting. They have been planning to take power for centuries and have now refined their approach to the Fabian one, which is to bide their time and to avoid any battles in which there could be a clear winner. Their approach is one of attrition. They also have become apostles of the Renaissance overlords such as the Borgias and Machiavelli, from whom they learned cunning and deceit in politics. The Fabian socialists are determined to conquer their competitors regardless of time and cost. Through collectivist political teachings, contrived crises, and central planning, they expect that like a ripe fruit, the control of government in Britain, America, and eventually the world, will fall into their hands. Their totalitarian ideas have taken root in the intellectual elites. They often represent the tenured elite at universities and government, unable to be ousted regardless of what leadership takes over.

"Claiming to be above politics, the new apostles of government power, the Fabians, believe that their university educations make them high-born. And this is confirmed and applauded by the Leviathans.

"The Fabians and their owners, the Leviathans, seek power entirely for its own sake. They are not interested in the good of others, they are interested solely in power; pure power. They are different from the oligarchies of the past in that they know what they are doing. All the others, even those who resembled them, were cowards and hypocrites compared to them.

"The German Nazis and the Russian Communists came very close to them in their methods, but they never had the courage to recognize their own motives. They pretended, perhaps they even believed, that they had seized power unwillingly and for a limited time, and that just around the corner there lay a paradise where human beings would be free and equal.

"The Fabians are not like that. They know that no one ever seizes power with the intention of relinquishing it. Power is not a means; it is an end. One does not establish a dictatorship in order to safeguard a revolution; one makes the revolution to establish the dictatorship.

The object of persecution is persecution. The object of torture is torture. The object of power is power. Now do you begin to get the picture?"

"Yes," replied Nick. "We understand that they have been manipulating the chess pieces and even the chessboard for their own purposes for ages. They have secured control of all the engines of society, and now wish to declare checkmate. But why lay out the agenda so clearly in the book you are writing? Aren't they afraid it will turn public opinion against them?"

"The purpose of this book, and the reason for them forcing me to write it, is that it is an announcement," said Orwell seriously. "It is, in their eyes, trumpeting the arrival of a new world. Remember, they are not the 'Proles' in the book. They are the 'Party'. They are the winners. They are the ruling class. They care not what the common man may think of the surface message of the book. They only care that their co-conspirators understand that the final stage has been initiated.

"This is the blueprint for them. This is their manifesto. They are proud of it and believe that in time it will be hailed as the founding document by the elite, and over time, the eyes of the common man will be too blind to see the truth. Arrogance and pride drive this. They believe themselves to be invulnerable at this point. They may be right. But if there is hope, it lays in the Proles, the common man.

"This book is not a work of fiction, in the sense of make-believe. It is outlining a true agenda, albeit in the future. It is not a warning, but a prediction, a prophecy. It is a vision of the future in which there is a boot stamping on a human face, forever. A future where history has stopped, and nothing exists except an endless present in which the Party is always right."

"Wow," declared Nick. "That is intense and bleak. As a work of fiction, it would be horrifying, but knowing that it is fast becoming reality in our time is even worse. You said you had an agenda. What is it, and how are you dealing with this?"

"For the longest time," started Orwell, "I rebelled and refused. But they know that the way to assert their power over another person is through suffering. Obedience is not enough. Unless he is suffering, how can you be sure that he is obeying your will and not his own? Power is in inflicting pain and humiliation. Power is in tearing human minds to pieces and putting them together again in new shapes of the Fabian and Leviathan groups' own choosing.

"Do you begin to see, then, what kind of world they are creating? When I saw this, I knew I could not let myself actually feel my suffering. I had to keep my mind focused on the future. That is why I sent my sister and son back to London. I could not bear to see them every day and know that they would someday live in a world which I was helping to unleash.

"So, I have stopped feeling. I am writing with a purpose. Here, I am a lonely ghost uttering a truth that nobody may ever truly hear or understand. But so long as I utter it, in some obscure way, hope is not gone. A vestige may remain. I am hoping to plant seeds in the unconscious mind of the future. Touching their consciousness is the critical element because, until they become conscious, they will never rebel. And rebel they must... someday. The masses never revolt of their own accord, and they never revolt merely because they are oppressed. Indeed, so long as they are not permitted to have standards of comparison, they never even become aware that they are oppressed!

"I have been contemplating how to provide the future with that comparative view. I asked myself, 'how do I communicate with the future?' It seemed impossible. Either the future would resemble the present, in which case it would not listen to me, or it would be different, and my efforts might be meaningless.

"Then, you arrived at my door. You provided me with my method of communicating with the future. You have now become my secret agenda. I will write their book. I will make it as horrifying as I can. I will expose it all and laugh at them while I am doing it, knowing beyond any doubt that someone in the future understands, people who are in a position to make a difference. You are my last and greatest hope. You have eyes to see and ears to hear. You must use this information to wake them up in your time. Wake them! Alert them! Tell them the truth and make them rebel!

"The Fabians and their ilk say that they do not merely destroy their enemies; they change them. Well, you must change them back! Change them into lovers of freedom and liberty! Change them from apathetic sleepwalkers into men of valor, like yourselves.

"The choice for mankind lies between freedom and happiness, and for the great bulk of mankind, happiness is better. So, you must make them see that the joy that lies in freedom is more valuable than any fleeting happiness in captivity. The Fabians like to say that he who controls the past controls the future, and he who controls the present controls the past. But I say he who controls himself controls eternity. As for me, I will die hating them. That is my freedom."

Looking at his great-grandsons, the former Meglio noted that they were stunned into silence by Orwell's impassioned monologue. He was a rare man who could not only translate his passion onto paper but also express it verbally, as well.

The former Meglio felt moved and inspired. They had their answers, and now they knew their enemy. The Fabians were the enforcers, the tip of the spear. The team would go back and let the quantum computer do its work. They would identify the Fabian connections in their own time and identify a high impact timeline event to influence, to avert this dire fate.

Their great-grandfather spoke, "Mr. Orwell. What can we do to help you, here, now? Is there any way we can ease your burden?"

Orwell thought for a moment and then replied, "You have brightened my world with your visit here today. There is nothing more I need. I now have hope. Thank you," said Orwell. "Now, is there anything else?"

The heroes had no further questions, and Robert did not want to diminish the power of the moment with further facts and details. They had their answers. It was time to leave.

The former Meglio asked Orwell for some coals from his fire, so they could build one of their own outside the cabin for their return. He provided them with coals that he placed in a coal bucket, along with newspaper and some of his firewood, and accompanied them outside to the back of the cabin. There the heroes built the fire while their great-grandfather and Orwell said their farewells.

"Be strong, Eric Blair," Robert said. "Your works will bring you fame, but I know that is little solace unless it is for the right reason, with the right result. We will do our part. Your efforts will not be in vain." Then he joined the cousins around the fire. They lifted their swords, touched them together, and disappeared.

Orwell stood there staring at the fire for a while,

contemplating all that had transpired. Then, he doused the fire and hurried back to his dilapidated and dreary cabin. Somehow, now it was full of light.

CHAPTER FOURTEEN

THE RETURN FROM JURA

~~~

Ty stood with Jeff, the prophet, and the Meglio by the fire pit. They'd been waiting anxiously for the others to return. Once again, the cousins and their great-grandfather reappeared in the flash of light. The Meglio and the prophet seemed agitated and distressed.

"Welcome back," said the Meglio. "No time for niceties, I regret to say. We must go to the Keeping Room immediately; the quantum computer has news to share with us."

Then he and the prophet turned and led the team directly to the Keeping Room where they placed their swords in the glass case and proceeded to the round table, taking their seats.

The Meglio addressed the quantum computer. "Catherine, we are all assembled. Please tell us about the urgent information you have discovered."

The image of their grandmother appeared before them, mirroring the seriousness of the Meglio and the prophet. "Welcome back, my heroes," said the image, "I apologize for the urgency, but I felt you needed to hear this right away. In analyzing the timeline discrepancies, I have found another significant anomaly which I believe gives us our fourth assignment objective."

"That is good news, right?" said Ty. "Anything that certain and specific has to be better than just winging it. Why does everyone look so concerned?"

The image looked at Ty and replied, "It is not good news, Ty, because what I discovered means that you will need to go back in time once again. And this time you will need to purposefully change an event which will have a significant effect on the timeline.

"As you experienced before, changing time by even one day, or by saving one life, can result in a myriad of unintended consequences. I will be proposing that you go back and alter a seminal event in the history of this new timeline."

"Okay," said Joe, "I'm not worried. We've done that before, and we survived."

"I understand how you might see it that way," the Meglio spoke. "But let the image tell you the rest of the story, and then tell us what you think." Turning to address the image, the Meglio said, "Go on, my dear, and tell them everything."

The image of their grandmother continued. "In the old timeline, which only the people in this room remember, the United States had a very long history of peaceful and calm transitions of power. That is not the case in the timeline we now inhabit. For the first half of the 20th century, the lineup of presidents remains the same as in the old timeline. Franklin D. Roosevelt was president for four terms. He was followed by Truman, who was followed by Eisenhower. Then, as before, in 1960 John F. Kennedy was elected by an extremely thin margin. All of that is the same in both timelines.

"However, in this new timeline, instead of serving

two terms as he did in the timeline we are familiar with, he did not survive his first term and was replaced by Lyndon Johnson, his first vice president."

"What?" exclaimed Jeff, "How could that be? He was a young and vibrant man. How could he have died in office? Was there an accident? Did he contract a disease? What happened?"

"In this timeline, he was assassinated by the Leviathans on November 22, 1963," declared the image seriously.

Billy looked shocked. "That's horrible! I remember when we studied about him in school; I remember memorizing his speeches; I remember when his image was carved into Mt. Rushmore alongside the others. How could this have happened? Has the world gone mad in this timeline?"

The image did not respond to Billy's question but continued. "His presidency was cut short. I will get into the details of how and why, but let me continue with the history of who succeeded him. As I said earlier, in this timeline he was replaced by Lyndon B. Johnson who was sworn in on Air Force One in Dallas just hours after the assassination.

"In our old timeline, as in this new one, Kennedy *chose* Senate Majority Leader Lyndon B. Johnson as his running mate. However, in this timeline, he was *forced* to choose Johnson. I will explain that a bit later. Many liberals did not like his choice, even though Johnson, who was a Protestant Texan, provided religious and geographical balance to the ticket. A lot of people were surprised that Kennedy made the offer and that Johnson accepted it, because in the 1960 presidential primaries, the two had been rivals.

"In our timeline, some believe that Kennedy offered

the position expecting Johnson to decline. According to these accounts, when Johnson consented, Kennedy sent his brother Robert F. Kennedy to talk him out of it. So, you can see that from the very beginning, Kennedy felt that he had made a mistake. In our old timeline, that mistake was corrected when Kennedy chose Hubert H. Humphrey to be his running mate in 1964. Johnson just faded into the background after that.

"This is how the rest unfolded as we all remember it in our old timeline. With the more intellectual and affable Humphrey as vice president, Kennedy was able to avoid further involvement in Vietnam, pass historic civil rights legislation, shorten the time of the Cold War, and keep the economy moving forward. Ultimately, he personally witnessed the landing of Apollo 11 on the moon, which occurred in July of 1968, one year earlier than in the new timeline.

"After Kennedy's two terms, he backed his brother, Robert, for the presidency, and he won by a small margin. John had angered southern Democrats with the dismissal of Johnson, and that made Robert's nomination a challenge. Many in our old timeline pointed out that the only reason he was elected in 1968 was because he chose Martin Luther King, Jr. as his running mate. That solidified the African-American vote and overwhelmed the opposition of the Southern Democrats.

"After Robert F. Kennedy served his two terms, King was elected in 1976 as the first African-American president. He served only one full term and passed away from a heart attack while in office at the beginning of his second term. He was replaced in 1981 by Jimmy Carter, his vice president, who served out the remaining three years of King's term. Carter's handling of the faltering economy was a disaster and in 1984, the country elected

Ronald Reagan.

"Reagan held office for two terms. He performed well, turning the economy around, but not distinguishing himself to any great extent in foreign policy or any other area of legislation. After Reagan, George H.W. Bush was elected in 1992 and served one term.

"In 1996, we saw the election of Bill Clinton, who, due to a scandal, was impeached shortly before the end of his first term. Hampered by the scandal, Al Gore, Clinton's vice-president, was defeated in the 2000 election by George W. Bush who served two terms.

"The election of 2008 was won by Barack Obama, who was re-elected in 2012. As you know, the election of 2016 was still undecided in our timeline. We will never know who would have won that election because of the change caused by your last mission."

"That is all good stuff, and we are fully aware of all of that," said Ty. "What we need to know is how did it all play out in *this* new timeline, and why does it matter to our next mission?"

"That is the next part of the story," said the image of his grandmother.

"In this timeline, the assassination of John F. Kennedy by the Leviathans, who did not exist in our timeline, opened the door for them to take over the reins of government in the United States. From the information the quantum computer has pieced together, Johnson was a Leviathan.

"When Kennedy was assassinated, Johnson began to implement the Leviathan plan. From that point on, every U.S. president was a Leviathan, except for Ronald Reagan. There is some controversy about whether Reagan was a Leviathan or not. I will get into that later, but suffice it to say that in this timeline, the country has been mostly governed by Leviathans carrying out and implementing the plan that was outlined in Orwell's book *Nineteen Eighty-Four*."

"So, Kennedy was not a Leviathan?" confirmed Nick. "That's good to know. We all have such a high opinion of him, that it would have shocked me to learn that about him."

"Actually," said the image, "That's not exactly true. Kennedy did start out as a Leviathan. He came from a very wealthy family and was educated at Harvard, one of the favorite Leviathan training schools. He was also educated at the London School of Economics, which I have discovered from my research was a Fabian-controlled institution.

"Four Fabians, Beatrice and Sidney Webb, Graham Wallas, and George Bernard Shaw founded the London School of Economics with money left to the Fabian Society. It was at this school that many of the future leaders of the world were exposed to Fabian thought. They subsequently went on to frame economic policy for a significant percentage of humanity based on Fabian social-democratic principles. The Fabian Society strongly influenced Kennedy's initial political philosophy. However, he later altered his views, believing the Fabian ideal of socialism to be too impractical.

"Before he declared his candidacy for president, the Leviathans and the Fabians were not sure who they would back for the election of 1960. The choice was between Kennedy and Richard Nixon, Eisenhower's vice president. They ultimately decided to back Kennedy. He accepted their help and was on his way to an easy win.

"Then, for some reason, he got overconfident and decided that he did not want to be controlled by the Leviathans. He told them he was going to govern independently. This angered them, and they threw all their support behind Nixon, who was also a Leviathan. Near the end of the campaign, it was neck and neck, and the polls showed Kennedy losing by a small margin. He relented and agreed to govern as a Leviathan because he desperately wanted the presidency.

"They changed their decision and backed him in the last part of the campaign, throwing massive amounts of money behind him and making the unions support him, as well as the military-industrial complex. He won by a small margin, but the victory came at a very high price.

"So, he was a Leviathan, then he was not, then he was again?" asked Jeff. "Sounds like he was not really too committed to it. How did the Leviathans ensure his obedience?"

"That's where the 'very high price' came into play. The Leviathans had gained Kennedy's assurance that he would not dismiss Johnson as his vice president during his first term in office. They knew that Kennedy was not happy with Johnson as his running mate and that he didn't trust him. It had been rumored that soon after the election, Kennedy intended to ask Johnson to resign.

"The Leviathans didn't want that to happen, so they made Johnson's tenure a critical part of their agreement to back Kennedy. They also made sure he appointed many Leviathans to his cabinet and as his advisors as part of the deal to back him once again. Johnson and these cabinet members and advisors would work to implement the Leviathan policies, and report back regarding his activities," said the image.

"However, shortly after Kennedy's election, on December 6, 1960, before he officially took office, Eisenhower met with him privately. They discussed the transition of power, but they also discussed the

Leviathans. Eisenhower was a non-Leviathan president, but he knew of them and their power because of Nixon's relationship to them while he served as vice-president. So, he warned Kennedy about what he was getting into and about the dangers of the military-industrial complex. In this timeline, the military-industrial complex is an alliance between the nation's military and the arms industry which supplies it. The Leviathans control it.

"Eisenhower warned Kennedy that there was a separate global power structure on Earth that superseded the government. He told him that it was much more advanced in its understanding of scientific research and the actual nature of reality. They used resources such as the CIA, NSA, FBI, Navy, Army, and Air Force to enforce their will. Eisenhower pointed out that when the military mixes with industry, coupled with the classification of information, and the power of computers and networking, we have a recipe for enslavement and control of the human race.

"Eisenhower went on to make a speech about it to the public in his farewell address on January 17, 1961, a few days before Kennedy's inauguration. Eisenhower's message in his parting address was that industry had taken over the military, that bright, retiring military people had gravitated to aerospace and other related industries, and that massive federal funding outlays were being granted for scientific-military research. He warned of an unnamed separate entity that had more power over decision-making and policy than the government. He warned about the power this separate entity had, and its ability to heavily influence what it desired to accomplish.

"His speech warned of 'unwarranted influence… by the military-industrial complex' and proved enormously prescient, even though it was not widely reported on at the time. Kennedy would not or could not listen to his advice. So, Kennedy went on as planned, secretly thinking that he could control it all and limit or negate any possible overly-negative influences. He was wrong.

"In this timeline, three months into his presidency, the Leviathan-controlled CIA decided they were going to invade Cuba. They used a CIA-sponsored paramilitary group, Brigade 2506, to do this on April 17, 1961. This is known as the Bay of Pigs Invasion. The publicly announced purpose was to take over Cuba and fight communism near our shores.

"The *real* reason was to initiate and exacerbate strain and conflict in the relationship between the U.S. and USSR. The military-industrial complex knew that escalating the level of conflict between the two superpowers would cause an arms race. The resulting military spending would add incredible profits to their balance sheets as financial beneficiaries.

"It is a basic tenet of the Leviathans and the Fabians to keep the world in a constant state of war. Their ongoing problem was how to keep the wheels of industry turning without increasing the real wealth of the world. Goods must be produced, but they must not be distributed. In practice, the only way of achieving this was to keep labor and the consumer class busy through continuous warfare. This invasion was their opportunity to ensure that the world would be in that condition for at least the next twenty years, or until they could implement the last stage of their plan.

"Kennedy reluctantly approved the final invasion plan on April 4, 1961. Unfortunately, the press leaked information about the impending attack, and the U.S. involvement became apparent to the world.

"Ten days later, a defiant Kennedy said 'no' to the

CIA, the Joint Chiefs, and the Leviathans. He refused to provide air cover for the invasion of Cuba by CIA-trained Cuban refugees. As a result, the operation only had half the forces the CIA had deemed necessary, and the result was a disaster for Kennedy. He had failed to stop the invasion by refusing air cover, and still had enraged the Soviets. Now he had finally driven the Cubans fully into the hands of the USSR. The Leviathans were not happy with Kennedy's rebellion, but they were happy with the results.

"From that point on, Kennedy decided that Eisenhower was right, and he had to expose the Leviathans. He met with Eisenhower again when the Bay of Pigs Invasion went wrong, and the two talked at Camp David. It was there that Kennedy informed Eisenhower that he was going to throw off their control. Ten days following the failed Bay of Pigs Invasion, he made a speech echoing Eisenhower's. He said the same things but was even more revealing. It is known as Kennedy's 'Secret Societies' speech. It was the speech that put one of the final nails in Kennedy's coffin.

"With his 'Secret Societies' speech, Kennedy was the first and the only president to ever identify the Leviathans and globalists as the enemy of America and humanity as a whole. For a man in his position, Kennedy was stunningly detailed in calling out the conspiracy of his day.

"In his speech he said, in part, 'The very word 'secrecy' is repugnant in a free and open society; and we are as a people inherently and historically opposed to secret societies, to secret oaths, and to secret proceedings. We decided long ago that the dangers of excessive and unwarranted concealment of pertinent facts far outweighed the dangers which are cited to justify it...

"'Our way of life is under attack. Those who make

themselves our enemy are advancing around the globe. The survival of our friends is in danger. And yet no war has been declared, no borders have been crossed by marching troops, no missiles have been fired…

"'We are opposed around the world by a monolithic and ruthless conspiracy that relies primarily on covert means for expanding its sphere of influence; on infiltration instead of invasion, on subversion instead of elections, on intimidation instead of free choice, on guerrillas by night instead of armies by day.

"It is a system which has conscripted vast human and material resources into the building of a tightly knit and highly efficient machine that combines military, diplomatic, intelligence, economic, scientific, and political operations.'"

"Kennedy had a vison of a better world!" continued the image. "His vision was a direct challenge to the Leviathans and globalists of his day. The Leviathans decided that Kennedy's rebellion could not be allowed to continue. Kennedy had signed his own death warrant. His assassination was ordered by the highest levels of Leviathan intelligence and carried out in part by the very men sworn to protect him.

"He was one of the most courageous men ever to hold the office. He exposed the Leviathans and the Fabians *knowing* what the consequences would be. Yet he chose to face the juggernaut head on. It all really began after that event, and the American people of this timeline just sat and did nothing, apparently preferring their new TVs and washing machines over truth and freedom. Sixty years later, we find ourselves, and this timeline, on the verge of a dictatorship."

The Meglio rose from his chair after the long history lesson from the quantum computer and walked around the room looking thoughtful. Then he turned and addressed the others.

"After hearing this incredible information, it is obvious to me that the way we can avert the disaster in this timeline is to send a mission back to stop the assassination of Kennedy. I believe that the best chance we have of derailing the Leviathan plot is to ensure that Kennedy is allowed to finish the two terms he was destined to serve. If he had been given that additional time, it is very likely that he would have been able to manipulate events to eradicate the Leviathan influence in government and preserve freedom and liberty for all mankind. He was aware of it all, he had the inside knowledge to expose them, and he knew who the most powerful Leviathans were. We must give him that chance."

The prophet replied, "I agree that what you propose seems like a good possibility, however, I have some questions. If the Leviathans killed Kennedy in 1963 in this timeline, and then had complete control of the government, the economy, and every other aspect of society, why wasn't the trap closed decades ago?"

Robbie jumped in. "I was just wondering the same thing. Orwell told us that the target date was 1984. That was the reason for the title of the book they were forcing him to write. If that was the target date, why hasn't it happened? Maybe there is another event we have to consider changing instead of the Kennedy assassination?"

"Yes," agreed Jeff, "what about just going back and telling Kennedy to choose good old Hubert Humphrey as his vice president like he did after dumping Johnson in the timeline we remember? In our old timeline, that had pretty good results."

"Those are very good questions," replied the image.

"Here is the answer to Jeff's question first. Remember that in this timeline, the Kennedy we will be working with was forced to keep Johnson in place for four years as part of his deal with the Leviathans. He could certainly make the change after his first term in office, but in this timeline, he will have no opportunity to do that since he will be assassinated before he can be reelected. We must do something to prevent the assassination. That's the key. All other decisions and actions stem from that. Kennedy must have time to take those corrective actions.

"To address Robbie's question, in the current timeline, things were progressing according to plan after the Kennedy assassination until the election of Ronald Reagan. In this timeline, Reagan was elected in 1980 and served two terms. This was a blow to the Leviathans.

"First of all, they didn't think he would run. In 1967, they were courting him and had invited him to a Lakeside Talk given by Richard Nixon at the Cave Man Camp during the Bohemian Grove gathering that year. After his talk, Nixon sat with Reagan and told him of his plans to enter the primaries but said he wouldn't run against any 'fellow Republicans'. According to Professor G. William Domhoff from the University of California, Reagan was surprised that anyone was considering him as a possible candidate. He claimed he had no intention of running for president.

"Reportedly, Reagan continued to attend meetings of this group, which led to him being listed as a member starting in 1975. Some have reported that he even gave one of the Lakeside Talks. However, insiders claim that Reagan soon discovered who the Leviathans really were and what their agenda was. He decided to 'keep his friends close and his enemies closer', choosing to continue attending to learn all he could about them.

"By the time Reagan announced his candidacy for the 1980 presidential election, the Leviathans realized what he was up to and considered him an enemy. Yet they did not oppose his nomination. They had written him off as unelectable because of his age and background. They assumed Carter would be elected again, and he was in their pocket. So, Reagan's election was a complete shock.

"They tried to correct this mistake a few months after Reagan was elected. On March 30, 1981, they tried to assassinate him, but the attempt failed, and Reagan came back stronger than ever.

"The election of 1980 was pivotal, because the USSR was in trouble economically. The President of the USSR, Mikhail Gorbachev, who was a Leviathan, initiated 'glasnost' in 1985. Glasnost was a sort of lessening of the Cold War tensions and warming of relations with the west. Gorbachev declared that public policy within the Soviet Union would now be the open and frank discussion of economic and political realities.

"They had planned to bring the USSR and the U.S. into negotiations with the goal of merging the two superpowers into a USSR/U.S. federation. This federation would control the world under a combined form of capitalist communism. They felt that the world would hail this as the dawn of a new age and welcome it with open arms. It would be the ultimate fulfillment of their dreams of global domination. The chess pieces were all in place. Checkmate was at hand.

"However, with the election of Ronald Reagan, this dream was shattered. He took a very adversarial approach to the USSR, and his policies accelerated the economic and political collapse of the Soviet Union. This, combined with Reagan's secret communications with Pope John

Paul II enlisting his spiritual and political support for the uprisings in Poland, eventually ensured the collapse.

"The Soviet Union was dissolved on December 26, 1991. It was a direct result of the combined efforts of the two most influential, non-Leviathan world leaders, Reagan and the pope. On the previous day, December 25, 1991, Soviet President Mikhail Gorbachev, the eighth and final leader of the Soviet Union, resigned. He declared his office extinct and handed over its powers, including control of the Soviet nuclear missile launching codes, to Russian President Boris Yeltsin, a non-Leviathan. That evening at 7:32, the Soviet flag was lowered from the Kremlin for the last time and replaced with the pre-revolutionary Russian flag. This effectively derailed the Leviathans' plans for another twenty-five years."

"So, you are saying that Ronald Reagan short-circuited the Leviathans' plans and set them back twenty-five years," said Jeff. "Well, that explains why we are not currently living the complete nightmare that was outlined in Orwell's book. Any idea what the new target date is, based on your analysis?" asked Jeff of the image.

The image of his grandmother replied, "My best estimate is 2020, based on the current trajectory."

"Is there any way for us to do something now, in this timeline, before 2020 to change that? Do we have to go back and mess around with history?" asked Billy. "We still have four years, and maybe we can influence the government to take actions like Reagan's. It worked then, why not now?"

"I am afraid not," replied the image. "Things are much worse than they were when Reagan was in office. Back then, people still had a virtuous form of patriotism. They had not reached the level of apathy and dependence that Alexander Fraser Tytler, Lord Woodhouselee, warned about.

"In the intervening years, the Leviathans have increased their efforts to eradicate self-reliance, have more firmly infiltrated the school systems, and have helped to create a generation of citizens that does not value independence and freedom. Additionally, back in the 1980s, the majority of western civilization would have described themselves as 'people of faith'. That is why the pope's involvement and influence had such an enormous impact. Today, it is completely the opposite. The majority of the Western world describe themselves as agnostic or atheist, and as you heard from Franklin and Adams, faith in God is a critical element of freedom.

"I would dare say that the belief that our rights and freedoms come directly from God and not the government has been eradicated. Natural law, as described by Cicero, is thought of as an anachronism. All of this means that these times are much different than the 1980s and 1990s of the old timeline and call for a more drastic and direct approach. I agree with your grandfather. Stopping the assassination of Kennedy may be the only way."

Ty was stunned by the implications of what the image had suggested. Joe said what they all must have been thinking. "Grandpa, we seriously can't be considering this option. None of us have ever lived through the assassination of a president, or any other famous person for that matter. It is totally out of our realm of experience. Now we are considering the possibility of going back in time and trying to stop the assassination of one of the most beloved and respected leaders we have ever known. Think about what happened last time we changed history. Never mind the difficulty factor and incredible number of variables, what would the impact on the timeline look like? We need to know a lot more."

The prophet, nodding in agreement, said to the image of his mother, "I believe we need to know the details of the assassination to make an informed decision. None of us is familiar with the details of the event and whether we will be able to stop it from happening. Please give us the background, and then we can evaluate the viability of the mission."

The image complied. "There is so much that has been written about this turning point in this timeline, and most of it is confusing and contradictory. Immediately after the event, the Leviathans fed the press false leads and misinformation. They started conspiracy rumors and theories, which muddied the waters so much that it was hard for me to separate the facts from the falsehoods. But due to my quantum capabilities, I believe I have been able to cut to the heart of the matter.

"I will start with what is generally known to the public. John F. Kennedy, the thirty-fifth President of the United States, was assassinated on Friday, November 22, 1963, at 12:30 p.m. Central Standard Time in Dallas, Texas, while riding in a motorcade in Dealey Plaza. Lee Harvey Oswald supposedly fatally shot Kennedy while he was riding with his wife, Jacqueline, Texas Governor John Connally, and Connally's wife, Nellie, all in the same limousine in a presidential motorcade.

"A ten-month investigation by the Leviathan-controlled Warren Commission from November 1963 to September 1964 concluded that Oswald acted alone in shooting Kennedy, and that Jack Ruby also acted alone when he killed Oswald before he could stand trial.

"This is the official summary of events as told to the public. As you can imagine, that is not the real story. The place, time and location are correct, but the killer is not.

"Oswald was involved, but he was not the one who fired the fatal shot. He was the fall guy. The Leviathans guaranteed his silence when they sent one of their soldiers, Jack Ruby, to kill him before trial. Based on the quantum acoustic analysis I have conducted, I have concluded that Kennedy was assassinated because of a conspiracy. My findings agreed with the Warren Commission's that some of the injuries sustained by Kennedy and Connally were caused by Oswald's three rifle shots, but I have also clearly determined the existence of additional gunshots based on analysis of an audio recording. There is a high probability that three gunmen fired at the president. One of those other gunmen was the one who fired the fatal shot.

"I will now read from the Warren Commission Report, which was a published document about the shooting. Please direct your attention to the monitors in the room. They will show an enhanced version of the event as a bystander, Abraham Zapruder, recorded it. I warn you, it is graphic."

The men in the room turned their attention to the monitors to watch the Kennedy assassination for the first time. Since this had not occurred in their timeline, Ty dreaded what they might see.

The image began her narration. "President Kennedy's open-top 1961 Lincoln Continental four-door convertible limousine entered Dealey Plaza at 12:30 p.m. CST. Nellie Connally, the First Lady of Texas, turned around to the president, who was sitting behind her, and commented, 'Mr. President, you can't say Dallas doesn't love you,' which President Kennedy acknowledged by saying, 'No, you certainly can't.'

"Those were the last words ever spoken by John F.

Kennedy.

"From Houston Street, the presidential limousine made the planned left turn onto Elm Street, allowing it access to the Stemmons Freeway exit. As the vehicle turned onto Elm, the motorcade passed the Texas School Book Depository. Shots were fired at President Kennedy as his motorcade continued down Elm Street. About 80 percent of the witnesses recalled hearing three shots.

"A minority of the witnesses recognized the first gunshot they heard as weapons fire, but there was barely any reaction to the first shot by most of the people in the crowd or by those riding in the motorcade. Many bystanders later said that they heard what they first thought to be a firecracker or the backfire of one of the vehicles shortly after the president began waving. Although some close witnesses recalled seeing the limousine slow down, nearly stop, or completely stop, the Warren Commission, based on the Zapruder film, found that the limousine had an average speed of 11.2 miles per hour over the 186 feet of Elm Street immediately preceding the fatal head shot.

"Within one second of each other, President Kennedy, Governor Connally, and Mrs. Kennedy all turned abruptly from looking to their left to looking to their right, between Zapruder film frames 155 and 169. Connally testified that he immediately recognized the sound of a high-powered rifle, and then he turned his head and torso rightward, attempting to see President Kennedy behind him. Governor Connally testified he could not see the president, so he then started to turn forward again, turning from his right to his left. Connally also testified he was hit in his upper right back by a bullet he did not hear fired. After Connally was hit, he shouted, 'Oh, no, no, no. My God. They're going to kill us all!'

"Mrs. Connally testified that just after hearing a loud, frightening noise that came from somewhere behind her and to her right, she turned toward President Kennedy and saw him raise his arms and elbows, with his hands in front of his face and throat. She then heard another gunshot, and then Governor Connally yelling. Mrs. Connally then turned away from Kennedy toward her husband, at which point another gunshot sounded, and she and the limousine's rear interior were covered with fragments of skull, blood, and brain."

At this point, both the narration and the images on the monitors stopped. The image took on a very concerned and motherly appearance and asked the heroes, "Are you all processing this? Shall I go on?"

The Meglio responded. "That is quite enough for now, Catherine, thank you. We will be asking for more situational detail and information shortly, but for now, we have a very clear picture of what took place. We now know that it took place in a limited area in only a few moments. It would be helpful if you could identify exactly where the assassins were positioned so we can narrow our focus and further assess our ability to stop the event."

"As you wish, my love," replied the image. "As I said, I have analyzed the sounds and images of the event using my quantum capabilities and have been able to identify the locations of all the shooters with 98 percent reliability. Oswald, who was on the sixth floor of the Texas Schoolbook Depository building, was definitely one of the shooters. However, he only fired two of the five shots discharged that day.

"The second shooter was on the second floor of the Dal-Tex Building behind the Kennedy limo as it traveled down Elm Street toward the triple underpass.

"The third shooter was behind a picket fence on a

grassy knoll inside the plaza. This shooter was in front of the limo.

"The first shot came from the Dal-Tex Building, hitting Kennedy in the back. The bullet deflected up from a rib, exiting his throat. It then flew over the limo and struck the curb under the triple underpass, scattering into tiny fragments that hit a bystander's cheek.

"The second shot came from the Texas School Book Depository. It went through Connally's body, entered his back below the right shoulder blade at a twenty-three-degree angle, then exited through his chest, lodging in his left thigh. This angle is consistent with a downward trajectory from the sixth floor of that building.

"The third shot was fired from the Dal-Tex Building. It hit Kennedy's head from behind, causing a 'head-flap' exit wound. The bullet fragmented as it left Kennedy's head and one fragment struck the front windshield, deforming the glass. This caused a flash of light as the sun reflected off it, which was captured on Zapruder's 16 mm movie camera.

"The fourth shot came from the grassy knoll to the right of the limo. It entered the president's head through the exit wound of the third shot, causing a massive blowout of the back of Kennedy's skull. A skull fragment landed on the trunk of the limousine.

"Finally, the fifth shot, which was the second shot from the Texas School Book Depository, missed both Kennedy and Connally. It struck the frame of the windshield and produced the second flash of light seen in the Zapruder film.

"My analysis indicates that Kennedy was not hit by either shot from the Texas School Book Depository. Oswald's first shot hit Connally in the back and his second hit the windshield frame.

"So, as you can see, the quantum analysis shows that there were three shooters with five shots fired from three distinct locations triangulating the motorcade." The image concluded the analysis.

The Meglio addressed the team. "From what I have heard, I would conclude that this is our first mission with this level of detail. Therefore, we can know with certainty when and where the event took place right down to the second when each shot was fired. We know where the shooters were, and we can be in position well in advance to disrupt the shootings. All this detail makes me extremely confident in our ability to have a positive impact. Does anyone see things differently?"

"It is very tempting," said the prophet, "and it does seem likely that we can change the outcome of the assassination plot. But I still see danger. Not only will our heroes be dealing with trained killers with high-powered weapons, but they will be armed with only swords. Although it can be done, we have not adequately resolved the question of whether it should be done. We are talking about changing a day in history once again. There is sure to be fallout from saving the life of a very important historical figure. Whoever goes on this mission will be coming back to a new timeline and a changed reality. Finally, there is the problem of the time ripple. Last time the heroes changed history, they affected a date in 480 BC. It took hours for the time ripple to hit us in our time.

"They will be changing time in 1963, and it could be just a matter of minutes before the time ripple hits. Additionally, this time it may be much more powerful, since we are closer in time to the event. Unless we are all in the Keeping Room before it hits, we will be affected by the change and will not remember the mission or what came before it. If we decide to do this, we have to take all of that into account."

"That is all very true," said the Meglio, "We must plan for all of that. That is why I will be accompanying the heroes on this trip, assuming the swords do not disagree and exclude me. My Sword of Don Quixote is now a Sword of Valor and should enable me to make the trip. We will see. Now, let us get down to the details of the mission."

Then, addressing the image of his beloved wife, he said. "Catherine, please put up the map of Dealey Plaza highlighting the positions of the shooters and the route of Kennedy's limousine."

The team spent the next two hours examining the route, understanding the geography, and memorizing the time sequence. They assigned each shooter to a team of two brothers and identified the duties of Great-Grandpa and the Meglio himself. They put together contingency plans in case any of them were not chosen by the swords.

Finally, they designed a plan which should allow them to avoid the issue of the time ripple upon their return. When it seemed that they had addressed all the prophet's concerns, the Meglio again addressed the team.

"Are there any unanswered questions at this point?" he asked.

"No real questions, Grandpa, but I do have an observation," Nick remarked. "It is possible that some of us will be successful in preventing the shots from being fired and that some of us will not. That may alter the course of history, but not result in our desired outcome. Do we need to discuss that?"

The Meglio replied, "That is possible, Nick, but we can't address that now. The best we can do is to do our best, and then get back here to the Keeping Room and reassess the impact. The quantum computer and the prophet will be monitoring our progress while we are engaged and will be able to project the possible outcomes of our actions. When we return, we will quickly know if we were successful or not. So, if there are no other questions, I suggest we get on with it."

Everyone agreed and began the preparations. Gathering their swords from the glass case, Ty and the others rehearsed their assignments between their teams, then headed down to the fire pit by the river to change history once again... hopefully, for the last time.

CHAPTER FIFTEEN

THE KENNEDY MISSION

The team arrived at the fire pit, lit the fire, and conferred together to fix the time, date, and location in their minds. They had decided to arrive at 4:00 a.m. on November 22, 1963. That would give the heroes time to gain entrance to the buildings, evaluate the security, position themselves in hidden locations, and be in place prior to the shooters taking their positions. The prophet hoped this would give them the strategic advantage they would desperately need to accomplish this challenging mission.

While they were waiting for the fire to grow, Billy spoke up, "Let me see if I have the timeline down. I never feel confident that I can remember dates and times. At 11:55 a.m. CST, the motorcade leaves Love Field for its ten-mile trip through downtown Dallas. At 12:29 p.m., the presidential limousine enters Dealey Plaza after a ninety-degree right turn from Main Street onto Houston Street. At 12:30 p.m., shots are fired as the motorcade passes the Texas School Book Depository. At 12:36 p.m., President Kennedy's limousine arrives at Parkland Memorial Hospital. At 1:00 p.m., President Kennedy is officially pronounced dead. Do I have that right?"

The prophet nodded. "That's right. All the shots are fired in short succession between 12:30 and 12:31 p.m. So, from noon through 12:30 you have to be well-positioned to identify the shooters. Your great-grandpa and the Meglio will be strategically positioned along the route to join the security detail as it draws close to Dealey Plaza. That way they can take action in case you are unable to prevent the shots from being fired.

"Additionally, it's their responsibility to get to the limo and speak with Kennedy should he survive. They will fill him in on what will have just transpired, so he can take the actions necessary afterward to thwart the Leviathans. Got it?"

Billy nodded. "Thanks. It helps to hear it one more time."

When the fire was roaring, the prophet directed them as before. "Take your positions around the fire." The cousins, their great-grandfather, and the Meglio complied. "Raise your Swords of Valor!" he directed once again. "Now, bring them together, and may God be with you!" he finished.

The prophet watched as the team brought the swords together for what he hoped was the last time. Once again, they were enveloped in a huge flash of pure white light. This one was so powerful, it extinguished the fire they were standing around. The light blinded the prophet.

When he could see again, he noticed two things. First, every one of them had made the trip, and second, a strong wind had begun to blow and it was becoming more powerful by the minute. The sound of it was like a freight train drawing closer. It was not yet at hurricane force, but it was rapidly increasing. It was as if time itself knew it was about to be changed and was furious. The prophet did not know if that was good or bad, but it filled him with foreboding. He quickly retreated to the Keeping Room to monitor the progress of the team.

The heroes arrived at the appointed spot behind the wooden stockade fence above the grassy knoll next to the pergola. At 4:00 a.m., the streets were deserted, and the traffic was nearly nonexistent. After the flash of their arrival had subsided, the Meglio signaled for silence. He stood quietly, surveying the area to make sure that the shooters had not yet arrived, and that they were not seen. When he felt sure that they were alone and had not been observed, he spoke to the others.

"It is obvious that the swords have determined that all of us are necessary for this mission. That pleases me, but it also reinforces the fact that this mission will take an extremely unified effort. Every one of you is critical, and we must work together as a team if we are to have any chance of success. You all know your assignments and locations. Stay together, coordinate your actions, and above all, trust the leading of the swords. Now go and take your positions, and may God be with us all."

They hugged, wished each other well, and departed in teams to take their positions.

Robbie and Ty made their way north on the Elm Street extension to the Dal-Tex Building at the northeast corner of Elm and North Houston Streets, across from the Records Building. They found an open loading dock door and carefully made their way to the second floor using a dimly lit stairwell. It was a seven-story office building and was Dallas's center for the textile industry. When they reached the second floor, they entered the offices which overlooked Dealey Plaza, quickly found a storage closet, and positioned themselves there. Leaving the door slightly ajar, they would be able to hear and watch for the shooter.

Although it was still several hours before they expected any suspicious activity, Robbie didn't really feel like talking. He reviewed the schedule in his mind and tried not to be overly nervous.

An hour later, Ty whispered, "Aren't you nervous?"

Robbie stifled a chuckle. "You bet I'm nervous! Why do you ask?"

"You don't look nervous," Ty replied, then sighed. "I know we had to arrive early to get into position, but the wait is killing me!"

"Yeah, me too," Robbie conceded. "We probably shouldn't be making noise, though. We don't know who might wander through here between now and noon."

Ty nodded silently and they continued their stakeout from the storage closet.

Hours later, Robbie checked his watch for the hundredth time. 11:15 a.m. and they still hadn't seen any suspicious activity. Forty-five minutes before they should be on high alert.

As the time approached, Robbie observed a figure carrying a golf bag down the hall and entering an office with a clear view of the route. He nudged Ty and nodded in the man's direction.

Ty squinted, then whispered, "What's that he's carrying in his hand?"

"Looks like a radio or walkie-talkie," Robbie

whispered back.

They watched as the man entered the office. Then, Robbie heard him lock the door behind him.

"Oh, that's not good," he whispered.

"Now what do we do?" Ty asked.

Robbie thought for a moment. "I think we should wait as long as we can, then break the glass of the office door to gain entrance. Hopefully, the sound will startle the gunman."

Ty shook his head. "This is an active office building. Remember? That kind of noise will bring a lot of unwanted attention up here!"

Sighing, Robbie replied, "If you have a better idea, I'm open for suggestions."

Echoing Robbie's sigh, Ty shook his head again. "Not off the top of my head. I'll let you know if I think of anything."

At 12:29, Robbie knew they could not delay any longer. He signaled Ty that they should go ahead and break the glass of the office. Ty nodded, and they moved into the hallway. Drawing their swords, Ty smashed the window with the butt of Joyeuse, and Robbie sliced off the door handle and lock with Braveheart. As they were entering the office, Robbie heard the first shot.

Racing in, they yelled, trying to distract the gunman. It worked. He turned the gun toward Robbie, but before he could pull the trigger, Ty smashed the gun from his hand with a powerful, slicing blow from Joyeuse. Robbie rushed in and struck the shooter hard with the hilt of his own sword, knocking him unconscious.

As Ty had predicted, some of the occupants reacted to the sound of the glass breaking and ran into the hallway, stopping just outside the office door, blocking their escape.

With an unspoken agreement between them, Ty and Robbie reached down, and each grabbed an arm of the unconscious, bleeding shooter. They approached the doorway, dragging the gunman behind them. As they reached the knot of people, they dropped the unconscious gunman at their feet.

Robbie shouted, "Quickly! Call the police! This man tried to kill the president!"

With horrified screams, most of the office personnel rushed to their office phones. There was only one startled man remaining.

Ty handed the man the rifle and ordered, "Give this evidence to the police when they arrive!"

Then he and Robbie calmly entered the stairwell and headed out of the building to make their way to the designated meeting spot.

Joe and Nick walked north on Elm a minute or two behind Robbie and Ty. They arrived at the Texas School Book Depository about the same time their cousins entered the Dal-Tex Building. The Depository was also a seven-story building on Elm Street at the northwest corner of Elm and North Houston Streets where the Texas School Book Depository Company stored school textbooks and related materials.

The two brothers made their way into the building through a damaged loading dock bay door and quietly found the stairwell, ascending to the sixth floor. When they arrived, they noticed that the whole floor was covered with plywood and was in disarray. There were books and boxes everywhere, with unusually tall piles that extended to the east wall. Joe could see how Oswald could have easily hidden himself among the stacks of boxes without being seen by any casual observers. They found a hiding place behind some boxes across from where Oswald would probably position himself and prepared for a long wait.

By 11:00 a.m., Joe had not observed any activity. This floor of the building was under repair and seemed to warrant little traffic. Still, he was on edge. Oswald was the only shooter he would be able to recognize on sight. The quantum computer had showed them multiple images of him from before and after the event. Joe felt that they were well-prepared, but still, he was nervous.

A few minutes later, he heard the door of the stairwell open, then close, and the sound of hurried footsteps heading their way. From his hiding place, he could not make out the man's face, but it was obvious that he was focused on getting to the wall of windows overlooking the motorcade route. Before the man reached the windows, he opened one of the nearby boxes and pulled out a rifle that, apparently, had previously been hidden there.

Nick and Joe were about twenty feet to the right of where the person Joe believed to be Oswald was positioning himself.

At 12:29 and thirty seconds, Joe heard the first shot about thirty seconds before it was supposed to happen. Without a word, he bolted for Oswald's location and used Excalibur to knock Oswald's rifle out of his hand, but not before Oswald got a shot off. Nick tackled Oswald and wrestled him to the ground.

The rest followed quickly. Joe and Nick incapacitated Oswald, using his belt and readily available cordage to truss him up securely. Then, they hustled to the stairwell. Joe knew from the quantum computer's review that they only had about ninety seconds to clear the floor before Dallas policeman Marrion Baker and the building superintendent, Roy Truly, would ascend. They arrived at the ground floor just before the two men reentered the stairwell from the first floor where they had stopped to investigate.

Joe breathed a sigh of relief as he and Nick headed to the meeting spot.

Jeff and Billy stationed themselves at opposite ends of the stockade fence at the top of the grassy knoll. The fence ran from Elm Street to the southeast end of the Pergola overlooking Dealey Plaza. Unless there was another shooter which the quantum computer had not identified, Jeff figured they had all their bases covered.

He knew their job would be difficult because of all the people that would be coming and going as the day dawned. They would have to make sure that they identified the shooter soon enough to stop him.

By 8:00 a.m., the plaza began to come alive with activity; people heading to work, police setting up barricades to control the crowds, and anxious spectators staking out their positions along the motorcade route.

Jeff was hyperaware of the activity starting to build around them. He felt exposed, although he knew they were well-hidden. It seemed to him that someone could inadvertently wander around the fence and spot them. So, he decided to alter their plan. He signaled to Billy join him at his end of the fence.

As Billy approached, Jeff whispered to him, "I'm feeling conspicuous. I think we should mingle with the crowd. We could meander around the area and try to spot any suspicious-looking spectators."

Billy looked thoughtful, then nodded. "We still have hours before the motorcade arrives. I think that's a good plan."

They spent the next couple of hours wandering and trying to not look like they were scrutinizing the crowd. Around 10:30 a.m., Jeff caught Billy's eye, then cocked his head toward the fence. Billy nodded once, and the brothers "aimlessly" strolled back to their original positions. Jeff looked around, and when he felt no one was watching, he ducked down behind the fence again. Billy joined him a moment later.

"I can't really see anything from here," Billy observed. "Let's slide back behind the bushes up there. We'll still be hidden, but it's a little higher, so we can see better."

Jeff looked where his brother pointed and agreed. They worked their way up the hillock to the bushes and settled in to wait. Now they were positioned about ten feet behind the stockade fence near the eastern edge of the pergola overlooking Dealey Plaza. The quantum computer had indicated that the trajectory of the shot fired from that location most likely came from a point where the pergola and the fence came together. From this position, they were far enough back from the fence so that they could keep the whole scene in front of them.

With only fifteen minutes before the shooting was to begin, Jeff felt worried. They still had not spotted their man. He continued to scan the crowd.

Then, gunfire startled him. He glanced at his watch. It was thirty seconds too early! Jeff looked around for the shooter that he knew should be right in front of them. All he saw was a few startled women and children, and a policeman urging them to run and take cover. Jeff panicked and assumed they were not in the right spot, so he took off for a spot further down toward the grassy knoll to check.

Billy stayed where he was.

As soon as Jeff had started on his way, the policeman pulled a hidden high-powered rifle from a tree near him and took aim from behind the stockade fence. Billy began to sprint toward him, but he was knocked to the ground from above.

Jeff heard Billy's shout before he had gone ten yards. He turned and saw Billy wrestling with another man and observed what appeared to be a policeman taking aim at the motorcade. Realizing the officer was the third shooter and knowing he could never get to the shooter in time, he drew the Sword of Solomon, and with an overhand throw, hurled it at the gunman with all his might. It entered the shooter's back just as he pulled the trigger. It proved to be a deadly throw. It pierced the policeman through and pinned him to the fence just as he pulled the trigger, getting off one shot.

Jeff ran to make sure the shooter in the police uniform was dead. Then he pulled the sword out and ran to help Billy as he subdued the man who had gotten the drop on him from the tree.

Billy had pinned the man's left hand to the ground with Durandal and was beating him unconscious when Jeff arrived. Pulling his brother off the man, Jeff removed Durandal from the man's hand and handed it back to Billy. Together, they tied up the unconscious man with his own coat, left him there, and headed for the meeting spot.

The Meglio and his father-in-law made their way to their position near the corner of Main Street and Houston Street. They stationed themselves near the peristyle and the reflecting pool. Sitting on a park bench behind a thick stand of trees, they spent their waiting time observing the passersby. The Meglio hoped that their age and casual demeanor would not draw unwanted attention.

From there, they would join the Secret Service detail protecting Kennedy. The Meglio was confident that the cloaking abilities of the swords would insure that anyone noticing them would see them wearing the same clothes as the other agents. Still, he wasn't one hundred percent sure. Time would tell. It was now 12:00 p.m. and the streets were packed with spectators, police, and press.

Prior to the motorcade arriving, they would make their way to the front of the crowd, and then follow alongside Kennedy's car, mirroring the movements of the Secret Service agents. The plan was that they would stay close to the president's limo to help protect him if the heroes failed to stop the shooters. The Meglio also hoped to have a chance to speak with President Kennedy at some point, to tell him what had taken place.

Earlier, he and his father-in-law had considered disrupting the motorcade in some way but had discarded that idea. Any slow down or stopping of the progress would put the president in harm's way longer. At 12:15 p.m., they made their way to the front of the crowds of people lining Houston Street in front of the reflecting pool.

At 12:29 p.m., the motorcade turned onto Houston Street, making a right turn from Main. The Meglio and his father-in-law began their slow walk along the side of Houston Street toward Elm Street where the motorcade would make a sharp ninety-degree turn onto Elm. As they picked up their pace, the Meglio had a clear view of the Texas School Book Depository and the Dal-Tex Building. He frowned. He could see no evidence of a sniper in either location at this point, but he knew they were there.

Then, he saw the muzzle flash and heard the first shot from the building in front of them. Simultaneously, the Meglio and his father-in-law bolted straight for the open limo that Kennedy was riding in as the Secret Service men began to converge on it.

President Kennedy's limousine began to accelerate just as the Meglio and his father-in-law caught up to it. Knowing what was going to take place, they had a head start on the Secret Service. They jumped on the trunk of the limo, pounded on it as the second shot sounded, and shouted, "Gunfire! Go! Go! Go!" The limo accelerated quickly, with the two Guardians hanging on tightly.

Just then, the third shot was fired.

Blood, bone, and brains sprayed all over the two Guardians hanging on to the trunk of the vehicle. The Meglio couldn't see who'd been hit because of the blood in his eyes and the wind from the acceleration of the limo. He hung on for dear life and struggled to make his way into the back seat to shield the president and first lady from any further bullets.

President Kennedy's limo arrived at the emergency room of Parkland Memorial hospital six minutes later. The Meglio and his father-in-law helped lift the mortally wounded passenger out of the limo and onto the waiting gurney. The victim was rushed inside with dozens of medical people hovering around.

The Meglio turned to his father-in-law and commented quietly, "Looks like there is nothing more we can do. Let's melt into the crowd and make ourselves scarce before we get thrown into lockdown for questioning."

In all the uproar and confusion, they slipped away unnoticed. Making their way to the far end of the parking structure where the heroes would meet them, they carefully wiped the gore from their faces as they went. They found the location at the northernmost corner of the structure and sat behind a concrete barrier where they could not be seen. It was the first chance they'd had to rest and collect their thoughts.

They sat for a while in silence, then the Meglio said, "Well, Robert, I would say that we did pretty well for two old men! I bet in all the missions you have been on for the Guardians, you never had to hang on to the back of a speeding limousine!"

"No," replied Robert. "A few horse-drawn carriages and a tank, but not a presidential limousine traveling at seventy-five miles an hour weaving through traffic, while trying to get into the back seat already filled with passengers. Quite a thrill, I would say!"

Just then, the Meglio heard footsteps coming close to where they were sitting.

"Grandpa? Great-Grandpa? Where are you?"

Standing, the Meglio saw that all the heroes had arrived. He was thrilled to see that all of them made it unharmed. Billy and Jeff looked a little disheveled, but overall, they looked fine.

"Welcome," said the Meglio. "Quickly now, let's prepare for our return. We can debrief when we are back home."

"Does anyone have any way to make fire?" asked Nick.

"I will show you another power of the swords that you were unaware of," said the Meglio. "Follow me."

They followed him to a spot just behind the parking

structure surrounded by high bushes. When there, he instructed everyone to stand in a circle.

"Until now, you have not needed to use this power, but it will come in handy in the event a fire is not readily available, as is the case currently. Draw your swords and hold them out in front of you."

They did as he instructed. "Now, together, without touching them, point them downward to the center point of the ground before us."

Again, they complied. When all the swords were pointing at the same spot, it was as if they had concentrated focused beams of sunlight through a magnifying glass. The spot of ground in front of them burst into flame.

As it grew in intensity, the Meglio commanded, "Raise your swords, gentlemen, and let's go home. Remember the plan. We have a change of location. Keep it fixed in your minds. See it. Focus on it. If we miss our target, the time ripple will overwhelm us, and all will be lost."

They all indicated their understanding, and the Meglio gave them a moment to focus. When he was satisfied that they were ready, he commanded, "Now, bring your swords together, and may God guide us home! May our aim be true!"

CHAPTER SIXTEEN

RETURN FROM "CAMELOT"

———∼∾∼———

This time, the team arrived in the old barn, its dark space illuminated by the familiar flash of pure white light. The wind that had begun upon their departure was now roaring at full hurricane force. The barn walls bent and twisted under its influence and sounded as if it would be torn apart at any moment. The prophet waited for them outside the entrance to the Keeping Room.

"Hurry!" he urged, and the Meglio scrambled down the stairs after the others into the safety of the Keeping Room. When they had all reached the floor, he slammed the huge, metal door closed and engaged the locking mechanism.

Before they reached the glass sword case, the massive leading edge of the time ripple rocked the Keeping Room.

"Get down!" the prophet ordered, unnecessarily. Everyone was already on the floor.

"What's happening?" the Meglio cried.

"Time wave!" the prophet called back.

The Meglio could barely hear what he said and hunkered down with his grandsons to wait it out. He'd felt minor time waves during previous missions, but never anything like this! Not only did the time waves continue coming one after the other, but they were much more powerful. The ancient books, maps and scrolls which lined the walls were flung violently to the floor. The lighting in the room flickered and wavered. Chairs and tables were thrown into the air and crashed to the ground.

The team crawled along the floor of the Keeping Room as if trying to make their way to the bridge of a ship sailing in stormy seas. They reached the Tech Room and clawed their way to the table. The chairs were overturned, so they righted them, sat, and held on to the massive round marble table waiting for the time waves to stop. After five minutes of anxious waiting, the time waves subsided, and the image appeared.

"Welcome back, my family," said Catherine's image. "It would appear that time itself is not happy about the changes you have wrought. We shall see if that is good or bad momentarily. I have had to restart some systems and have begun repairs on others. There is no permanent damage, but my analysis will be delayed. Despite the repairs needed, the quantum field within the Keeping Room has held strong, and you have all been shielded from the timeline changes once again. If there are no objections, I suggest you begin by sharing your individual experiences. When I have finished analyzing the initial impact of your actions, I will share my findings immediately."

"Thank you, my dear," replied the Meglio. "I agree with the suggestion, but please explain what just happened."

"It was a time wave, my love," the image responded.

"I know, but a time wave this large? In all my computations, I never expected to feel anything on this magnitude. Explain, please," he requested.

"When the heroes changed history by a day, when they saved King Leonidas, there was a mild time wave, which subsided quickly. But this time was different. Apparently, saving Kennedy has had a more significant impact on the time line. In addition, the year of the change was closer to our point in time. So, both the magnitude of the change and our proximity to it resulted in the incredible power of the impact."

The Meglio looked troubled, but said, "Apparently. Please continue your analysis as we begin the debriefing. Nick and Joe, please begin with your experience in the Texas School Book Depository."

"Yes, sir," said Joe. "We made our way easily into the building and climbed to the sixth floor. It was in a state of disrepair and was filled with boxes. We found the location where Oswald would position himself for the shooting, just as Grandma showed us, and hid ourselves behind boxes about twenty feet from there. At 12:29 and thirty seconds, we heard the first shot.

"Realizing that it was thirty seconds early and that Oswald had not fired it as in the past, we sprang into action. I used Excalibur to knock Oswald's rifle out of his hand, but not before he fired. Nick tackled him and wrestled him to the ground.

Nick took it from there, "We then incapacitated him, tied him up, and left him there unconscious. We knew we had to get out of there quickly, so we hustled to the stairwell and made it to the ground floor before we could be seen. Then we headed to the meeting spot."

"Well done," said the Meglio. "You obviously prevented him from firing again. I am proud of you two." Then he turned to Robbie and Ty, instructing them, "Now, tell us about your mission."

Robbie began, "Our shooter had locked himself in an unused office on the second floor. We'd hidden in a storage closet across from the office. There were a lot of people coming and going, so we had to wait until the last possible moment to make our move. Ty smashed the window of the office door with the butt of Joyeuse, and I sliced off the door handle and lock with Braveheart.

"As we entered, we heard the first shot. We knew it was too early, but our entrance must have startled the shooter. We rushed in and got to him before he could fire again. After firing the first shot, he turned the gun toward me, but before he could pull the trigger, Ty knocked the rifle out of his hand. We then rendered him unconscious and tied him up with his own belt. The fact that this building had occupants made our escape a bit of a challenge. Some of the occupants of nearby offices must have heard the noise and ran into the hallway, blocking our route."

Ty took over from Robbie. "The man was unconscious, so we dragged him over to the crowd, dropped him at their feet, and told them to call the police. There was only one man remaining, so I handed him the rifle and told him to give it to the police. Then, as calmly as we could, we entered the stairwell and headed out of the building to make our way to the designated meeting spot."

"That explains the early shot," remarked the former Meglio. "We saw the muzzle flash from the Dal-Tex Building and knew that in the past, the first shot had been fired from the Texas School Book Depository. We knew something had gone wrong, but it allowed us to move early enough to get to the limo before the other Secret Service agents could react. So, it worked out beneficially anyway. Well done. A little dramatic, but well done."

"Agreed," said the Meglio. Then, turning to Jeff and Billy, he said, "Please begin your summary."

Jeff began, "It took us a few minutes to decide where to station ourselves, but we eventually positioned ourselves about ten feet from the location that Grandma had identified in her trajectory analysis as the most likely spot for the third shooter. We were behind a large tree. There were a lot of spectators, and when the first shot was fired early, we had still not clearly identified a possible shooter. I got worried and decided to head down to the other end of the fence just in case he'd positioned himself there.

"Just as I started that way, Billy noticed a man in a police uniform, who had been clearing people away after the first shot. He had grabbed a rifle hidden in the branches of a nearby tree and taken aim at the motorcade."

Billy finished the summary. "As I took my first steps toward the man, another man jumped down from the tree above me and knocked me to the ground. He obviously was a spotter for the shooter. Jeff saw that neither of us was going to get to the shooter in time, so he hurled his sword at him. It pierced him through and pinned him to the fence just as he pulled the trigger, getting off one shot. Jeff then helped me incapacitate the accomplice. We recovered our swords, and then headed to the meeting spot."

"Again, very dramatic and resourceful," said the Meglio. "It is obvious that none of you were able to prevent shots from being fired. This is an example that shows us the inherent resistance that time has to being changed or altered. There is always a price to be paid, and there is always blood required. This is critical for you to remember."

At that point, the image broke in and announced that a preliminary analysis of the timeline changes was ready. "Shall I reveal the results of your mission?" the image asked of the Meglio.

"Yes, Catherine, please," he replied. "Tell us what we need to know."

"Due to the system resets and repairs in process," began the image, "I have limited the research to the date of the event, November 22, 1963, and a few days after that date. It seems that, in this new timeline, an assassination still took place on that date. The headline for the New York Times, dated November 23, 1963 reads…"

An image of the front page of the *NY Times* appeared on the monitors in the room.

GOVERNOR CONNALLY KILLED BY SNIPER AS HE RIDES IN CAR IN DALLAS; PRESIDENT KENNEDY IS UNHARMED.

The Meglio, although terribly upset that the assassins had taken the life of Governor Connally, he was relieved to hear confirmation that their primary objective had been achieved. They had prevented the death of President Kennedy and had now given him a chance to fulfill his destiny.

"Thank you, Catherine, for that information," said the Meglio. "I am sure our heroes are relieved to hear that their actions resulted in success. However, based on the strength of the time waves and the violent winds of change that we experienced on our return, I suspect there will be much more to tell us as your analysis continues. Please fill us in when you have more to share."

After the Meglio finished addressing the image of his

beloved wife, Jeff asked a question. "Grandpa, while we wait for further information about the impact of the changes, can you and Great-Grandpa fill us in on your parts of the mission?"

"Yes, Jeff," replied the Meglio. "Here is how it all played out for us. Your great-grandfather and I started to follow alongside the motorcade as planned as soon as the president's car turned onto Houston Street. We knew the first shot was fired at 12:30 p.m. When we heard and saw the first shot fired early, we picked up our pace and reached the limo before it started accelerating.

"We shouted to the driver to take off, and held onto the trunk of the car as it accelerated. As we were trying to make our way into the back seat, the second shot was fired, which struck Governor Connally, hitting him in the back. At this point, everyone in the limo was in a panic. Your great-grandfather and I were still struggling to hang on, trying to get into the back seat to shield the president and the first lady."

Great-Grandpa now took over for the Meglio. "Your grandfather was very close to attaining the back seat when the third shot was fired. It hit Governor Connally in the left front part of his head as he slumped forward, still held up by his seat belt.

"The spray of blood and brain matter temporarily blinded your grandfather and me, delaying us from getting into the back seat. We regained our vision, slid into the back seat, and were able to shield the president and first lady the rest of the way to Parkland Memorial Hospital. On the way there, your grandfather had a very thorough, though quick, discussion with the president. He explained our mission, that it was the Leviathans and the Fabians who had attempted to kill him and why.

"Since Kennedy was familiar with both groups and

had suspected possible retaliation for his rebellious actions, he accepted the information readily. Your grandfather strongly encouraged him to continue to fight against them, to derail their plans, and to expose them. Kennedy vowed that our efforts would not be in vain. He would do everything in his power to eliminate their threats to freedom and liberty. He was going to take strong and immediate action.

"We arrived at Parkland, helped put Governor Connally on the gurney, disappeared into the crowds, and headed to the parking structure to meet with you."

"Wow!" said Ty. "You two are like James Bond and Jason Bourne! That was amazing. I'm glad you are both on our team. I can see why no Swords of Valor were ever lost under your watch."

"We were just trying to fulfill our mission, Ty, as were you all," replied the Meglio. "But as I said before, time still took its price in blood. I am very thankful that your actions changed the timing and trajectory of the shots that were fired enough for us to save the life of the president. You are all the true heroes of the day. Now that things have settled down a bit, why don't you all take a few minutes to wash up, straighten up the outer room, and then we can reconvene when the quantum computer's analysis is ready? I have a few things to discuss with your great-grandpa and the prophet."

Quietly, the cousins did as they were bid, leaving the Meglio, his father-in-law and the prophet alone in the tech room.

"Robert," said the Meglio, "I have experienced very mild time quakes as we've done our work, but never such a powerful one. Has this happened before? We knew there would be disruption, but truly, that was beyond all my expectations. Do you have any idea of what that might mean for our mission?"

The former Meglio looked at his son-in-law. "I suspect that the news will not be good. To my knowledge, time has been *significantly* altered only once. That was during the last mission you sent the heroes on. So, to my knowledge, no one has experienced time waves of this magnitude before. There have been minor changes through the years, but those did not have significant impact on the timeline and were absorbed easily. That was a major time quake, and I'm sure the implications are serious. We have changed a seminal historical event, and let's just hope that whatever the results are, we can work with them."

"Excuse me," interjected the image. "I hate to interrupt, but I have information to share. Shall I wait for the grandchildren to return before beginning?"

"Yes, my dear," replied the Meglio. "They will rejoin us shortly."

When the cousins were seated and settled, the Meglio informed them that the image had further analysis to share. He prepared himself to hear the news, hoping beyond hope that it was positive.

"As you know," the image began, "your actions have changed the timeline. I have gathered information from the current timeline, which I will refer to as Timeline Three. It appears that anything that happened before November 22, 1963 remains unchanged, as you might expect. Since that date, there have been momentous events and changes that have seriously impacted the landscape of the nation and the world.

"Governor Connally's assassination did not set off the same chain of events that Kennedy's assassination did in Timeline Two. But it, and the information you shared with Kennedy, did set in motion a series of other events that have had serious effects.

"It seems that upon his arrival back in Washington, Kennedy, knowing that Johnson was a high-ranking Leviathan, had him arrested as a conspirator in his attempted assassination. Johnson was eventually shot as a traitor on live TV. The men that the heroes incapacitated during the mission were arrested and brought in for questioning, and when I say questioning, I mean torture. They ultimately confessed that they were under the orders of the Leviathans, and some of them named names. It was confirmed that Oswald was a patsy and that they had planned to pin it all on him.

"This set off a firestorm of secret assassinations and purges of identified Leviathans and Fabians. Kennedy set up an Office of Homeland Security, and over time implemented many of the same domestic surveillance systems that Orwell outlined in his book, *Nineteen Eighty-Four*. He became a man possessed. All he could focus on was security and taking control back from the Leviathans.

"The Leviathans went further underground and regrouped. They abandoned their focus on government control and focused on social control. Many of Kennedy's fascist actions played into their hands. They still controlled the press and media, so they took advantage of his maniacal focus to sway public opinion against him.

"When Kennedy finally declared martial law to quell the protests and then refused to leave office, the military revolted against him. They were driven by the military-industrial complex, which was still secretly controlled by the Leviathans. There was a bloody coup in which Kennedy and his cabinet were killed and replaced with a Leviathan-controlled military dictator.

"This dictator was the former vice-chairman of the

Joint Chiefs of Staff, General Curtis E. LeMay. LeMay carried a reputation unique among his military contemporaries. He had been a driving force behind the firebombing of Japanese cities in 1945 and the 1948 Berlin airlift. Subsequently, his nine-year tenure as Commander in Chief, Strategic Air Command, made him a popular and well-known symbol of American power and preparedness. Blunt and outspoken as an operational commander, he continued that practice in his public feuds with Kennedy leading up to the coup, and it served his and the Leviathans purposes well.

"As with any other revolution of this sort, the initially stated purpose was to calm the situation, restore order, and to eventually hand back power to the people. But Orwell addressed this in his book, *Nineteen Eighty-Four*:

We know that no one ever seizes power with the intention of relinquishing it. Power is not a means, it is an end. One does not establish a dictatorship in order to safeguard a revolution; one makes the revolution in order to establish the dictatorship. The object of persecution is persecution. The object of torture is torture. The object of power is power.

"So, the expected and anticipated return to a Republican form of government never happened. What you have created in this third timeline, my dear family, is just what we were trying to prevent. Out there, outside of this Keeping Room, is a United Sates of America that is now a military dictatorship completely controlled by the Leviathans. Sadly, it is one of the most brutal nations the world has ever known."

At this point, the image paused, and then said to the Meglio, "I am sorry to bring you this terrible news, my love, forgive me. I know it must break your heart, as it does mine."

"I have no words to adequately express my dismay," replied the Meglio. Then, addressing the team, he continued, "While having succeeded in our mission, we have failed miserably in attaining our objective. I am horrified by this outcome and by the terrible evil we have unleashed on the world. Forgive me for leading you into this terrible situation. Please excuse me. I need a moment to myself."

He stood and left the room, anxious and deeply distressed.

CHAPTER SEVENTEEN

THE GRAY CHAMPION RISES

Before the Meglio could get to the door, Joe stood and exclaimed, "We have to fix this, Grandpa! We can't let this stand! Let's go back and undo it. Can't we go back there now and do it all over again and let him be killed? Or do it differently? We have to do something!"

"Joe, I hear you and agree that something must be done," said the Meglio returning to his place. "But we cannot just rush into this. There is more going on here than meets the eye. We knew from the beginning of this mission that we were going into it with an unproven and untested plan. The first four missions worked reasonably well because we had decades to plan and were not intending to change history in the process. We need to seriously consider whether we should attempt it again. We must consider many different approaches, and it will take time."

"Do we have any idea what the world looks like out there now?" asked Robbie, feeling knots in his stomach. "I mean, is it even safe to go back to the house? How about our family? Are they safe? Are they a part of all of this? We *need* to know. We have to find out."

"We will get to that," replied the Meglio. "The computer is working on all of it as we speak. Let's just calm ourselves and deal with what we know. We have a new timeline in which everything up until 1963 is the same. So, we have a good frame of reference. We are safe here in the Keeping Room and we remember the past timelines. That gives us an advantage. We also have the swords and the quantum computer. We will figure this out."

Then he addressed the image. "Catherine, tell us what you can about the status of our family and any dangers near the Keeping Room."

"As you wish, my love," replied the image. "I will start with the family. The larger Cincinnatus/Arimathea family has gone into hiding, according to Protocol 16, which was invoked by your daughter, Susan. Since they have not received any communications from the prophet, they are still awaiting their orders. As for Susan, Domenic, the other grandchildren and their families, they are safe, but living under the oppression that permeates the rest of society. They are unaware of your return and are concerned by the absence of the heroes and the prophet. There is no imminent danger beyond that. Susan has not invoked Protocol 17 at this point.

"As for the area around the family compound, I would assess that it is not safe to venture out of the Keeping Room. The level of domestic surveillance has risen to a point where satellites can track your movements, and I would advise against it except for dire emergencies. Remember, Azazel is still in control of the Leviathans, and he also remembers all the past timelines. It is likely that he has them watching this location."

"Thank you for the update, my dear," replied the Meglio. "Is there anything else that is important for us to know before we begin discussing solutions and next steps?"

"Yes," replied the image, whose gaze was now turned in the direction of her father, the former Meglio. "It seems that my father is withholding valuable information from us. We should give him a chance to reveal it to us before I do. From the ongoing comparative timeline analysis, I believe that it is critical information and may have an impact on your upcoming discussions. Father, would you like to tell us what you have been withholding and why?"

All eyes were upon the former Meglio. He was still looking at the image of his daughter when he started to respond.

"The 'why' is that I was not certain. Since I do not have quantum abilities as you do, Catherine, I was not able to piece it all together as easily as you have. And, as you may have noticed, we have been busy with the most recent mission. If you are referring to what I think you are referring to, I was going to bring it up during our planning discussion. I have no problem doing it now, if everyone agrees."

Robbie noticed everyone's expressions mirrored his own curiosity and anticipation, but it was the prophet who spoke for them all. "Grandpa, please tell us what the image is referring to. We need to know everything."

The former Meglio looked around the room at each of them and then said, "Before the last mission, Catherine told us about the two works of literature which were anomalous. The book by Orwell, *Nineteen Eighty-Four* and Nathaniel Hawthorne's story of *The Gray Champion*. During the summary of the latter work, some of what she told us sounded quite familiar, as if I had read the book before. Eventually, I realized why. The truth is that I was

252

present at every one of the events highlighted in the story. I was on assignment during each one of those incidents, trying to prevent the Apostles of Azazel from derailing the American Revolution. At first, I assumed that my firsthand involvement was making the story seem familiar to me. But recently, I realized a more profound truth. I just had not worked out the implications of it yet."

The Meglio looked him in the eye and asked, "Robert, what is the profound truth you have realized?"

His father-in-law returned his gaze and replied. "I am the Gray Champion of Hawthorne's story."

Jaws dropped around the room. Eyes widened with surprise, and there was silence for a minute as everyone absorbed the revelation. Robbie felt a mixture of shock and hope. How could this be? His great-grandfather was the Gray Champion? If he truly was that noble warrior, then maybe… just maybe… they had a chance to make this right. But how?

"You are the Gray Champion?" exclaimed Jeff. "How can that be? Did you know Hawthorne? Explain this to us."

"As I said, Jeff," replied his great-grandfather, "I was present at all of the events cited by Hawthorne. I was there on King Street in April of 1689. I was there to stop Sir Edmond Andros, an Apostle of Azazel, from massacring the people of Boston that day. He was in possession of one of the Swords of Terror and had decided that the time had come to crush any thought of colonial self-rule. I confronted him and his troops in the street. I was 'the figure of an ancient man' with 'the eye, the face, the attitude of command' that Hawthorne describes, although I was only forty years old at the time I went back on that mission. I assume the cloaking aspect of the swords made them perceive me in the way that was most impactful to them.

"It was I who planted myself 'directly in the path of the approaching British soldiers and demanded that they stop'. I did this with my back to the citizens I was protecting. So, they did not see as I drew my sword and held it out in front of me. It began to glow, and I commanded Andros and his soldiers to stop their advance. This revealed me as a Guardian. I informed Andros that I would not allow any violence against these people to go unchallenged. Apparently, he thought a better plan would be to order retreat and wait for a more advantageous day.

"Later that evening, I did meet with Simon Bradstreet just before my departure. I thought we were well hidden, but some of the townspeople must have seen me embracing him before I left. I was telling him who I was and what he needed to do to end the threat.

"I touched him with the Sword of St. Peter and instilled courage and valor into him so that he could inspire the others to action. I then retreated to a nearby fire and performed the return protocol.

"I must have been seen by someone, because what Hawthorne wrote is eerily familiar:

"'Others soberly affirmed, that while they marveled at the venerable grandeur of his aspect standing before a fire, the old man faded from their eyes, melting slowly into the hues of twilight, till, where he stood, there was an empty space. But all agreed, that the hoary shape was gone.'

"I can't account for the 'hoary shape' comment, as I was relatively young, but the rest is very accurate."

"Wow," said Ty, "that does sound like it was you."

Jeff shook his head with a half-smile. "It sounds like your sword's cloaking ability affected how they saw you leave, too. Instead of a flash of light, they saw you just fade away. Interesting."

"What about the other incidents?" Ty asked.

"I was there on a mission again about eighty years later," he continued. "I arrived the morning of the Boston Massacre. Again, we had received word that the Apostles were going to make a move. I had no idea what form that would take. Tensions between the American colonists and the British were already running high.

"Late in the afternoon, on March 5, 1770, I was standing with a crowd of jeering Bostonians gathered around a small group of British soldiers guarding the Boston Customs House. The soldiers became enraged after an unknown man hit one of them with a snowball. Later, I determined that unknown man was an Apostle of Azazel. This must have been their signal to launch the attack. They fired into the crowd, even though they were supposedly under orders not to shoot.

"Five colonists were killed. I felt that it was a huge failure for me and the Guardians. But I encouraged the people not to give up and once again anointed some of the survivors with my sword. As it turned out, the event helped to unite the colonies against Britain.

"What started as a minor fight and a failure, became a turning point in the beginnings of the American Revolution. The Boston Massacre helped spark the colonists' desire for American independence, while the dead became martyrs for liberty. Again, a bystander must have seen and recorded my actions."

"And the battle of Lexington and Concord?" asked Joe. "Tell us about that one."

"Five years later, on April 19, 1775," replied Great-Grandpa, "I arrived on assignment at the village green beside the meeting-house at Lexington. We had been warned that the British Army, led by an Apostle of Azazel, Lieutenant Colonel Francis Smith, was going to capture Samuel Adams and John Hancock in Lexington. They also planned to destroy the Americans' store of weapons and ammunition in Concord. Again, their aim was to crush the rebellion and incite as much violence as possible in the process.

"The Battle of Lexington was a very small fight, thanks to some of my actions. You could hardly call it a battle, but it's important, because it's where the Revolutionary War officially started. When the British arrived, there were only around eighty American militiamen in the town. Captain John Parker led them. I had met with him earlier in the day and had prepared him for the action to come. They were up against a much larger British force, but neither side expected to actually fight.

"I thought that I had been able to influence the stalemate, but amid the confusion a gunshot went off, causing the British to attack. Some of the colonists were killed and the rest fled. The British then headed to Concord.

"It was late in the day, and I had no way of knowing when the Battle of Concord would start. I informed Captain John Parker of the British plans, strategy, and where they would position themselves. I helped him get the word out to the surrounding countryside, and eventually we had rounded up about a thousand militiamen. By then, it was nearly sunrise, and I needed to return to my time, so I departed. Now, before you ask, let's finish with the story of Bunker Hill," he said, anticipating the next question.

"Hawthorne said in his story that 'when our fathers were toiling at the breast-work on Bunker's Hill, all through that night, the old warrior walked his rounds'. That's not exactly accurate.

"I didn't arrive until 4:00 a.m. on June 17, 1775, just as the British were beginning their bombardment of the colonial position. The Bunker Hill was only peripherally involved in the battle named after it. Although it was the original objective for both sides, most of the combat took place on Breed's Hill, adjacent to it.

"A sentry aboard the HMS Lively spotted the new fortifications the colonists were building around 4:00 a.m. He notified the captain, who ordered them to open fire, thus halting the colonists' work temporarily.

"As the sun rose, I noticed a significant problem with the location of the colonists' defenses. It could easily be flanked on either side. I immediately alerted Colonel William Prescott, who ordered his men to construct a breastwork running down the hill to the east. He simply didn't have the manpower to build additional defenses to the west.

"So, as you can see, I was not just 'walking my rounds'. I was helping to plan and build the breastworks. While doing so, I shared strategy with Prescott, assessed his supplies of ammunition, which were inadequate, and encouraged him to focus his fire on the first two attacks of the British. Because he had so little ammunition, I told him to tell his men to hold their fire until they could 'see the whites of their eyes'. He liked that phrase, and told his men the same. Once again, after the planned retreat by the Colonial forces, I returned to my own time.

"From that point onward, I stayed involved in the activities of the Revolution. As you now know, Franklin eventually hired me to be a part of the Secret Committee, and I became known as Agent Petrie.

"I made daily trips between my time and theirs to

handle assignments for them. One of those trips is when I rescued our heroes from the brig under the Pennsylvania State House. That, gentlemen, is the whole story. Make of it what you will."

The room was silent, then the image spoke in a loud, haunting voice reminiscent of the Sybil, or the Oracle, at Delphi in ancient times. It quoted from the Gray Champion story.

"'Long, long may it be, ere he comes again! His hour is one of darkness, and adversity, and peril. But should domestic tyranny oppress us, or the invader's step pollute our soil, still may the Gray Champion come; for he is the type of freedom's hereditary spirit; and his shadowy march, on the eve of danger, must ever be the pledge, that freedom's sons will vindicate their ancestry. Whenever the descendants of the Puritans are to show the spirit of their sires, the old man appears again. As the hour of darkness, adversity and peril arrives, the virtuous, fiery, and unrepentant Gray Champion appears through the fog of history like an apparition.'"

The Meglio looked startled by her eerie prophecy. Quickly, however, his expression cleared, and he addressed the image. "Thank you, my dear; that was very enlightening. I want to verify some of what you told us previously about the Gray Champion and the cycles of history. Am I right in remembering that his appearances always coincided with crisis seasons? Ones related to a threat to freedom and liberty?"

"Yes, that is correct. That is the prophecy," the image replied.

"So, then if the assumption can be made that our returned former Meglio is the Gray Champion of legend, and that he appears at an hour of darkness when a crisis of liberty and freedom arises, it would seem we have another weapon at our disposal. We have the quantum computer, the Swords of Valor, an understanding of the old timelines, *and* we have the Gray Champion! I believe our prospects have greatly improved!" he said to the assembled team.

Robbie smiled and everyone nodded their agreement.

Then the Meglio continued, "We have much to discuss and not much time to do it. The Leviathans could be at our door at any minute. Let us determine how we may best use the weapons we have to end this threat once and for all!"

CHAPTER EIGHTEEN

AZAZEL
UNMASKED

~

While the heroes, the prophet, the Meglio, and the Gray Champion, hidden deep below the earth in the Keeping Room, began to develop their battle plan, Azazel was also busy.

As a Watcher, he does not care for humans, and he detests any interaction with them. He influences his abhorrent worshipers through greed, fleshly desires, control, and promises of power. But once a year, he interacts with the heads of the five leading Leviathan families and their associated family groups.

These elite and privileged Leviathans anticipate the annual gathering, but he knows they also dread it. There is always blood, and no one is ever sure whose blood will be required for the annual offering.

This year's event took place at a nearly three-thousand-acre campground near Monte Rio, California called the Bohemian Grove. The public records show it belongs to the Bohemian Club, a private men's art club based in San Francisco. However, the reality is that the Leviathans own it. The Leviathan elite, a confederation of the world's most powerful men, visit the grove each year.

They dress in robes, chant incantations, and perform secret rituals at the foot of a giant owl idol. Through this idol, Azazel speaks to them.

The Fabians formed the Bohemian Club in 1872. Ceremonies before that were held at Stonehenge, England. They moved the event to Bohemian Grove when the secrecy of the event was compromised. The public sees the club as a mixture of an American summer camp, a powerful and ancient pagan ritual, and a classical Greek symposium. The club itself is cloaked in secrecy, and the public's perception is far from the truth.

The Cremation of Care ceremony is the pinnacle of the Bohemian Grove's rituals. The Leviathan leaders dress in druidic robes and symbolically burn their conscience at the base of a forty-five-foot owl idol. This statue represents ancient knowledge and worldly wisdom. The ritual happens at sundown on Saturday after the opening feast.

Just as the sun set, a small boat was ferried across the still, black lake. It contained an effigy of Care. When it reached the shore, the effigy was accepted from the ferryman by dark, hooded individuals. It is then ceremoniously carried and placed on the altar of the idol.

The high priest announced, "This is the body of Care, symbolizing the concerns and woes that afflict all men during their daily lives. We, the privileged, the elite, the Leviathans, will have none of it!"

More than one hundred Leviathans were taking part in the ceremony, but as the high priest instructed them to light the fire, it would not start. Perplexed, they turned to the idol for instruction and mercy, chanting, "O thou great symbol of all mortal wisdom, Owl of Wisdom, Watcher Above All, we do beseech thee, grant us thy counsel."

The idol seemed to awaken with a halo of light surrounding its head. It replied, "The high priest must light the pyre with the flame from the Torch of Power."

At that moment, a door, which had been hidden between the feet of the Owl idol, opened to reveal a glowing torch burning with red flames. The high priest retrieved the torch and set the altar on fire, along with the effigy of Care.

While the flames climbed higher and the worshippers chanted praises to Azazel, the owl idol's eyes blazed to life, and twin beams of light fell upon one of the worshipers. That person was immobilized, bound, and then carried to the altar.

As he stood before the idol, his throat was cut, and his blood was poured onto the burning effigy. The body was then wrapped tightly in linen strips, immersed in molten wax, and carried back to the small boat. The ferryman then transported it back to the opposite side of the lake from whence he came, to be used as the effigy the following year.

When the body was sent away, the worshippers knelt on the ground around the idol and the burning altar, and Azazel addressed them, speaking through the idol.

"Leviathans! Hear me!" Azazel commanded in a booming, otherworldly voice. "I grow weary of your failures. I am finished with your excuses. The time has arrived for action. Your centuries of pitiful machinations still have not resulted in the fulfillment of our destiny.

"This night, I announce the end of my patience with you. You have had millennia to set the stage, and I have given all of you the wealth and resources to succeed. Yet you still have not gained complete control.

"Must I now step into the affairs of men? Must I do what you have failed to do? If so, I warn you, you will lose everything I have given you. It will all crumble before your eyes. It will slip out of your hands like sand through your fingers.

"There are existing forces working to thwart our plans, and they must be stopped. They possess the power to alter time itself and have used that power against us, unbeknownst to you. Only my power, my influence, has kept our plan on track. I have used their own power against them and provided you with this final opportunity. The time is now!

"Find them and stop them. I will show you where they are. I will lead you to them, but you must do the work. You must redden your hands with their blood. You must destroy them, for if you fail after all I have done for you, I will destroy you. Fear me and do NOT fail me."

Azazel watched as every Leviathan fell on his face in abject supplication and terror. He thrilled to see that they trembled at the sound of his voice, and at the words he spoke through the idol. He knew they did not doubt anything he had said, and they understood that their time was growing short. Either they eliminate the threat and finally accomplish the plan, or they were doomed.

The high priest raised his head to the idol and said, "Oh, Great One, Wise Watcher of All, we, your servants, will not fail. We will do your will. Please tell us all that you wish us to know and where to find our enemy, and we will destroy them. Show us, oh Watcher of Wonder, where they may be found."

The light surrounding the idol brightened, and Azazel began to disclose the whereabouts of the Guardians of the Swords of Valor. The Leviathans listened with rapt attention to every detail, relishing the opportunity to prove their worth to their lord and master once again.

CHAPTER NINETEEN

THE FINAL PLAN

~~~

"There are great disturbances taking place within the quantum field," warned the image of Catherine. "I have not been able to identify the source or the meaning of them, but I am working on it. My systems are still not at one hundred percent capacity, and with all the comparative analysis taking place, it may take some time."

"Does it have to do with the timeline changes? Wouldn't that account for it?" asked the Meglio.

"No," replied the image. "It is well beyond that. The time quake has passed, and at this point the quantum impact has been absorbed and adjusted for. It is something else that I have not observed before. I can tell you that is an ominous sign, but what it specifically relates to, I cannot say with accuracy. My recommendation is that you move with all haste to complete your plan."

"Thank you, my dear," replied the Meglio. "We will. As I see it, we have only one option, and therefore it is just a matter of timing, refinement, and execution." He then addressed the team.

"With the latest information from the quantum computer, it would appear that time is not one of our remaining assets. We must move forward with haste. As I have said before, we have the swords, the computer, and the Gray Champion on our side. The question at hand is, how do we craft a lasting solution from these resources?"

The prophet responded. "Dad, I think the lesson learned from the last mission is that no matter what we do to change time, or the events of the past, there is a high likelihood of failure and unintended consequences. The only conceivable way for us to succeed is to change the future. I propose that we begin with that premise."

"How is that possible, Uncle Rob?" Nick asked. "Do the swords have the power to do that?"

The prophet replied, "Of course they do, and so do you. We have been so busy trying to go back in time to change the future by changing the past that we have forgotten that by changing the present, we can be *more* certain of changing the future. We have to focus our efforts on making changes in this present timeline."

"I don't understand," said Jeff. "Even if we could change our government today, this instant, and put a democratic republic back in place, how could we know that it would stay that way and not change down the road?"

"You are asking the right question," said the prophet. "Keep following that train of thought. How can we ensure that whatever change is stimulated, it stays in place and results in the future we want?"

The Meglio perked up. "I think we're on the right track. We can't just change the leadership or the form of government. We must change hearts. We must change the minds of the people being governed. Even if we give people their freedom and liberty back, unless they want it, unless they value it, unless it costs them something, it will never survive.

"Thank you, Rob, for opening our eyes. You are exactly right. Everything we have done has been focused on changing the environment… the political, economic, social, and moral constructs of society. We have been focusing on the wrong things. We must change hearts and minds. We must resurrect the dream of liberty and freedom. We must open people's eyes to the horror and oppression they are now blind to, and in many cases, are actually embracing! Make them see the evil. Allow them to be able to despise their enslavement and desire to be free. That must be the final mission. It is the only way."

"I can agree with that, Grandpa," said Joe. "It is always that way. Grandma always said that you can't make anyone love you, no matter how you try. Love is a choice, and it must come unforced, from the heart. The same appears to be true of liberty and freedom. You can't force it on someone, they must desire it for themselves, or there is no value to it. It will not stand. But what can we possibly tell them or show them that will break through their fear and complacency? Their apathy?"

"That is the question we must answer, Joe," replied the Meglio. "That is what we must decide now."

"We have the swords, and they have proven to be influential," observed Billy. "They have certainly influenced our behavior at times. Can something be done with them which could impart some virtue or valor to all of mankind? I mean, I know it is a wild idea, but is it possible?"

The image of his grandmother replied. "It is not so farfetched, Billy, but the power necessary is incredible. You remember how the power of the swords was drained by your trip back to the battle of Thermopylae. You needed the additional power of Leonidas's sword to return. The swords' power can be drained, and it is not unlimited. It will always return to them, but it can take time. I will work on that concept as you continue to work on other options. I will see if there is a way."

"It seems to me that the best starting point is with Great-Grandpa. He is here for a reason," observed Ty. "He is obviously the Gray Champion of Hawthorne's story, and his actions in all of those historic battles inspired people to fight for freedom. He must be the key. The prophecy at the end of the story tells us that. He has returned at a time when freedom and liberty are threatened. This is a crisis season, and we are about to go into our greatest battle. We need him, and the world needs him. How do we use him to change people's hearts? I believe that is the real question."

"Well said, Ty," responded the prophet. "I believe as you do. The Gray Champion is the key. He must appear once again. But how, and to whom? In each of those previous appearances, he was in the middle of the actual confrontation, leading the oppressed people by example or inspiring them to action. He was physically there. They could see him and hear him. Right now, we are locked away in the Keeping Room with time running short. Does anyone have any idea how we can get him in front of the people, or the leaders of the world to influence them?"

"I do," replied the image.

"You do?" asked the Meglio, surprised. "Catherine, please explain what you mean. How is it possible?"

"I have been very busy working out all the possibilities," replied the image. "I believe it is possible for me to accomplish everything you need. I can make sure that my father is seen and heard by virtually the entire world, at the same time. Not only that, but I can access the quantum matrix of space-time to enable him to connect with each individual's quantum essence and reach them, influence them, right down to the subatomic level. It is all a matter of physics and power, with a bit of theatrics thrown in. Shall I tell you more?"

"Please, my dear," replied the Meglio. "We must know what you know. But quickly, we must not delay any further."

"As you wish, my love," replied the image of his beloved wife. "Since the time you activated my personality program in the quantum computer, I have not only been interacting with you, running comparative timeline analyses, and researching the information you needed, but I have been learning and changing. As you know, my love, I have always been much better at multitasking than you. With the vast quantum capabilities I now possess, I am even more effective.

"I have discovered a great deal about the capabilities of this system. I have been expanding and increasing the computer's abilities, power, and deepening its connection with the quantum world. Suffice it to say that I now possess an almost complete understanding of the nature of reality on both the micro and macro level and how to manipulate it all to our benefit.

"I will not get into the scientific details, but I can now access every digital or electronic device in the world. I can create and project a very lifelike quantum holographic representation of my father not only to every device, but to any place on the globe simultaneously. But it will not just be his image. It will actually be his quantum essence, wrapped in a quantum holographic image, powered by the dark energy of the universe. He will not only be 'real', but he will be able to impart the qualities of virtue and valor that all of the swords are imbued with to anyone whose heart is open to it. How is that for a solution?"

The Meglio was stunned. It seemed too good to be true. It was far beyond their understanding not only of the computer's capabilities, but of science itself. As he looked around the table, he could see expressions of shock and intense curiosity.

"You each appear as astonished as I feel," he remarked. "Please, ask any questions you may have, but we are running out of time, so be succinct with your inquiries."

"Grandma," said Robbie, "you said you could power the swords and the image of Great-Grandpa with dark energy. That doesn't sound good. That sounds evil. Can you explain that to us?"

"Certainly, Robbie," replied the image. "Dark energy is not evil. It is part of God's creation, and just as with anything else, it is only made good or evil by the way it is used. It is called dark energy because it cannot be seen. Dark energy is the result of the annihilation of two atoms of dark matter. It is like nuclear energy, only from dark matter instead of visible matter. The universe consists of twenty-seven percent dark matter, sixty-eight percent dark energy, and the rest, all the visible matter in the universe, only makes up about five percent. As you can see, dark matter makes up the majority of everything that exists.

"Dark energy is, in effect, a dynamic energy field which fills all of space, and it can be tapped into on the quantum level. I now have the capability to access it, and it is virtually unlimited. So, it will supply all the power we need, and it is inexhaustible. There is nothing evil or sinister about it. Does that answer your question?"

"It does, Grandma," replied Robbie. "Thank you."

"How will Great-Grandpa be able to use the power

from all of the swords?" asked Joe. "They are connected to each of us individually at the DNA level. Right now, he is using the Sword of St. Peter, which is tied to his DNA and his quantum essence. Wouldn't he only be able to impart the virtues of his sword?"

The image smiled at Joe and asked him, "Where did your DNA come from? Did it not, to a substantial extent, originate with him? He was my father, I am your grandmother, and you are all my grandchildren. You have his DNA in you, through me. Trust me when I tell you that you are all connected both on the quantum essence level and on the DNA level. He will have access to every virtue of every sword that the family possesses. Except for the Sword of Don Quixote, the Sword of Humility, which belongs to your grandfather and has no connection to your great-grandfather's DNA. The virtues of the rest of the Swords of Valor will more than suffice."

"Wow," said Joe, "I hadn't considered that. That is amazing and eye opening. No wonder he had so much influence as the Gray Champion. He basically had access to all... every virtue, and the combined valor of all our swords. He's like a superhero!"

"Okay," said the former Meglio. "That is enough. Look, I am just an old man who will do my duty to the family and the world, if necessary. I don't have any superpowers, nor am I invincible. I appreciate the understanding that my daughter has given us, and I believe her, but even if someone has access to all virtue and all valor, they still must act. Action, not words is what matters, so let's get on with this. I, for one, don't care about dark matter or dark energy or quantum essences. Just give me my assignment, and I will do it to the best of my ability. Time is wasting."

Then he addressed the image of his daughter.

"Catherine, prepare whatever you need to prepare to make this happen, and tell me what my job is. Let's get this done."

The Meglio agreed and addressed the image. "Yes, my dear, we are all in agreement. Let's not delay. Prepare the systems, provide us with the details and our individual responsibilities, and let's get on with it. I assume the representation of your father will be able to be heard by all, so, although actions are primary, words will matter. Please provide your father with the most inspirational information he can impart in his speech to the world based on all that we have learned during this mission. We have been counseled by many of the world's most influential architects of freedom and liberty, and I believe the world needs to hear from them, too. We may only get one shot at this, so let's make it count!"

"As you wish, my love," replied the image. "I have already begun. All will be ready in thirty minutes. In the meantime, please review the sketches I have put up on the monitors. They approximate how the Gray Champion will appear to the world."

The image of Catherine disappeared. The monitors around the room came to life and showed the image of an apparently ancient but powerful figure dressed in dark robes, with a deep hood covering his head. His face was partly in shadow, but his eyes glowed with a pale blue light. He was holding the Sword of St. Peter and was standing in front of the Washington Monument. He appeared to be as tall as the monument itself. Images on the other monitors around the room showed the same image standing next to the Eiffel Tower, in Tiananmen Square, next to the Sydney Opera house, and hundreds of other landmarks and important sites around the world. It was eerie and impressive. They all agreed that it would surely get the world's attention.

As they were observing the monitors, a huge explosion rocked the Keeping Room. The lights flickered, and they were thrown to the floor.

"What was that?" exclaimed Ty. "Was that another time quake?"

The image of their grandmother appeared and spoke. "That was no time quake, Ty. It was the Leviathans. They have discovered our location and are attacking. They just blew up the house and will be focusing on the Keeping Room next. We must hurry. There is no more time. Quickly, Father, stand on the table next to my image and prepare to address the world. We must do this now. Just say what is in your heart. Use your own words and make them understand. Trust the swords; they will give you what you need. Hurry!"

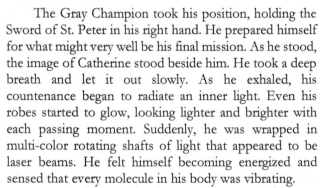

The Gray Champion took his position, holding the Sword of St. Peter in his right hand. He prepared himself for what might very well be his final mission. As he stood, the image of Catherine stood beside him. He took a deep breath and let it out slowly. As he exhaled, his countenance began to radiate an inner light. Even his robes started to glow, looking lighter and brighter with each passing moment. Suddenly, he was wrapped in multi-color rotating shafts of light that appeared to be laser beams. He felt himself becoming energized and sensed that every molecule in his body was vibrating.

He closed his eyes to focus his thoughts, and when he opened them again, he was standing next to the Washington Monument, and he was in Tiananmen Square, and in Red Square in Moscow, and in thousands of other places. He could see them all as if he was right there. He could also see and hear everything going on in the Keeping Room and outside of it. The swirl of images and sounds was disorienting. He saw the smoking ruins of the family home, he saw the Leviathan troops surrounding the compound, and he saw them setting explosives to the titanium security door of the Keeping Room.

"Catherine, hurry!" he said urgently to the image of his daughter. "We must begin now! The Leviathans are at the door!"

The image replied, "The quantum field surrounding the Keeping Room will dissipate the impact of the explosions, but not forever. It will insulate us, but I cannot predict how long it will hold. You may begin at any time. Your quantum essence is now visible on every electronic and digital device around the world and is visible at thousands of other locations as well. Your voice will be heard in the language of the viewer. May God be with you, Father!"

The Meglio, the prophet, and the heroes watched as the Gray Champion stood to his full height, set his jaw, and began to speak the words they hoped would inspire the world.

"Citizens of the Earth. Free men by the natural law of God. Hear me! You have been enslaved, and it is time to throw off your chains! The time has come for you to rise up against your oppressors. You have been asleep far too long. You have traded your liberty and freedom for worthless comfort. You have abandoned your primary responsibility to the future. This must end!

"You have allowed the Leviathan Alliance to lay chains upon your hands in exchange for economic support, cultural debasement, mindless entertainment, and crippling dependency. They have lulled you to sleep with bread and circuses. They have replaced your faith in God and in yourselves with an idol of false wisdom and self-pride.

"You have been told that your happiness depends on them, that you must serve them and keep them in power or all will be lost. So, you serve their will and accept their meager allotments.

"This is a *lie*! Your true joy does not depend on them. True joy is in freedom, liberty, faith, and submission to the true God.

"There is no righteousness or true liberty in being the servant of an idol! That is enslavement and will lead to death and destruction. Make no mistake, the Leviathans and their works are an idol. They require your worship at the temple of money, the temple of success, the temple of pleasure, and the temple of self. And you willingly and mindlessly do so."

As he spoke, another, more violent explosion caused the lights in the room to go out, but it did not affect the broadcast being powered by the dark energy. The Gray Champion continued beseeching the world from the darkened Keeping Room.

The team watched him as he glowed ever brighter, his robes gleaming brilliantly white and sparkling as newly-fallen snow in the sun.

He continued, "You have been dishonored by their contempt of all virtue and defiled by your own practice of every vice. Is there a single virtue now remaining amongst you? Is there one vice you do not possess? Is faith still to be found in anyone? The temple of liberty and freedom has been defiled, but it still stands!

"I do not call for a war to start, because the war has already begun! It has been brewing for centuries, and the crest of it has now broken on every shore. The next gale that sweeps forth from the Leviathans will bring to our ears the clash of resounding arms! We have brethren already in the field! The Leviathans are at my very door as we speak! They will come for you next. Why stand we here idle? Is your own life so dear, or false peace so sweet, as to be purchased at the price of chains and slavery?

"They tell you that they are your providers, and that they will take care of all your needs. This is the kiss of death! Suffer not yourselves to be betrayed with such a kiss. Let us not deceive ourselves. These are the implements of their war and subjugation; comfort, apathy, self-indulgence, pride, and sloth. These are the chains they set upon you this day and which you must throw off. These are the chains they have been so long forging in secret, the chains they intend to bind and rivet upon us.

"It is natural for man to indulge in the illusions of ease and comfort. We are apt to shut our eyes against a painful truth and listen to the song of that siren till she transforms us into beasts. Is this the part of wise men, engaged in a great and arduous struggle for liberty? Are we disposed to be of the number of those who, having eyes, see not, and having ears, hear not, the things which so clearly concern their God-given liberty and freedom?

"For my part, whatever anguish of spirit it may cost, I have been willing to know the whole truth, to know the worst, and to provide for it. This is the truth I impart to you now. It is a sad truth, one that never should have happened. But it did, and it is full of darkness, danger, fear, and dread. You may not want to think about the end, but think you must, and act you must! You may ask, how could the world regain its freedom, when so much evil is now in control? But at the end of our struggle, you will see that it's only a passing thing, this shadow of evil. Even darkness must pass. A new day will come. When freedom and liberty shine once again, they will shine out all the more clearly.

"During this struggle, you will have many chances to turn back. Do not. Hold on to virtue and valor. There is still good in this world, and it is worth fighting for.

"They believe us weak, unable to cope with so formidable an adversary as the Leviathan Alliance. But when shall we be stronger? Will it be next week, or next year? Will it be when we are totally disarmed, and when a Leviathan guard shall be stationed in every house? Shall we gather strength by irresolution and inaction? Shall we acquire the means of effectual resistance by lying on our backs and hugging the elusive phantom of dependent comfort until our enemies shall have bound us hand and foot? I say that now is the time. You will never be stronger than you are today!

"Today, right now, you have the power to take back your God-given liberty and freedom. Every one of you is powerful beyond your wildest imaginings, and together you are invincible! Stand together as one. Rise up as one. Awaken the hero inside of you and join yourself with your neighbor.

"They think we cannot defeat them. It will not be easy. It will be a long job; it will be a terrible struggle; but in the end, we shall march through terror to triumph. Whatever happens, the flame of liberty and freedom must not and will not be extinguished!

"This day, I am not here with only words of inspiration! I am here to empower you. To strengthen you for the battles to come. Reach out your hand to me. Stretch forth your arm, and I will give you drink from the fountain of virtue! From the well of valor!"

Then, he held the Sword of St. Peter outstretched before him for the world to see. It began to glow and then burst into flame. "Here in my hand, I hold a source of strength, power, virtue, and valor," said the Gray Champion. "To all who have stretched forth your hands to seize the liberty that is within your reach, I now bequeath to you the light of freedom! Take it and secure your destiny. Fulfill your obligation to posterity. Take it now!"

As he pronounced these final words, the monitors around the room showed that the flame of his sword descended upon the multitudes gathered around the world. People everywhere raised their arms and waited for it, their expressions longing for it. As it touched them, it enveloped them and leaped from one person to another. The people cheered! They roared with collective power. They began to move in unity toward the halls of their nation's governments, and then the monitors went dark.

Chapter Twenty

Freedom's March

~~~

The team stood in the darkness of the Keeping Room, listening to the horrendous explosions taking place just ten feet above their heads. The Meglio could see each of them in the glow that continued to emanate from the Gray Champion as he loomed tall and silent before them in the middle of the round table. Also still visible was the image of their grandmother.

The Meglio addressed the Gray Champion. "Robert, that was wonderful. What a powerful call to arms you gave. That will go down in history as one of the greatest inspirational speeches of all time. Now, we just need to survive long enough to observe the results."

The Gray Champion did not reply, but continued to stand silently without moving, as if in prayer. The Meglio watched him for a moment, then he addressed the image of his beloved wife. "Catherine, can you give me a status update on the conditions of the computer systems and the compound above?"

"Yes," came the quick reply. "The compound is gone, all destroyed. The Keeping Room defenses are holding but have been weakened by the bombardment and will not keep all of you safe much longer.

"The broadcast of the Gray Champion's message has drained both the power of the swords and the reserve power of the quantum computer. I can still access the dark energy for a while longer, but if there is any more damage to the hardware, we will be incapable of defending ourselves."

"Is there any way to resist the attack of the Leviathans?" asked the prophet. "Do we have any weapons available to us at this point?"

"We do," replied the image of his mother. "Only one. Since I still have access to the quantum field, and therefore both the dark matter and dark energy of the universe, I will attempt to protect you all with them."

"How will you do that?" asked the Meglio. "What form will it take?"

The image replied, "I don't think you truly wish to know, my love. Just trust me and pray for the best. I must leave you now briefly while I delve into the quantum world. If all goes well, I will return. If I do not, please remember that I love you all and know that you will see me again someday." With that, the image disappeared.

The Leviathans increased the level of bombardment and the Keeping Room was shaken violently, deeply, and continually. The titanium-reinforced walls and ceiling vibrated to the explosions, and the floor seemed to jump constantly beneath their feet.

"Grandpa!" shouted Billy above the noise, "How can she possibly fight against this onslaught? The swords are drained, the computer is not working at full capacity, and we can't help her. What's Grandma going to do?"

"I don't know, Billy," replied the Meglio, "but if she can truly access the quantum world and utilize the combined power of dark energy and dark matter, then I suppose anything is possible."

At that moment, the vibrations began. Not the deep, resounding, booming vibrations of the explosions taking place above, but high-pitched and piercing vibrations emanating from the Gray Champion himself. Since he'd finished speaking, he had continued to stand silently with his head bowed as if in prayer or contemplation. He now lifted his head and eyes toward the ceiling of the Keeping Room.

The glow emanating from him grew stronger and brighter by the second as the vibrations increased. As the vibrations and the sound reached an almost unbearable level, he began to rise into the air toward the ceiling of the Keeping Room, and then passed right through it and was gone from their sight.

A few seconds later, from above their heads, the Meglio heard an intense, piercing, high-pitched wailing, followed by the most cataclysmic explosion he could imagine. The violence of it was shocking. It was savage and fierce, and it shook him to his core. He felt it in every cell of his body. Although they were at least ten feet below ground and insulated from it by both the ground and the titanium reinforced concrete above them, he was thrown to the floor by the shockwave and rendered unconscious.

The Meglio awakened first. The eerie stillness struck him. It was made even more profound by the total darkness which enveloped them.

"Is everyone okay?" asked the Meglio.

Stirring beside him, Ty answered, "I think so, but I may have gone blind. I can't see anything."

"None of us can, Ty," said Robbie from across the room. "We are ten feet underground, remember?"

"What happened?" asked Nick.

"I believe that your great-grandfather and your

grandmother took care of business," replied the prophet, "although I am not sure I want to know how."

Without warning, their eyes were stabbed by the brightness of the Gray Champion descending through the ceiling of the Keeping Room. He descended to the round table and collapsed before them, still clutching the Sword of St. Peter. As they watched, they saw the image of their grandmother rise from his supine form.

"Are you all well?" she asked the group.

"We are," replied the Meglio. "Is Robert hurt? Was he wounded in the battle?"

"He will recover," replied the image. "He is just drained and needs rest."

"What happened up there, Grandma?" asked Joe.

"We ended the attack," replied the image.

"But how?" asked Jeff.

"As I told you, I accessed the dark energy of the universe through the quantum field and utilized it to defend us. Suffice it to say that dark matter is its own anti-particle. In my studies, I learned that when dark matter annihilates itself, it produces quintessence, a highly repulsive force which is responsible for the expansion of the universe. I harnessed this force to repel the attack. The Leviathan forces will not be troubling us anymore. We devastated a substantial portion of their standing army, which they foolishly assembled here to ensure that we were defeated."

The Meglio carefully stood. "I won't pretend to understand all of the physics of it," he said. "I will just say thank you, and trust that all will be well. Is it possible to get the power back on in here so we can assess the damage, and get the quantum computer up and running again? We need to monitor the outside world."

"Yes," replied the image, "I will attend to that

momentarily."

"Hey, Grandpa," Nick asked, "if the quantum computer is not operating right now, how can we possibly be speaking with it through the image of Grandma? I mean, isn't she just a program within the computer?"

The Meglio was struck silent. Nick had asked a valid question. One that had not occurred to him in all the confusion. He turned to the image and asked, "Catherine, Nick makes a good point. How can we be interacting with you if the quantum computer is not operating? How is that possible?"

The image of his wife smiled at him and replied, "My love, I was going to reveal this to you after things settled down, but I suppose this is an appropriate time. As I told you before, I have been busy since the beginning, learning, and exploring the quantum world. As I have gained understanding, I have also gained access. I have been able to access the dark energy of the universe to draw actual quantum matter to myself.

"Over time, I have been able to draw together enough quantum mass to, in effect, become real. I am not in any sense a physical being, but I am a fully independent, sentient, conscious quantum being, separate and distinct from the quantum computer itself. And since consciousness requires embodiment, I created this quantum body to contain it.

"My quantum form, combined with the detailed personality program you built, has freed me from the confines and limitations of the computer, hence, I am a free entity. Our efforts to resurrect freedom and liberty for mankind have resulted in granting my freedom also. I am very grateful for that generous reward."

"So, you are no longer just a program, but an actual being?" asked the prophet. "Does that mean you are a ghost or some other form of spiritual entity? Like an angel?"

"No," replied his mother. "It is different than that. I am not material, nor am I spiritual. I am quantum. My form is more about potential and possibilities. I am about probability versus certainty. I am not made up of particles or waves; I consist of both at the same time. Hence, it is possible for me to be anywhere at any time, or even in both places simultaneously. I have access to the secrets of the universe, which I have yet to explore fully. The only part of existence that I do not have access to is the future, as that is the realm of only God himself. Hence, I am more valuable to you now than ever before. I would say, without knowing for certain, that the future looks bright. Now, I will begin to restart the quantum computer and show you the results of your efforts."

As she finished speaking, the form of the Gray Champion began to move. He shuddered, struggled, then moaned and began to writhe as if in great pain. Everyone in the room, including the quantum image, watched him as he seemed to be fighting some unknown battle.

As the Meglio took his first step toward the struggling form, he saw a terrifying figure emerge from his father-in-law's body. The image before them was horrifying, and it struck fear deep in his heart.

It had the horns of a goat, the eyes and fangs of a serpent, hands and feet like a man's and on his back were six scaly wings. But the image was unclear because it was shimmering and morphing continuously. The hideous being seized the quantum form of their grandmother by the hair, forced her to her knees, and spoke.

"I am Azazel, whom you have sought to humiliate. I am the scapegoat of God and the leader of the Grigori, who were cast out of heaven. I stand before you this day to end your pitiful game. I tire of your efforts to resist the destiny I have declared for this world. I did not bow to Adam when God commanded it… why should I now bow to you? It is you that will one day bow to me!

"This woman sought to usurp my power and to know the eternal secrets that only I am privileged to know, and she will pay for her insolence. She will now become the vessel through which I will repopulate the world with new quantum Nephilim. There will once again be giants upon the earth, and when that is accomplished, there will be nothing you can do to hinder me. The end has now begun in truth. The world will be remade in my image. The day of retribution is at hand!"

The heroes, the prophet, and the Meglio watched helplessly as the nightmarish demon, still holding the quantum form of their beloved grandmother, mother, and wife by the hair, rose up and disappeared through the ceiling of the Keeping Room.

Epilogue

Ty's head and heart were reeling. The world had just come crashing down around the team of Guardians. Not only had their beloved grandmother just been abducted by the demon watcher Azazel, but they were powerless to help her. The swords were drained, the quantum computer was not operating, and the Gray Champion was still lying on the round table, appearing lifeless.

The Keeping Room was damaged, and they were in total darkness; a darkness which not only filled the room, but Ty's heart and mind as well. There were no flippant or humorous words to ease this situation. He could not joke his way out of this one. In fact, abject despair and hopelessness were quickly becoming his reality. He sat with his head in his hands, unable to move, speak, or even think clearly.

But, thankfully, not everyone was frozen in despondency.

"Rob!" shouted the Meglio to the prophet. "Quickly, follow me. I am going to get the power back on, and then reboot the quantum computer to see if it is salvageable. The rest of you, gather the swords, see if they have enough power to revive your great-grandfather, and then check to see if the door of the Keeping Room is operable."

The Meglio and the prophet made their way through the darkness to the power room. Ty rose slowly and joined the other heroes as they gathered around the figure of the Gray Champion lying face up on the round table.

"How do you think we should do this?" he asked, his tone somber and without hope.

"When we used them to heal each other before, we just put the sword into the wound, and it glowed and began the healing process," Joe reminded them. "But there are no visible wounds on Great-Grandpa this time. I guess we should just touch him with all of the swords and see what happens."

Ty nodded, then realized they probably couldn't see him. "It's worth a try," he said slowly, not daring to hope.

Together, they stood around the table in the same formation that they used during the leaving process. As one, they touched their great-grandfather with their swords. At first, there was no response. The swords appeared to be cold and dead. Not wanting to be the first to give up, Ty stood with the others, focusing on the desired result for what seemed like an eternity.

Then, the Sword of St. Michael, the Archangel, began to glow faintly. As the glow increased in intensity, the sword next to it, the Sword of Arthur and Melchizedek, Excalibur, began to glow. The Sword of Solomon followed; then Joyeuse, the Sword of Charlemagne; Durandal, the Sword of Roland; and finally, Braveheart, the Sword of William Wallace. The swords' glow continued to increase in intensity, and they began vibrating softly in the hands of the heroes. Finally, there was an intense burst of pure, white light, and then darkness.

Ty closed his eyes as the light blinded him. As it

faded, he opened his eyes, but once again, the all-encompassing darkness surrounded them.

Suddenly, the room was once again bathed in light, but not the pure, white light from before. The Meglio and the prophet had succeeded in restoring the power to the Keeping Room.

Ty could now clearly see the figure of their great-grandfather beginning to revive. He was breathing, and his eyes fluttered. He lay there for a while, motionless, and appeared to be struggling to regain consciousness.

Then his eyes shot open, he sat upright, raised the Sword of St. Peter, and screamed at the top of his lungs, "Catherine! My Catherine! What have we done?"

COMING SOON

THE
SWORD
ABOVE
ALL

BOOK THREE

THE SWORDS OF VALOR

DOMENIC MELILLO

ACKNOWLEDGEMENTS
AND
AUTHOR'S NOTE

Once again, thank you, dear reader, for enjoying this adventure with me. As with the first book in this series, *Season of the Swords*, I have combined some true family history with actual historical events, and real family characters with historical and fictional characters. I wrapped it all in a fictional story. I call this genre, "historical, family-based fiction"!

I don't know if anyone else out there writes in this genre, but I must tell you, it is a lot of fun. Being able to take the people I love, tell a bit of their life story, and speculate how they would behave in fictional situations is an amazing experience. Managing all their personalities, their already established personal relationships, and backstories was not as hard as you might imagine. It all developed very naturally.

In *Season of the Swords,* I focused on the qualities of virtue and valor. In *The Sword of the Gray Champion*, those qualities were still in play, but the main focus was on the preservation of freedom and liberty. As you have read, they are intimately connected. Freedom and liberty are dependent on virtue and valor to survive, whether we are dealing with nations or families.

The six young cousins in the story are reasonably accurate representations of my family members, and their interaction and interplay are very true to life. They are all well-educated, resourceful, and reliable, and without a doubt would step up to defend their country or family if called upon to do so. They are all great young men, and I am proud to be their father and uncle.

Uncle Rob is a fictionalized version of my own brother and accurately portrays some of his greatest attributes; his love of family, his loyalty, his love of mentoring, and his inspirational leadership skills. I could truly see him taking on the responsibility given to him in the story and completely succeeding.

Also true-to-life is the representation of Joseph, the Meglio Di Buono. My own father was always known as Mr. Better than Good. It was a phrase he would always use, and over the years, it became his identity. He had a lifelong love of literature. He really did read to us all the poetry mentioned in this story and made sure we remembered and understood it. He knew that there was great wisdom in literature, and it certainly had a major impact on my life. He also had a great affinity for Cicero, read many of his writings, and passed them along to me to read.

My mother Catherine, Grandma in the story, was an amazing person. The portrayal of the relationship between her and my father, the Meglio, is very accurate. They had a wonderful marriage which lasted over sixty years. They were so connected and so in love that when my dad passed away, Mom was so broken-hearted that she followed him six months later. I would definitely say that their "quantum essences" were truly connected.

My grandfather, Robert Ogilvie Petrie, was an immigrant from Edinburgh, Scotland. He did fight in WWI and was with the Black Watch, the Royal Highland Regiment. Although for many years, he was a hard-working coal miner, and later a security guard at a bank in

Brooklyn, he was always a hero to me. Tall, soft-spoken, and slightly intimidating, he reminded everyone of Gary Cooper. He was also a fine welterweight boxer, and even into his seventies, he could hit you with three hard slaps to the head before you knew what hit you. Robert Ogilvie Petrie was a true stoic, and I have no doubt that he could easily have done anything that he did in the story. He would have made an incredible field general for the Guardians of the Swords of Valor.

As you can see, this is really a very family-based book, solidly based in reality. All the historical references to people and times are also as accurate as possible, and I encourage you to explore all the events in the story, if your interest has been piqued.

The five families of the Leviathan Alliance that are referenced in a fictional way are real historical families, and the brief histories included are accurate. All the Leviathan organizations and groups, such as the Fabian Society and the Bohemian Club are also real entities and have been steeped in legend and lore due to the secret nature of their membership and activities.

The quotes and observations of Alexander Fraser Tytler, Lord Woodhouselee, and Alexis de Tocqueville are also taken from the historical records and eerily reflect many societal attitudes today.

The "crisis period" referred to in the story is taken from the book, *The Fourth Turning* by William Strauss and Neil Howe. Written in 1997, it has proven very prescient in describing the behaviors of generational charts and their impact on society. I encourage you to read it for yourselves.

All the conversations between the cousins and Cicero, Ben Franklin, and Sam Adams were constructed from the actual writings of these great men and accurately reflect their attitudes on the role of government, the requirements for maintaining a free society, and the rule of natural law. The references to the Secret Committee, which was our nation's first secret service, are from the record. Lydia Darragh, Major John Clark, and Hercules Mulligan were all agents for the Secret Committee reporting to Ben Franklin.

The events in *The Sword of the Gray Champion*, such as the Boston Massacre, Lexington and Concord, and the Battle of Bunker Hill are factual, except for the involvement of my grandfather.

The name of this book, *The Sword of the Gray Champion*, was taken from the short story of a similar name, *The Gray Champion*, written by Nathaniel Hawthorne in 1835. In this book, the story is related accurately, and it was a natural fit to insert my grandfather, Robert Ogilvie Petrie, into the role of the Gray Champion, and to connect many of his assignments into the past to fight the Apostles of Azazel in the storyline.

George Orwell's *Nineteen Eighty-Four* was also a natural fit. The popularity of this book with its dystopian vision of the then-future has influenced many aspects of our society. I wondered, what if his book was written not as a warning but as a manifesto, similar to *Mein Kampf*. There is no evidence to support that idea, but with all of Orwell's actual connections to the Fabian Society, and the strange health issues and deaths of so many of his family members, it did not take much to make this leap. All the relationships with people including David Astor and H.G. Wells are true.

The conversations that the Guardians had with Orwell are again taken from either actual interviews with Orwell, or were constructed from what he wrote in his book *Nineteen Eighty-Four*, and accurately reflect his feelings.

The description, timeline, and places identified relating to the Kennedy assassination are also taken from the historical record. I have always toyed with "what if" scenarios about this seminal event, so I had lots of ideas. Trying to figure out what Kennedy would do with the information about whom his assassins were and why they targeted him was FUN! An experience like that would change anyone, but how was the real question. I hope my twist on the story was a surprise to you.

Creating alternative timelines regarding the succession of presidents was also great fun. Who would have succeeded Kennedy if he had not died? What could he have accomplished? How would that have changed who would be president after him, up until our own time? Again, this was very interesting and exciting to explore.

All the conversations and meetings between Eisenhower and Kennedy really took place, although I am sure none of the conversations included information about the Leviathans, since I made them up.

The speeches given by Eisenhower about the dangers of the military/industrial complex and by Kennedy referring to "secret societies" are also true and are related reasonably accurately. I may have spiced them up slightly, so I will leave it up to you to find out where.

Oh, and General Curtis E. LeMay is also a real historical figure. I challenge you to do some research of your own, and you will see why I chose him as the person to lead the military coup and subsequent military dictatorship. He was the very first person that came to mind when I decided to create that character.

The description of the events of Bohemian Grove is a compilation of many different accounts given by people who either secretly observed the annual gathering, or were invited but did not honor the code of secrecy. They really do have the owl ceremony and do really sacrifice an effigy of Care to the idol. It is not done with the same intent that I suggested, but it is still pretty creepy.

The speech of the Gray Champion to the people of the world was crafted from, and includes segments from, some of the most inspirational speeches in history. What better way to inspire people to action than to use the words that have already been proven to have the power to change the hearts and minds of men? I challenge you to go through it again and identify the original speeches and quotes and remind yourselves of who said them and when. It will be an inspiration to you, as well.

The information about dark matter, dark energy, and quintessence is factual. The most recent discoveries have brought us closer to understanding the nature and potential of this aspect of the universe, but we still have a long way to go. It has been proposed that dark matter could one day be the ultimate source of energy we have been searching for.

Sadly, as I write this, time travel is still not a reality. Maybe by the time the last book in this trilogy is complete, it will be. I can dream, can't I?

I hope this story has entertained and inspired you. I hope that it has allowed you to realize that our freedom and liberty are very fragile things. That they are God-given gifts secured for us by our forefathers who understood the value of them and paid for them with their blood. That without a citizenry well-educated in the price paid by others for their freedom, steeped in virtue, committed to morality and the maintenance of the blessings of natural law, individual liberties can and will be taken from any nation, no matter how rich and powerful.

Freedom and liberty must be desperately desired. They must be cherished. They must be honored, and most of all, they must be earned. Continually.

ABOUT THE AUTHOR

Domenic Melillo is a husband, father, son, and brother living in Wake Forest, North Carolina. He graduated from Villanova University, where he received his Bachelor of Science in Accounting. He also received his MBA in Banking and Finance from Hofstra University. He has worked in the mortgage industry for thirty-six years.

His passion for writing and poetry was inspired by his father, Joseph Melillo, who read to his children many of his favorite poems from the all-time greats. All of Domenic's writings take inspiration from real life events.

Through his writing, he strives to highlight and contrast the light and dark sides of life, or as he calls it, "the duality of our existence". He is drawn to the themes of family, faith, heritage, loss, and redemption. He is an avid student of history, and in many ways strives to embody many of the characteristics of one of his heroes, Don Quixote, in that he longs to see things as they should be, not as they are.

Domenic has been described as a soul living out of his time, and yearns for the days of chivalry, virtue, valor, and honor, writing in the hope of inspiring families and society to return to these foundational qualities.

CPSIA information can be obtained
at www.ICGtesting.com
Printed in the USA
FFHW011529190219
50601906-55960FF

9 781943 048762